"Mrs. Cavanaugh? Just One More Thing Before You Leave."

"What would that be?" she snapped, facing him.

"I've never liked doing business with people who try to hide things from me. I'm just naturally suspicious at heart, I suppose."

"You know all that you need to know about me."

"No, Mrs. Cavanaugh," he disagreed, drawing so close to her that their bodies touched. "You're hiding something and I intend to see for myself what it is." Then without warning he lifted her veil and allowed his eyes to scan every feature, every facet of her pale, startled face.

Standing in rigid, breathless anticipation, she waited for his next response. Without her veil to protect her, she felt vulnerably naked and totally at his mercy. He could destroy her in an instant if he wanted to.

Dear Reader,

We, the editors of Tapestry Romances, are committed to bringing you two outstanding original romantic historical novels each and every month.

From Kentucky in the 1850s to the court of Louis XIII, from the deck of a pirate ship within sight of Gibraltar to a mining camp high in the Sierra Nevadas, our heroines experience life and love, romance and adventure.

Our aim is to give you the kind of historical romances that you want to read. We would enjoy hearing your thoughts about this book and all future Tapestry Romances. Please write to us at the address below.

The Editors
Tapestry Romances
POCKET BOOKS
1230 Avenue of the Americas
Box TAP
New York, N.Y. 10020

To Sharon Bickel and Maryann Miller,
who began it all.

To Betty Henrichs, Billye Johnson,
and Fayrene Preson,
for lending me their
constant support and encouragement
during my more trying periods.

And to Laura Parker Castoro;
never has an "I told you so"
meant so much. Thank you!

Lady
Raine

Chapter One

July 1888

MACAO'S BUSY HARBOR SWARMED WITH A THOUSAND different sights, sounds and smells. Ragged sampans bobbed like ungainly corks atop the murky waters, while their tiny decks overflowed with the many generations of Cantonese who knew no other way of life. They entered into this world and departed from it aboard their floating homes, leaving them for dry land only when necessity demanded it. On the nearby dock a myriad of nationalities bartered, haggled and conversed in their own native dialects: Spanish with English; Mandarin with Portuguese; English with Russian. And surrounding this Babel-like confusion was the ever-present heat, its haziness overpowering the entire scene.

Acutely aware of her surroundings, Raine carefully picked her way up the narrow dirt lane that led away from the teeming harbor and into the squalid, poverty-ridden area where shanties abounded. The people here weren't as fortunate as their fellow countrymen down below. Here they had much more to contend with than noisy, inconsiderate neighbors. They had violence, corruption and danger to live

1

with as well. But it was here, amid these dilapidated buildings that she hoped to find the American captain who would aid her.

With her thoughts channeled on what lay ahead and on the role she would soon be portraying, she paid scant attention to the questioning glances passersby tossed her way. She was very different from them, and she knew it.

Dressed in a long, white silk cheongsam with high collar and modest slit up the leg, she had the outward appearance of a Eurasian, though her slender height clearly belied this fact. That had been the one thing she hadn't been able to alter. Her full breasts had been bound tightly and her pale skin had been covered with makeup to make her appear less European. But her height, unfortunately, still remained its statuesque five feet seven inches.

At last, and much to her relief, the faded red door of the shack she sought came into view. She approached it with caution, clenching her gloved hands into tight fists before flexing her fingers and running them down the sides of her gown. It was a nervous gesture, but then she had just cause to be apprehensive. Lord, no case of opening-night jitters had ever been quite as bad as what she experienced now. No performance she'd ever given had been as important, either.

Inhaling deeply, she forced all of the unimportant thoughts from her mind and concentrated totally on her role. The curtain was about to rise and she was the solo performer.

Lifting her fist, she rapped twice on the shaky wood panel.

"Yeah?" A masculine voice barked from inside.

"Captain Slade?" Her inflection held no note of apprehension; it was oddly calm, well-controlled and very cultured, just as she had intended it should be. "I wish to speak to you."

"Oh, hell. Go away!" the voice growled. "It's too damn early."

"Captain," she persisted. "It is extremely important that I speak to you. I can assure you it is. I—I will be glad to make it worth your while if you will spare me your time."

"Oh, damn!" he growled again. "Su-ling? Wake up, Susie. You gotta get up now."

Su-ling obviously didn't care for being awakened, because Raine heard a definitely feminine voice utter a complaint. Approve or not, though, the rustle of clothing and the squeak of rusty bedsprings from inside soon assured her that the American had succeeded in rousing his nocturnal companion.

Raine wasn't embarrassed in the least at having interrupted the American's tryst. She had been told of his weaknesses for gambling, drinking and loose women and had expected as much. A pirate, her source of information in Hong Kong had called him. A pirate who was trustworthy as well as scrupulous —if there was such a combination.

"Captain Slade, I do not have all day to wait out here," she informed him, darting a quick glance over her shoulder at the growing crowd of gawking Cantonese.

"For Crissakes, lady, keep your corset on. I'm coming!"

Suddenly the door swung open, forcing Raine

back as a man's menacing form filled the narrow opening. His face, rumpled and creased from sleep, instantly contorted into an agonized wince as the bright sunlight made contact with his sensitive eyes. His discomfort was probably well deserved, she thought with a smile. No man should carry on as he did and not expect to suffer some consequence.

A moment after he opened the door, a diminutive woman in wrinkled trousers and coat, pushed past him, tossing a grumpy look in Raine's direction before turning her slanted black eyes away. The tall American bent over, muttered something into the woman's ear, then swatted her playfully across the behind as she scurried away, giggling.

"I ain't got all day either, lady," he grumbled sourly, his good humor suddenly lost as he straightened to his impressive height. "What do you want?"

"If you don't mind, Captain, I would prefer to discuss our business in private. May I come in?"

With a grunt, Slade stepped back, holding the door open wide so she could enter. It was then, as she went to pass him, that she realized just how large he truly was. Well over six feet, by her estimation, and quite powerful if his build was anything to judge by. His hair, a dark shade of brown highlighted with blond streaks, was shaggy and unkempt as were his untrimmed beard and mustache. And when he suddenly yawned, she noted the deep grooves in his cheeks, a sure sign that he possessed dimples when he smiled—if he ever did, that is.

Raine wrinkled her nose in disgust at the musty odor that assailed her nostrils. It left her in little doubt of what had transpired here last night. Hearing about his weaknesses was one thing, but discovering them firsthand was something else. It caused her to remark stiffly, "I have been informed that you have a ship for hire, Captain."

"Yeah," he nodded, pulling on a wrinkled shirt over his broad, hairy chest. "The *Mary Ellen*. She's docked here in Macao."

"Yes, I'm aware of that. What price are you asking for her services?"

"Depends," he retorted, stumbling toward the unmade bed.

"On what?"

"On how far you want to go and on how long it takes us to get there." With a groan, he dropped onto the bed's thin mattress and held his aching head with his hands.

"Well, it shall be for quite a long while, I imagine," she declared, unwilling to sympathize with his condition. "You see, I wish to sail to San Francisco."

Slade's head shot up, sending a pain through him like the lash of a whip. "Good God, lady! Regular ships make that run out of Hong Kong all the time. Why in hell don't you just take one of them?"

"I don't wish to make that long voyage with a lot of other passengers. I would prefer to make the crossing alone."

Through his pain-wracked brain, Slade slowly began to notice certain details about her and it gave him cause to wonder just what her real reason was for wanting to go that great distance—and with him of all people. She was all decked out in white, from the top of her veil-covered head to the tips of her high-buttoned shoes. Having lived in the Orient as long as he'd done, he knew that women here wore that color, rather than black, when they were in mourning. Good God! Maybe that was it. Maybe she wanted to take a stiff to San Francisco with her.

"Uh, lady, I don't carry no corpses on the *Mary Ellen*. They're bad luck, for one thing, and for another, they smell."

"It's not my intention to transport a body, Captain. It never was."

"But you're in mourning, aren't you?"

"Not over a recently deceased person," she assured him after a short pause. "Now are you willing to charter your ship to me, or aren't you?"

Slade thought about it for a moment, weighing the advantages against the disadvantages. The advantages won hands down. If he did take her to Frisco, it would get him out of this neck of the woods for a while and he wouldn't have to worry about Fong's boys pulling a fast one on him when his back was turned. Hell, why not? As long as he didn't have some stinking stiff on board, he couldn't see any reason not to hire out to her.

"When do you want to leave?" he asked.

"How soon can you have your ship ready to sail?" she countered evenly, her tone void of the joyous elation she felt.

"Well . . . I'll need to round up a crew. Then I got all the supplies to buy—after I get an advance, that is. Oh, two, maybe three days, I guess."

"No, no," she frowned, shaking her head. "That's much too soon. I couldn't possibly be ready by then."

then please tell me now so that I may look elsewhere for suitable transportation."

"I don't object to you being divorced, Mrs. Cavanaugh." Why should he? Her money was as good as a married woman's. But Lord, she sure was bitter about it. The hard edge of her husky voice clearly said as much. He couldn't rightly blame her, though. Divorced women were looked upon as outcasts, social lepers in more proper circles.

With this matter settled, they stepped out of the dark shanty into the bright light of day. Slade's wince returned as the pain in his head once again accelerated, but he kept his discomfort to himself and led her down the dirt lane toward the dock where the *Mary Ellen* was anchored.

"Are you staying here in Macao?" he asked when they had walked a short distance.

"Why do you ask, Captain?"

"Well, I'd like to know where I can get in touch with you if something should crop up before we sail."

A brief pause ensued before she quietly admitted, "No, I'm not in Macao at present. I'm staying with . . . friends in Hong Kong. You aren't to worry, though. I shall send one of my servants over frequently, if you wish it."

"No need, Mrs. Cavanaugh. I can make it easier on the both of us and move the *Mary Ellen*—"

"No!" She stopped abruptly, whirling about to face him. "We will leave from *here*, Captain. Under no circumstances are you to move your ship from this harbor unless I give my permission first. Is that understood?"

Slade had never liked taking orders from someone else, especially when that someone was a woman. The sudden tautening of his features mirrored this fact. "Let me tell you something, lady. The *Mary Ellen* is *my* ship. I don't give a damn how much you pay to charter her, she's still mine. You got that? If I decide to move her, goddammit, I'll move her!"

Raine maintained a tight leash on her temper. She couldn't afford to have him rescind his services to her now—she was in too great a need of them. "I understand perfectly, Captain," she replied with strained calmness. "I fear I must beg your forgiveness for having sounded so presumptuous. That was not my intention, I assure you. But I would ask you . . . plead with you even, not to move your ship until I have been notified beforehand. It truly is important to me."

Slade gave her a long, assessing look then lowered his bearded chin; the only indication she could see that he had acknowledged and accepted her apology. *For God's sake,* a little voice cautioned her, *don't slip out of character again. No well-bred Eurasian lady ever raises her voice to a man.*

Turning, they started toward the dock again, but Raine's sense of ease vanished and her irritation mounted when he suddenly challenged, "You're up to something illegal, aren't you?"

"Illegal?" *Just stay calm,* her little voice warned. *Don't lose control. He's only guessing.* "No, Captain, you're mistaken."

"I don't think so. You're up to your aristocratic little bu—uh, neck in something shady. If you weren't, you'd have found a ship closer to home, in

10

Hong Kong. You wouldn't have come all the way here to Macao."

Slade tried to read the expression on her face, but her heavy veil wouldn't permit it. He could only see the rigid angle of her dark head, but it was enough to assure him that he was right. "You know, Mrs. Cavanaugh, you can trust me," he went on with lazy assuredness. "What you're up to is your business. I won't try to interfere or blow the whistle on you. But I would like to know if your scam is likely to get sticky so I can plan ahead for it. You see," he added, angling his head closer to hers, "I've transported contraband aboard the *Mary Ellen* a time or two, so it's not like you're dealing with a greenhorn. I do have some experience."

"You're too observant for your own good, Captain," she mocked icily. "But you could not be farther from the truth. I am not *up to*—as you so aptly put it—anything remotely illegal. I merely wish to leave China from the port of Macao rather than Hong Kong."

"Okay," he conceded with a wave of his hand. "Have it your way. But I'll tell you, if we run into trouble along the way, and I find out you're the cause of it, you'll pay." And pay dearly, he thought. Hell, women had been nothing but trouble for him most of his life and it didn't look like she would be any different.

They continued toward the ship in a stiff, uneasy silence, both occupied with their own impressions and thoughts. Only once, just as they stepped onto the dock and an errant breeze blew aside Raine's veil, did she show any outward sign of vexation. But just as quickly as the heavy silk lifted, she tugged it back down into place again, her steps never faltering.

In that brief moment, though, Slade caught a glimpse of her profile and found himself curiously intrigued. Her delicate features—what he'd seen of them—were more European than Eurasian. And her accent, which was pure English upper class, seemed to add reinforcement to this belief. Yet her mode of dress and her mannerisms clearly said she was of mixed blood. No doubt about it, she was an enigma all right. A confusing mass of contradictions as were many Eurasians and Orientals. One thing was certain; he would have to watch his step when he was around her.

"There she is," he announced proudly when they reached the end of the dock. "The *Mary Ellen*. She may not be the biggest or the fastest barkentine in the Pacific, but she's the soundest."

"How long have you been her captain?" Raine queried, moving toward the gangplank, her surprise evident in her tone. Whatever she had expected the *Mary Ellen* would be, it certainly didn't come close to matching this clean, seaworthy-looking vessel.

"Oh, ten years or thereabouts. I won her in a poker game off an Australian *gentleman merchant,*" he ended on a note of sarcasm.

"Did you now?"

"Yeah. He should've stuck to his business and left the card playing to those who knew what they were doing. Are you familiar with games of chance, Mrs. Cavanaugh?"

"No, Captain, I'm not. Perhaps, though, if our voyage should grow tedious, you might find time to teach me your . . . poker, was it? I'm afraid the only card game I'm acquainted with is whist."

"Mmm." He nodded noncommitally. Whist! Good Lord, that kind of parlor game might suit the likes of her, but it sure as hell didn't suit him.

"Pa!"

The unexpected summons caused Raine to turn sharply. A tall, gangly youth approached them. No older than thirteen or fourteen, she saw that he possessed a head full of silky black hair and the high, slanted cheekbones of an Oriental. But his eyes, which were clear and green, told her that he was definitely of mixed parentage, and that his father, who also possessed green eyes, was none other than Captain Slade.

Dread instantly consumed her. God in Heaven, why hadn't she been told of this son? As unimportant as it might seem now, it *could* make a great deal of difference later on.

"I thought I'd taught you better manners, Davey," Slade admonished gently, dropping his arm around the boy's shoulders before mussing his already unruly hair. "You should've said hello to Mrs. Cavanaugh first."

"Sorry, Pa," the boy mumbled sheepishly. "How do you do, ma'am?"

"Very well, thank you." She smiled nervously. "Is your name David or Davey?"

"David, ma'am. But Pa and the rest of the crew call me Davey."

"If it's all right with you, may I call you David?"

The boy nodded, his flushed face turning to look at his father. "Cookie was just about to send me after you when you boarded, sir."

"Is something wrong?" A frown pulled Slade's heavy brows together.

"No, he just wanted to know if you were going to be ashore again tonight."

"You tell Cookie I'll be here," Slade directed the boy.

"Yes, sir. Is there anything else you want me to tell him?"

"Uh, yeah. Ask him if he would make us some tea. You do drink tea, don't you, Mrs. Cavanaugh?"

"Of course I do, Captain. But I wish you wouldn't go to so much trouble on my account. I shall probably be leaving shortly, as soon as I've inspected my rooms."

"Quarters," Slade corrected, guiding her toward an opened door near the rear of the ship.

"I beg your pardon?"

"A ship has quarters or cabins, Mrs. Cavanaugh, not rooms."

"Oh," she responded flatly.

And they were very adequate quarters at that, she soon discovered. Though not as large or as roomy as she might have wished, they were adequate nonetheless. Both possessed a single window hung high on the wall to allow for ventilation, a wide berth built firmly into the bare wood floor with storage space beneath, and a built-in cabinet with a sturdy latch to lock it.

14

"Do you think it might be possible for you to put a door in this wall?" she asked when she had examined the second cabin. "I would like for the two cabins to be adjoining if possible."

"No, we can't do that without weakening the upper structure. And it's a bulkhead."

"What?"

"This isn't a wall, it's a bulkhead. This is a deck, not a floor. And that's a porthole, not a window. You haven't done much sailing, have you?"

"Why, I sailed here all the way from England, Captain," came her stilted retort.

"Yeah, probably aboard a luxury passenger ship."

"As a matter of fact, it was."

"Well, I'm afraid you're in for a big disappointment if you expect your voyage aboard the *Mary Ellen* to be anything like that one was."

"I don't expect that at all, Captain."

"You won't have any luxury at all, and not a whole lot of comfort, either."

"I know, but—"

"There won't be any orchestra aboard to entertain you in the evenings, and there won't be any stewards to wait on you hand and foot. Not only that, you'll find that our meals are as plain as they come."

"Captain Slade," she broke in determinedly. "I can assure you that I was not expecting an elaborate setup when I came looking for you."

"I hope not. And I hope you're not above lending a hand if and when it becomes necessary."

"In what capacity would I be expected to help, may I ask?"

15

"Depends," he evaded with a shrug. "On a ship this size, everybody has to pull his—or her—own weight. We can't afford to pander to freeloaders."

"Well, for your information," she snapped, "I'm not completely helpless, and I thoroughly abhor being pampered. I will be more than willing to offer my, or my staff's, assistance when and if we are needed. But for what I am paying you, Captain, I should hope that isn't often." If he expected her to take on the crew's more difficult tasks, he had a surprise in store. She had other, more important responsibilities—or would have when their voyage began.

"Just what *can* you do, Mrs. Cavanaugh?" Slade challenged as he stepped closer to her.

"More than you might imagine, Captain." She took a backward step in order to maintain the distance between them, but a bed suddenly loomed up behind her, ending any progress she might have made. She was forced to stand there with his awesome body nearly touching hers. Lord, but he was arrogant and much too presumptuous for her liking. And the lazy perusal he was now giving her all but bordered on the insulting.

"I doubt it," he mumbled at last, stepping aside.

"Doubt all you wish, Captain, but I can assure you I am not a helpless ninny. I can sew *and* cook, and I can keep myself adequately entertained, thank you very much. I can even care for the ill and infirmed on the simplest of levels if I have to."

"You can?" His thick brows arched in dubious speculation.

"Yes, I can!"

16

Before she could avoid his next move, Slade reached out and grasped her arm, surprising her even further by peeling off her glove and examining her hand. "I don't believe you for a second," he snorted and dropped her wrist.

"Well, for ten thousand dollars, you had better try, Captain Slade!" Jerking on her glove again, she turned on unsteady legs and started for the door.

"Mrs. Cavanaugh? Just one more thing before you leave."

"What would that be?" she snapped, facing him again.

"I've never liked doing business with people who try to hide things from me. I'm just naturally suspicious at heart, I suppose."

"You know all that you need to know about me."

"No, Mrs. Cavanaugh," he disagreed, drawing so close to her that their bodies touched. "You're hiding something and I intend to see for myself what it is." Then, without warning, he lifted her veil and allowed his eyes to scan every feature, every facet of her pale, startled face.

Standing in rigid, breathless anticipation, Raine waited for his next response. Without her veil to protect her, she felt vulnerably naked and totally at his mercy. He could destroy her in an instant if he wanted to.

But he didn't. Something, some nameless flicker of emotion darted behind his eyes, assuring her that discovering her identity had never been the intent of his action. There was no sign of recognition visible in his expression that she could see; only unconcealed admiration.

17

Slowly, reluctantly, he let the veil fall with a whisper back over her face. Releasing her breath, Raine dug down into her handbag and extracted the promised advance they'd agreed upon. She thrust it out at him then fled out the door.

Slade didn't follow her. He could only stand there, bewildered and surprised by what he'd seen to even move. She was a beautiful woman, her face flawless to the point of perfection. But she was *too* beautiful, in his opinion, to be hiding her loveliness from the world beneath that silly veil.

As beautiful as she was, though, there was something about her that continued to puzzle him. It wasn't her age—which he assumed was about twenty-four or five—but everything else. Her coarse, dark hair; her slanted, deep violet eyes; her short, straight nose; her pale, porcelain complexion —when all were appraised separately, they were unquestionably perfect. Then why didn't they fit together? It was as if she had been given the finest of features with the wrong pattern to arrange them by.

"Oh, hell!" he spat with disgust, moving to stand before the porthole. He wasn't about to let a woman get to him now, and he certainly had better things to do than stand around, thinking about her!

Oh, he would still take her to Frisco, but as soon as he had his money, he would leave with the tide and not give her a second thought. He hadn't lived to be thirty-eight without learning a few things. One of them being—women like her spelled trouble!

Chapter Two

Slade relaxed atop the quarterdeck, enjoying life and the world in general. With his long legs stretched out before him, he lit up his first cigar of the day. It was just one of the nice courtesies Mrs. Cavanaugh's generous advance allowed him. All the ship's stores had been bought, his crew had been signed on, so now he had nothing better to do than sit and wait until her ladyship decided she was ready to sail. Watching the smoke curl up from the cigar and into the blue sky above him, he hoped she wasn't in any hurry. He wouldn't mind enjoying this easy way of life for a little while longer.

Taking a deep drag, he savored the cigar's taste as if it contained the most expensive opium available in Macao, rather than the exorbitantly priced tobacco from Cuba. Lord, he hadn't had a cigar that tasted as good as this in years. Not since the time he'd hauled all those damn idols out of Angkor Wat in Cambodia. He'd bought his own smoke that time as well, now that he recalled.

Angkor Wat. How long ago had that been? Four, five years? Just thinking about it now made his skin crawl. All those ruined temples and huge stone heads covered in jungle growth was as clear in his mind now as if it had been only yesterday. And that shifty-eyed little weasel, Fong—how he had known the gold idols were buried in the heart of that one temple, Slade couldn't imagine. Hell, not even the local villagers had known about them, and they'd helped unearth Angkor back in the sixties.

That trip had been pure hell from start to finish; not at all the pleasure jaunt this voyage with Mrs. Cavanaugh promised to be. But he had needed money, and needed it badly, or he wouldn't have gone with Fong. They hadn't anticipated half the dangers they'd encountered along the way—the least of which had been those damn, slimy green snakes that dropped out of overhanging trees just as they walked beneath them. *Hanuman,* the locals had called them. Those who were unfortunate enough to be bitten had died.

By the time he'd made it back to Bangkok, where the *Mary Ellen* was anchored, he'd earned himself a tidy little bundle from his share of the loot. Unfortunately, he'd earned the everlasting hatred of old Fong Chiang as well, the ungrateful little bastard. He had refused to go back to Angkor on a second expedition and Fong had sworn that he'd get even with Slade if he ever got the chance.

Blowing out a stream of smoke, Slade wondered what ever possessed him to remember all that now? It was ancient history and Mrs. Cavanaugh wasn't even remotely connected to it. Although, come to think of it, she was about as hard to figure out as Fong had been.

"Pa?"

Davey's voice intruded on Slade's musings, bringing him back rudely to the present. "What is it, son?"

"We got cargo waiting to come aboard."

"Cargo!" Puzzled, Slade swung his legs over the side of the quarterdeck and dropped lightly onto the main deck below. "I'm not expecting any cargo. All our supplies were loaded aboard yesterday."

"Well, the man on the dock said he had orders from Mrs. Cavanaugh."

"Oh, Mrs. Cavanaugh, huh?"

Slade ambled over to the port railing and peered down to the dock below, wondering if this was her way of telling him that she was getting ready to sail? A heavily laden ox-drawn cart caught his eye, as did the sandy-haired giant who stood beside it. "She don't believe in traveling light, does she, son?"

"No, sir," the boy agreed with a smile. "It appears she don't."

"Mr. Dennison!" Slade called out as he crossed the deck, capturing the first mate's attention. "Ready the hoist! More cargo coming aboard."

"Aye-aye, sir!" Dennison responded.

"Davey, stand clear. I don't want anything falling on you."

"Yes, sir."

Slade descended the gangplank in three long strides, his cigar clenched tightly between his strong teeth. His intention was to examine the cargo, because nothing came aboard his ship until he looked it over first.

"I understand you got a load of goods for me," he addressed the cart handler.

"Aye, that I do, if you're Captain Quentin Slade." The handler spoke with a heavy Scottish burr.

"Yeah, I'm Slade. What all have you got here?"

"I wouldn't be knowing that, sir. I just haul what I'm told and don't ask questions." He shoved a manifest toward Slade and grumbled, "Sign here."

Slade scratched his signature on the allotted spot, then turned to look over the loaded cart. Three big trunks hugged the front while a dozen or so smaller bags and valises filled the rear.

"It looks all right to me. We'll accept it."

Before he could order the first mate to begin hoisting it aboard, the burly Scot thrust an envelope at him. "The sister wanted me to see that you got this personally."

"The sister?" Slade frowned.

"Aye. The nun who brought these goods over on the ferry from Hong Kong. A right bonnie wee lass she was."

Bonnie or not, Slade wondered what a nun was doing associating with Mrs. Cavanaugh, a self-confessed divorced woman? Still confused, he slit open the envelope and extracted the note from within.

"Captain Slade," it began in a flowery scrawl. "These are but a few of my possessions that I will be taking with me. More will follow later. The trunks are unimportant to me at the moment, but if you would be kind enough to put them into your hold until I am in need of them, I would be most grateful.

The other bags I should like to have in my quarters. Yours truly, Mrs. Cavanaugh."

Lord help him, she even wrote as uppity as she talked.

After stuffing the note and envelope into his shirt, he jammed his cigar into his mouth and puffed on it angrily. Damn that woman. No mention at all of when she wanted to leave—not even a little hint.

"Dennison!" he barked. "Get this stuff on board."

"Aye-aye, Captain!" the mate acknowledged from the deck.

When the cart was at last empty and all the cargo had been hoisted aboard the *Mary Ellen*, Slade motioned for the handler to leave.

The Scot saluted. "Be seeing you, Captain."

"Not too soon, I hope," Slade muttered as the cart lumbered slowly up the quay and out of sight.

Slade stood in his quarters, leaning over his deck where an array of charts and maps were spread. Why he was bothering with them now, he wasn't sure. Two days had passed since her ladyship had sent over her trunks and he hadn't had a word or sign of her since as to when she wanted to leave. Just what the hell was she up to? Well, he wouldn't concern himself too much, so long as the money and the weather continued to hold out.

A knock sounded at his door.

"Enter," he ordered, turning away from his desk.

"You're needed on the dock, Cap'n," Cookie told him through the crack in the door.

"What now?" he groaned, following the squat, bandy-legged man topside.

He made his way to the port railing and saw the same dour Scot who had brought down Mrs. Cavanaugh's first load. But instead of more trunks and valises, the cart now possessed a wide assortment of goods so outrageous that Slade growled in anger.

An ornate, china hip-bath, complete with flowers and naked cherubs painted on its side was perched atop the cart, capturing the entire dock's attention. But if that weren't bad enough, numerous crates of wine, champagne and gin rested beneath it, as well as cartons of expensive tinned foods.

"Son of a bitch!" he bellowed, leaping down the gangplank. It was his job to buy the stores, dammit, not hers! She had enough food here to feed a whole damn army!

When the manifest was offered to him, he jerked it out of the Scot's hand and scribbled his name in the proper space. "Did she send a note along with all this?"

"No," the Scot replied. "The Chinaman didn't have one with him."

"Chinaman! What happened to the nun?"

"I'd not be knowing that, sir. It was a Chinaman who came on the ferry this morning."

Slade muttered an obscenity beneath his breath, wishing he knew what was going on, then yelled, "Dennison!"

"The hoist is already being readied, Captain."

Slade threw the gawdy hip-bath a baleful look before letting his eye wander over the crates of champagne, wine and gin. What in God's sweet name was she going to do with the stuff? Bathe in it?

"Do we put it in the hold, Captain?" Dennison asked him when the last crate was lifted aboard.

After giving it some thought, Slade smiled slyly. "You can put that damn tub in her ladyship's quarters. The wine and champagne can go in the hold. We'll break open the gin and sample a bottle of it later." Unless she was a lush, there was no way she could drink all of it by herself. Surely she wouldn't miss the one bottle.

The mate grinned. "Aye-aye, sir."

"Pa," Davey spoke up. "If you put the tub in her cabin, she's not going to have much room to move around."

"We'll let her worry about that, son."

"But, Pa—"

"Not now, Davey. Leave it."

"You know, Captain," Mr. Dennison remarked, eyeing the dated crates with a speculative gleam. "That sure was a fine year for champagne."

"Was it?" Slade glanced down at the containers. "I wouldn't know a good year from a bad one, to tell you the truth. I prefer the taste of beer and bourbon, myself."

"Well, so do I, sir," the mate agreed. "But that was still a very good year."

"Mrs. Cavanaugh should be commended for her good taste then, shouldn't she?"

"You don't suppose she'd object too much if we—"

"*She* might not, but *I* would," Slade interjected

when he saw the direction Dennison's more cultured thoughts were headed. "The gin will suit us just fine."

"It was only a thought, Captain."

"There's never any harm in thinking, Mr. Dennison. Now see that this gets stored below." Without a backward glance, knowing that his orders would be carried out, he strolled across the deck toward his cabin.

Heavy clouds rolled in from the ocean, drenching Macao in a hot summer rain. The typhoon season would be arriving soon, and Slade knew that if he didn't get away he would find himself caught in the middle of it. The last thing he wanted was to be stuck here in this stinking, godforsaken part of the world when there were other, dryer ports to be at.

Puffing angrily on his cigar, he paced the distance of his cabin like some jittery, caged animal. He felt like his nerves were going to snap any minute. Hell, being at the mercy of someone as unpredictable as Mrs. Cavanaugh would grate on anyone's self-control. No two ways about it, he'd been his own man for too long now to find it comfortable conforming to some silly woman's whims.

But giving in to Mrs. Cavanaugh wasn't his main worry at the moment, it was his own restlessness. Why, only a week ago he was enjoying this lazy, carefree existence after delivering the last of his previous cargo, and now he couldn't wait to get back out on the open seas.

He wasn't the only one itching to set sail. His crew had sat idle aboard the *Mary Ellen,* growing so bored they finally demanded shore leave. Not having any good reason to refuse them, Slade had given in. Now he wished he had gone with them. Being stuck here in this floating cage was finally getting to him.

Pulling his timepiece out of his pocket and noting the hour, he realized that it still wasn't too late. Dennison had had leave last night, so it was his turn to man the bridge. Cookie, who never left the ship after dark anyway, could handle anything else that cropped up. If he hurried, he could find Su-ling before some other sailor hired her for the night. And even if she wasn't available, he could always look around for some other clean, docile girl.

Starting to head out the door, to find Cookie and inform him where he was bound, he flinched when it suddenly opened. Davey rushed in, water dripping from his new hat.

"Pa, I think you'd better come topside," the boy said breathlessly.

"What's the problem?" The seriousness of his son's expression caused the hairs to stand up on Slade's neck.

"You'd best see for yourself, sir."

All sorts of visions, ranging from minor to catastrophic, raced through Slade's head as he grabbed his slicker and hurried topside. As soon as he stepped out into the miserable drizzle and heard the loud commotion, he knew what was happening. His blood boiled at the sight of the pair of live nanny goats being led aboard by the small, wet Chinaman, who smiled and bobbed his pigtailed head at him. Then Slade's angry gaze shifted to the stout woman dressed in brown bombazine who had just hurried on board, carrying an open umbrella in one hand and a covered birdcage in the other.

Not trusting his temper at that moment, Slade gritted his teeth and stormed over to the railing. A sonorous lowing sound from below told him that more surprises were coming.

"Good God Almighty!" he roared. Below, the dour Scot was unloading crates of live chickens from his cart. "What the hell does that woman think this is? An ark?"

Davey stepped away from his father, fearing where his wrath might lead. He tried to huddle near the mainmast, but in backing up, he accidentally bumped into the stout woman and soon found himself in possession of her birdcage.

"Here, boy, take this below to Miss Sher . . . er, Mrs. Cavanaugh's suite."

"Yes, ma'am," he agreed hastily and made himself scarce.

"I say," she called out. "Are you Captain Slade?"

"What?" Pivoting at the sound of his name, Slade glared at the woman who had addressed him. "Who the hell are you? Part of *her ladyship's* staff?"

"Her ladyship? Oh, I see! You must mean Mrs. Cavanaugh. Well, yes, actually I suppose I am. I'm Miss Henrietta Carlisle, but you may call me—"

"Where is she?" Slade interrupted, his mustached lip curling into a snarl.

"She will be aboard later . . . before we sail."

"Before we . . . ?" A goodly portion of Slade's teeth and gums were bared through his tight, menacing smile. "You mean, her *highness* has made up her mind to go *now* . . . tonight?"

"You don't have to snap at me, young man. I am neither deaf nor hard of hearing."

Slade ignored the rebuke. "Jesus Christ! I've been stuck in port for nearly a week and *now* she—"

"Mrs. Cavanaugh has been extremely busy, Captain," Miss Carlisle staunchly asserted. "If she hadn't been, I am sure she would have informed you of her schedule. Not that there was any need, mind you. She was under the impression that you would be ready to leave at her notice."

"*Her* notice!"

"Must I remind you not to bark at me? I am not one of your doltish crewmen that you can order about."

"Then where the hell is *she?* I'll be more than happy to bark at her!"

"I've told you already, Captain," Miss Carlisle retorted stiffly. "She will be aboard later. You are to be ready to depart the very instant she arrives."

"Oh, I will, will I? Well, we'll just see about that! It's high time her ladyship learned what it feels like to be kept waiting. *Cookie!*"

"Aye, sir?" The bandy-legged cook turned away from the crates of squawking chickens he'd been inspecting and hurried toward Slade.

"Inform Mr. Dennison that he is to be in charge of the watch tonight. *I'm* going ashore." Not once during his scathing speech did his glare waver from Miss Carlisle's astonished face.

"Captain Slade! You aren't honestly thinking of leaving *now,* are you?"

"I sure as hell am!" He grinned malevolently.

"But, sir, you cannot!"

"Just watch me."

"But, Captain, we will be leaving as soon as—"

Her voice trailed off and was forgotten as Slade turned and stalked down the gangplank, past the dour Scot, past the huge snuffling ox and on up to the dock and the dirt path where the promised calm of Su-ling beckoned him.

Damn that woman! Damn her *and* her ten thousand dollars. There wasn't enough money in the world to force Quentin Slade into following some silly female's stupid whims.

Minutes later he slammed into the first tavern, hoping to find Su-ling there. His anger, having grown rather than lessened, reached its zenith after he drank a stiff shot of liquor. After a second shot it began its inevitable decline.

By the time he'd searched through two more local watering spots, sampling the weak brew in both places, he found himself oddly calm and somewhat numb. He wasn't drunk, he told himself, but he sure was close to it.

Through a pleasant haze, he finally spotted the lady he'd been searching for, sitting with another man. There was only one thing left for him to do—he would have to entice her away from the fellow, because he sure as hell wasn't in any mood to fight for her. No woman, not even gentle Su-ling, was worth going to that much trouble for.

Bottle in hand, he stumbled across the tavern toward the table Su-ling and her suitor shared. "Let me have the honor of buying you a drink, friend," he mumbled slowly, his tongue strangely thick in his mouth.

Su-ling's companion, a sailor by the looks of him, glanced at Slade, puzzled. *"No comprender, señor."*

"Ah, a Spaniard!" Slade announced, jerking out a chair and falling into it. "Wonderful country, Spain is. Wonderful!"

"Señor?"

"Uh, Spain—wonderful! You know, uh, mar-marve-*marvillo!*"

"Ah!" The other man beamed suddenly, nodding in agreement. *"España, maravilloso! Si, si!"*

Slade pushed his bottle forward and filled the Spaniard's glass. "To Spain then!" He gestured dramatically with his upraised glass.

"Si! España!"

Su-ling, remaining curiously quiet, let her black eyes dart from Slade to the Spaniard and back to Slade again as they downed their drinks.

"A-me-rica!" The Spaniard toasted when his glass was refilled, clinking it against Slade's.

"Well, hell, I'll drink to that," Slade agreed with a blurry, patriotic grin. Then after gulping down the drink, he lifted his glass once again. "To the Armada!"

"Qué, señor?"

"Oh, that's right. You all lost that one, didn't you? Well, never mind, it's not that important. To Madrid!"

More than slightly confused, the Spaniard sipped hesitantly to that toast.

Two hours and many toasts later, Slade succeeded in spiriting Su-ling away from the other man, who didn't appear at all distraught over his loss. Hugging the tiny woman to his side, they wandered out into the miserably wet night, Su-ling leading them to their intended destination.

"You don't know what a priceless creature you are to a man like me, Susie girl," Slade slurred drunkenly, trying to focus on the dark head resting against his waist. "You're so good. You never cause trouble. You never bring a man worries or heartache. You just make him feel comfortable and needed. Not all women are like that, you know."

Su-ling's head tilted up, her round face stretching into a smile.

"And, thank God, you don't talk much. I believe I admire that more than anything else. Jeez, some women can't keep quiet, no matter what. They yammer away and harp at you until you feel like smashing them in the teeth. But you're not like that, are you, Susie honey?"

Continuing to extol her praiseworthy attributes, they finally reached the weathered red door of her shack. Once inside, he allowed her to undress him, her small hands gliding over him with gentle expertise. At last, fully naked, he lay back on her narrow bed and watched sleepily as she unfastened the satin frogs of her cheongsam. It fell to the dirt floor in a quiet whisper, forming a pool at her tiny feet.

She wasn't much bigger than a child, he thought as she lay down beside him. Her dusky-tipped breasts were little better than buds and protruded impudently from her chest. Her waist was so small he could almost span it with one of his large, callused hands. She wasn't as lovely or as sexy as Mrs. Cavanaugh, but what she lacked in size, she more than made up for in other areas. For she was all woman, and knew the feminine art of pleasing him.

Sliding a hand down the length of her back, Slade's mouth closed over hers so that he could savor the familiar flavor of her kiss. When his ardor began to increase, he pulled her closer, allowing his fingers to rest on the jutting bone of her hip while his thumb drew lazy circles into the hollow of her belly.

Lord but she was soft. And talented too, he was forced to admit when her tiny hands began their exploration of his hairy body, bringing him fully to life.

"Su-ling," he groaned. "Oh, Susie girl, you're so sweet."

Aroused to the point of no return, his lips left hers to nibble down the column of her slender neck, rolling her over and under him. He inhaled sharply when her hands closed over him, preparing to guide his aching need into her soothing warmth.

Chapter Three

THE DOOR CRASHED OPEN WITH A BANG, COMPLETELY shattering the tense, erotic moment. Su-ling shrieked in alarm and shoved Slade aside. Caught off balance and unprepared, he almost fell off the bed, but saved himself in time by throwing a foot down to the damp floor below.

"What the hell . . . !" he roared as his stunned gaze finally focused on the form of a Chinese man, silhouetted in the doorway.

"Oh, my word!" exclaimed the intruder in an unmistakable English accent.

"Who are—?" Slade started, hugging the sheet tightly to his bare loins. What a helluva predicament; being stark naked and having to fight for his life. But then the Chinese intruder stepped forward and Slade realized that the face beneath the black sailor's cap wasn't Oriental at all, although the dark trousers and coat implied it. "Mrs. Cavanaugh?"

"Captain Slade, this is *most* unforgivable," Raine proclaimed in a trembling voice. The sight of him naked and erect was off-putting to say the least. "You are supposed to be with your *ship*, not . . . not servicing this woman!"

"Mrs. Cavanaugh?" he repeated, still unable to believe it was really her in man's clothes. "What the hell are you doing in that getup?"

"I haven't time to explain. We must set sail immediately!"

"We *what?*" Jerking the sheet around his waist, he shot to his feet. "You want to go *now?* Right this minute? You couldn't wait ten or fifteen—? Dammit, now you listen here, lady, I—"

"Pay your consort, Captain, and let's go!"

"Like hell I will!" He looked back at Su-ling, who was crouched into a tight ball, her knees drawn protectively to her chest. "It's all right, Susie girl. Don't be scared. I know this . . . *woman.*" Then, glaring at Raine, he growled, "You make me wait for a whole damn week, then have the nerve to show up here, scaring the wits out of people and making demands? Well, I got news for you, lady, I'm a far cry from being ready to go!"

"You have to, Captain."

"No, I don't have to," he mocked bitterly. "This time, *you* can do the waiting. Ten minutes won't kill you."

"I said *pay* her, Captain, and get your clothes on," Raine snapped, unimpressed with his defensive challenge. "Or I will leave without you."

"That's the idea, lady. You got it. Now go!"

"All right." Her sudden calm was almost frightening. "We'll do it your way. I'll leave. I'm sure your first mate will be more than capable of handling your duties as captain." And with that, she turned and slammed out of the shanty.

Loosening the sheet, Slade turned with a relieved

35

sigh and started toward the bed. But he froze in his tracks a scant second later.

"Son of a bitch," he breathed, her parting words registering in his muddled brain. "Son of a bloody bitch! She'd really do it. She'd sail the *Mary Ellen* without me!"

Without a word of explanation to Su-ling, he pulled on his clothes more quickly than he ever thought possible and rushed out into the night after Mrs. Cavanaugh.

The rain, still drizzling, had turned the dirt path outside the shanty into a muddy course. But Slade was not deterred. Slipping as he ran, it took him a matter of moments to catch up with his quarry, intercepting her halfway to the dock.

"Now you listen to me, lady—"

"Oh, save your breath," she bit out without breaking her stride. She had probably half of the bobbies in Hong Kong after her and *he* wanted to give her a lecture. "I'm in no mood to listen to your dull-witted jibbering."

"You're in no mood! Who the hell do you think you are?"

"I am the person who hired you, Captain. *That's* who I am! I expect to receive that which I have paid for—not be forced to wait while you have a dalliance with your . . . your loose woman."

She turned the corner and stepped onto the dock, her steps faltering slightly when her mud-covered slippers slid across the boards.

"I didn't spend any of your precious money on Su-ling, lady," he growled, skidding up beside her. "I spent my own."

"I should hope so. But if that is supposed to assure me of your reliability, I can promise you it hasn't."

"I don't give a damn if it did or not. You chartered my ship—not me! I'm not for sale at any price, and I'll be damned if I'll throw aside my needs just to dance to your tune whenever you decide to whistle. I'm still the captain, remember."

"Then I wish to God you would behave like one."

"That does it!" Abruptly he stepped in front of her, halting her progress, and grabbed her arms. "Lady, the deal is off!"

"Oh, please!" she groaned impatiently. "We don't have time to stand here and quarrel."

"Yes, we do . . . because we're not going anywhere."

The horrible reality of his taunt finally hit her. "No!"

"Ah! That got your attention, didn't it?"

"You can't possibly mean to back out of our arrangement now. You—you can't!"

"Lady, I can do anything I damn well like."

"But, Captain, you . . ." She broke off lamely, her determination and control visibly crumbling. "You can't," she whimpered. Somehow, and quickly, she had to get him to change his mind. Her very life could be at stake! "My God, if you only knew what I've gone through—what I've done to get *this* far, you wouldn't do this to me now. Please believe me, I have *got* to leave Macao tonight!"

Apparently losing the last threads of her self-control, Raine began to sob pathetically.

Though he did his best to ignore her, Slade wasn't altogether unaffected by her reaction. He had anticipated another angry outburst, but he was totally unprepared for her pitiful-sounding tears. God in heaven, what should he do now? She was obviously at her wit's end and scared to death.

"All right, all right," he relented with a groan. "If you'll just stop that damn crying, we'll . . . we'll talk about it when we get to the ship."

Her sobbing stopped abruptly, her head snapping up as the tears still trickled down her dirty cheeks. "Couldn't we discuss it after we're out to sea?" she queried in an oddly calm voice.

Slade's eyes narrowed suspiciously. "Look, don't push your luck with me, lady. I'd just as soon forget I ever even met you, let alone take you aboard the *Mary Ellen* again. God only knows what you're up to, because I sure as hell don't. I've got an idea I'd be better off staying out of whatever it is."

"Captain," her voice wavered tremulously. "I will do anything . . . *anything* if you'll just please get me out of this country tonight."

Slade stood his ground for as long as he could, then with a low groan, gave up. "Jesus Christ, I gotta be crazy," he swore, stalking toward the ship, his grip on her arm tightening as he pulled her along after him. Momentary insanity was the only explanation he could think of that would account for his giving into her.

"Prepare to weigh anchor, Mr. Dennison!" he ordered the instant they stepped on board.

"Captain?" the mate returned with astonished surprise.

"You heard me, mister!"

"But, Captain, half the crew is still ashore."

Slade shot Raine a narrow, sidelong glance, her tear-streaked face visible in the lanternlight. Gritting his teeth, he growled, "We sail without them, mister. Now prepare to get underway."

"Aye-aye, sir."

"You," he snarled at Raine, "get below to *my* cabin and stay there. I'm not through with you by a long shot!"

Raine stood at the porthole, her arms wrapped protectively about her waist. Macao was slowly disappearing into the distance, fading away into nothingness in the heavy mist. Thank God, they were finally away from that place.

Knowing she should feel safe now, more secure, she didn't. After what had happened tonight in von Koenig's villa above Hong Kong, she seriously wondered if she would ever feel completely safe again. Well, maybe when she joined Rory in San Francisco.

Rory. Dear, wise, understanding Rory.

Why hadn't she listened to him? Why hadn't she heeded her big brother's well-intended warning instead of trusting her own silly, naive heart? If she had, perhaps none of this would have happened.

God, what a fool she had been. Wanting so desperately to be something she was not, she had believed every one of Roger's weak promises. But where she had so innocently believed, Rory had doubted, had openly questioned her young lover's true motives. Somehow—through his intuition perhaps?—he had sensed what the truth was and had told her of his suspicions. But she hadn't listened to him, much to her everlasting regret.

A vision flashed before her and she shuddered uncontrollably. If she lived to be a hundred, she would never be able to erase the horror she'd left behind in Hong Kong. It was still so very clear—the blood and the flames that seemed to lick out from the overturned lamp, devouring everything in its path. But her retaliation had been necessary, she told herself. All of her carefully made plans would have literally gone up in smoke like the villa if she hadn't struck out at Roger.

Knowing she should rid her mind of these unpleasant thoughts, Raine turned only to catch a glimpse of her reflection in the mirror atop the sea chest. A mirthless laugh bubbled through her parted lips, stopping before it could become a full-blown hysterical cry.

She looked awful! Surely that wasn't her face, staring back at her. No, it was merely the mask of the character she'd created for tonight's performance. The mask of a poor, pathetic little clown with great tormented eyes and a dirty, rain-streaked face.

No more! she vowed, reaching for nearby water cask and bowl. No more wearing masks! No more costumes! No more acting out the parts of characters so that she wouldn't be recognized. From now on, with God's help, she would be no one but herself— Raine Sheridan!

She was busy scrubbing away the last of the grimy makeup when Slade entered. His reflection in the mirror told her that he was as tired as she felt. Why hadn't she seen it before? As she did, he too wore a mask to hide his vulnerability.

"We're out to sea," he stated curtly, moving across the cabin to drop wearily into his chair.

"Yes," she acknowledged, drying her face.

"Is that all you've got to say, lady?" He snorted with disgust and shook his head. "Hell, I've just left more than half my crew behind, I'm sailing into God knows what kind of weather, and all you can say is 'yes'?"

"What else do you expect me to say, Captain?"

"I want to know *why*, dammit! You've got me where you want me, now I demand a few explanations. I deserve that much after all you've put me through."

"Ah," she breathed on a sigh, crossing to his bunk and lightly dropping onto it. "Explanations. I wouldn't know where to begin."

"Try the beginning," he muttered through clenched teeth. "That's usually the best place to start."

"All right." She inhaled deeply and began, "Twenty-two years ago, I was born—"

"Goddammit! I don't mean that far back and you know it! Now either you start giving me some straight answers, or I'll kick your larcenous little tail off this ship so fast, it'll make your head swim."

"Larcenous? You're still obsessed with the notion that I'm involved in something illegal. But I'm not, Captain. I never have been."

"I don't believe a word of it, lady."

"Nevertheless, it's the truth."

"Then why all the secrecy? If you weren't up to something shady and underhanded, why did you

41

wait till the last minute before letting me know you were ready to sail?"

"I didn't have any other alternative. To tell you the truth, I didn't know myself until this morning that we could be leaving China tonight. I wanted to send word to you—really I did!—but too many other factors were involved and I decided I couldn't take the risk."

"Risk, huh? Just what kind of risk are you talking about?"

Raine gave him a long, measured look, her full lips compressed into a tight, thoughtful line, then she rose slowly to her feet. "Come with me, Captain. I have something I want to show you."

She was already halfway out the door when he decided to follow her. And when he next joined her, she was standing before her cabin door, her hand resting lightly on the latch.

"Please, you will be quiet, won't you?" she whispered. "He's had an extremely trying night, and I don't want him disturbed."

"Him?" Slade demanded.

"Captain, please. I swear, all of your questions will be answered in due time." The promise made, she entered the small cabin and crossed to her bed.

"Good God in Heaven!" Slade muttered, both amazed and frightened at what he saw laying there. "You stole a *kid?*"

"No, I didn't steal him. And he's not a kid," she pointed out patiently, dropping down beside the sleeping baby. "He's my son."

"*Yours?*"

"Yes, mine." Her long fingers wove lovingly through the baby's pale touseled curls, a sweet, maternal smile curving the corners of her lips. "My little boy."

"But you said you were divorced."

"I am. I have been for quite some time, but that doesn't make him any less my son, does it? After all, *I* nurtured him inside my body for nine months. *I* gave birth to him." A brief pause followed as a flicker of pain crossed her face. "And *I* had to stand by while my former husband was allowed to take him from me when the courts proclaimed me unsuitably fit to be his mother."

Her voice trembled with the emotion she was unable to hide. When she turned and looked up at Slade, there were angry tears shining in her eyes. "Oh, I didn't give him up willingly, Captain, if that's what you're thinking. God knows, I fought them with everything I possessed, but what I had just wasn't good enough. Roger, my husband, was much stronger than I. He had very important connections, you see, in very high places. He had our marriage— and I use the word very loosely—he had it annulled within a matter of weeks after he learned I was expecting his child."

"But I thought an annulment wasn't allowed if the marriage had been consummated." His gaze shifted deliberately toward the baby.

"Oh, yes, I know. Adam's existence alone is proof enough to anyone that we did indeed consummate the marriage, but that wasn't the reason behind our annulment. Roger produced a stranger with a document which declared me married to another. I was made to appear a bigamist and he was awarded custody of the baby.

"Roger never wanted me for his wife. He didn't want *any* woman," she whispered bitterly. "He only wanted a healthy female receptacle in which to breed his child. Too late, I learned that his constant companion, von Koenig, provided many things for him, but an heir wasn't one of them."

Slade's look of disgust assured her that he understood the sordid explanation which she chose to leave unsaid.

"I began to plan the moment they left my apartment with my son," she continued, looking down at the baby. "I began plotting and scheming how to get him back. I wasn't going to allow the two of them to raise my child. Adam might become as twisted as they were if I did. You do see that, don't you?" She pleaded and received Slade's understanding nod.

"When I learned that they'd hired a nanny and had left London, I followed them here, a half a world away from any help I might have been able to find. I discovered that they'd set up house in a villa overlooking Hong Kong, and with a lot more time and a good deal of patience on my part, I soon made friends with members of their household staff . . . Adam's nanny in particular. The moment I knew she trusted me and that I was in her confidence, I began looking for a way out for us.

"That's where you and your ship came in, Captain. You were far enough away from all the activity Roger and von Koenig were involved with in Hong

Kong, yet close enough for my hasty departure to be convenient.

"Tonight, when I was assured that Roger and von Koenig would be out for the evening, I paid a call on my friend, Adam's nanny. I slipped a sleeping draught into her cup of tea when she wasn't looking and then tried to get my son out of the house."

"Something tells me you didn't make it," Slade observed huskily, his emotions caught up with her tale. He, too, had a son.

"They came back early," she confessed on a painful whisper. "I had Adam in my arms and a small case filled with his clothes. I was coming down the stairs when they walked in. Dear God, for a moment I just stood there, not knowing what I should do, or what they would do to me. Then Roger lunged toward me and I . . . I did the first thing I could think of. I kicked him as hard as I could in the stomach. He rolled down the stairs and knocked over an oil lamp, setting the villa ablaze. The last I saw of him, von Koenig was bending over him in that blazing room.

"I—I killed my husband to save my child, Captain Slade. I didn't plan or mean to do it, believe me! But I did it nevertheless. And I'm not in the least bit sorry for what happened. I'd do it again if I had to."

Toward the end of her impassioned speech, Adam stirred. With a soft grunt, he rolled over onto his belly, his round bottom arched into the air as his chubby thumb found its way home into his rosebud mouth.

Raine dropped a loving kiss on her son's damp

cheek before reluctantly leaving the bed. Without looking at Slade, she started back to his cabin across the passageway. The weighty burden she'd been carrying for so long was now gone from her shoulders.

At last the truth was out. But at what price, she wondered, reentering Slade's cabin. He was a father himself. Maybe he understood her plight. Then again, maybe he didn't.

Dearest Lord, why must she always be at the mercy of some man? Why couldn't she, for once in her life, be in total control of her own destiny?

With a frustrated groan, she ran a hand over her forehead, her fingers encountering the cuff of her black knit sailor's cap. With all that had happened, she'd forgotten it was still on her head. Amused at her own forgetfulness, she quickly pulled it off, releasing her long hair from its tightly drawn-back coil.

It was this vision which greeted Slade when he entered his cabin a scant second behind her. Her waist-long, honey blond hair was such an unexpected surprise, Slade could do nothing but stand there and admire it. It was the most beautiful shade of blond he'd ever seen. Pale honey strands mingled with even paler silvery locks from the crown of her head to the curve of her hips where it ended. He longed, for some reason, to reach out and touch it, caress it, feel its silky texture fall through his fingers. It didn't seem possible that this slender, ethereal, fragile lady was the icy, regal woman he'd first met.

"So that's why you didn't look right," he murmured almost introspectively. He'd thought her hair was at odds with her features. Now he knew he was right.

"I beg your pardon?" She turned in confusion.

"Nothing," he grumbled, reerecting his defenses. "You got anymore secrets you're keeping from me, Mrs. Cavanaugh?"

"No, Captain. No more secrets. My son, Adam, was it, I'm glad to say. Oh, there is one other unimportant thing I think you should know, though."

"I can't wait to hear what it is." He strolled toward his desk and lit a cigar.

"I'm not Mrs. Cavanaugh."

"Well now," he snorted through the smoke. "Just who are you?"

"My real name is Sheridan. Raine Sheridan."

"Raine, huh?" It was a strange name, but it suited her. Sort of special and unique, like the lady herself. "Well, Raine Sheridan, it's getting late and I'm worn out. If you've got any more little secrets up your sleeve you can save them until tomorrow. Maybe I can handle them better after I've had a good night's sleep."

"Captain!" she demanded sharply, refusing to be dismissed so offhandedly when so much still hung in the balance.

"What is it now?" he groaned.

"I have to know what you're going to do."

His expression twisted with speculation. "Well, I was going to bed . . . alone. But if you've got a better idea—"

"No! I didn't mean *that*." The truth she'd given him was a powerful weapon. He could turn around

47

and take her back to Macao if he wanted. "I want to know what you intend doing with me and my son."

"Oh. That." Shrugging the suspenders off his broad shoulders, he slowly walked toward her. "I'll have to give it some thought."

She stood there under his disturbing study, realizing that he was toying with her, much like a cat toyed with a helpless bird just before the kill. Lifting her chin defiantly, she turned and started toward the door. "Well, you will let me know when you've reached a decision, won't you?" she snapped.

"Maybe," he admitted with a wry grin. "We'll see. Oh, uh, close the door behind you on your way out."

Raine did more than close it. She slammed it as hard as she could.

Chapter Four

GERHARDT VON KOENIG STOOD IN THE DOORWAY OF
his once elegant drawing room and muttered a
disgusted oath at what he saw there. It looked
horrible, not at all like the room he'd designed so
carefully. Worse still, it smelled abominably. The
carpet beneath his feet was half burned away, its
once sharp-colored fibers now blackened and ruined
beyond repair. The entire room was saturated with
water as well. What the fire hadn't destroyed, the
water had.

God, what a mess Roger's little creature had
wrought, he thought. Who would have thought the
little trollop had had it in her? Not he! And certainly
not Roger.

Hearing footsteps in the hallway behind him, he
turned just as Roger descended the stairs. The
younger man's clothes were spotted with blood and
about his head was a bandage, covering the wound
he'd received when Raine had kicked him down the
stairs.

"I've got Nanny Simpkins calmed down," Roger
professed wearily. "She's agreed to leave in the
morning."

"Good. How's your head?" Gerhardt lifted a hand to touch the sloppily wrapped bandage.

"It'll be all right." Frowning, Roger managed to dodge the German's touch.

"Just look at this room, will you?" Waving a hand at the rubble, Gerhardt shuddered. "Why, we'll never be able to replace the Aubusson."

"My God, Hardy!" Roger's sudden oath surprised the other man. "My son has just been stolen out from under my nose, and *you're* concerned about the goddam rug!"

Gerhardt placed a consoling hand on the younger man's broad shoulder. "We'll get the boy back—it's just a matter of time. That little nobody couldn't have gotten very far with him, not at this time of night. Chances are she's holed up somewhere down the mountain, waiting for a ship to take her back to London. Unimaginative women like her are so easy to predict."

Roger merely grunted, neither agreeing nor disagreeing with Gerhardt's supposition. He ran a hand through his dark blond hair, his fingers gingerly touching the small bump on his scalp.

"She's more imaginative than either of us gave her credit," he murmured. "I never thought this would happen when we . . . when *I* tricked her. God, if I *had* known, I'd have taken suitable precautions."

"We did our best," Gerhardt assured him.

"Did we?" Roger was only now seeing the error in his folly of bringing an innocent girl into their sordid scheme and hurting her as he'd done. The damnable irony of it was, he'd actually loved her for a while. Hardy didn't know that, of course, and probably never would. Raine had been the only girl he'd ever known who had made him laugh, who had given to him freely without asking for something in return as other women had always done. She had loved him, too—he was sure of it. But he had hurt her beyond belief by divorcing her and taking their child. Now, God help him, she was extracting her revenge.

"One thing is certain," Roger said, putting aside his guilty thoughts, "I'm going to get my son back."

"Of course you will, and I'll help," Gerhardt responded. "We certainly didn't go to all that trouble and embarrassment just to have a little nobody of a slut foil our plans."

At this Roger chose to remain silent, but inwardly he castigated Hardy for his use of the word "slut." She hadn't been a slut when he married her. She had been an innocent blossom ripe for the plucking, and he'd been the one to deflower her. There were times, like now, when his shame over what he'd done to her almost overwhelmed him.

"I know just the man who will find her for us," Gerhardt informed him with a confident nod.

"Who would that be?"

"Wu Chi."

"Oh, for God's sake, Hardy! I only want my son back. I don't want anyone murdered!"

"I know, but it might actually come to that. If she's gone to this much trouble once, she's likely to do it again. And frankly, I would prefer to have her out of our way for good rather than run the risk of repeating tonight's fiasco. We simply cannot afford the notoriety. If your cousins ever got wind of this and challenged old Percy's will . . ."

Hardy was a master at planting thoughts and leaving them to germinate on their own. But Roger knew what he meant without having to be shown a detailed diagram. He'd gotten his title and inheritance only by the skin of his teeth, and if any doubts were raised, he could lose them just as easily.

"You might be right," he admitted grudgingly, one hand rubbing his aching forehead. "But I still don't like the idea. If it's at all possible, I do not want Raine harmed. Is that clear? And I don't want little Percival hurt either! God, I still remember the last time you involved Wu in one of your schemes. The little maniac nearly murdered three innocent people. He's a sadist of the first order."

"I'll agree that he's somewhat unpredictable, but he does do what he's told. You can't deny that."

"No, I can't."

Gerhardt smiled at the younger man. "Whatever you wish. We can't do anything more tonight. Why don't we go to bed?"

"I don't think I'd be able to sleep," Roger murmured, the vision of his precious little son coming to his mind. He hadn't thought it was possible to love someone as he loved his son. He loved him more, perhaps, than he loved Hardy, whom he'd always adored.

Gerhardt chuckled. "I wasn't thinking about sleep."

With a resigned sigh, Roger followed Gerhardt up the stairs, his mind still preoccupied with what had happened. "She even took time to pack his clothes, Hardy. If she hadn't done that, she would have been gone long before we returned."

Gerhardt's smile slowly faded as they reached the landing at the top of the stairs. "What did she pack Percy's things in?"

"His leather valise," Roger replied. "What else? It was the only thing in the nursery large enough to hold all his things."

Gerhardt's face turned a sickly ashen shade. "Oh, my God!"

"What's the matter?" Roger frowned in concern.

"She has the Hindu collection!" the German gritted out angrily.

"The *Hindu—?* What was it doing in my son's valise, Hardy? It was supposed to be safely locked away in your office!"

"I know it was, but I—I moved it," Gerhardt confessed lamely. "Now, don't look at me that way. I moved it to the nursery because I thought it would be safer there. After all, it's the last place anyone would ever think of looking."

"You fool!"

"Now, Roger, don't—"

"You stupid, stupid fool! That collection is worth a fortune."

"I know, Roger," Gerhardt declared sarcastically. "I'm the one who stole it in the first place, remember?"

"Yes, against my better judgment. Well, that settles *one* thing. We can't hire Wu! He'd kill Percival, Raine and anyone else, then steal the collection for himself. *We'll* go after them ourselves. How could you have been so stupid, Hardy? It would have been more safe tucked under your bloody mattress."

"Come, come now," Gerhardt sneered. "You're not exactly a paragon of intelligence yourself. After all, *you* made the mistake of choosing that little actress for the mother of your son and look where that's got you."

Silently seething at one another, both men wandered down the hall to the bedroom.

Chapter Five

THE MORNING SUN BEAT DOWN UPON SLADE'S BACK AS he leaned over the bowsprit, checking the jib. By the looks of it, the day was going to be a scorcher. Sweat trickled down his neck and he ran a hand inside his shirt collar to wipe the moisture away. Straightening to ease the kink in his back, he removed his hat and mopped his forehead. It was then that he glanced back at the stern and saw someone appear in the quarterdeck hatchway. It took him a quick, second look before he finally realized it was Raine.

He'd told her to save her other surprises until he could handle them, but he hadn't expected her to take him so literally. She looked an altogether different woman this morning from the bedraggled, dirty-faced urchin he'd brought aboard last night. In fact, the only thing that remotely resembled the old, short-lived Mrs. Cavanaugh was her pale blond hair, now coiled into a regal-looking knot atop her lovely head. Gone was her flat, shapeless figure encased in baggy Oriental clothing, and in their place was a simple blue skirt and white blouse which more effectively enhanced her well-endowed curves. Just looking at her now caused his imagination to run wild as his lusts began to consume him.

A quiet whistle of admiration escaped his lips. Her husband must've been crazy not to have loved her. Any man worth his salt would have.

Slade put an abrupt halt to his thoughts and cautiously glanced around to see if his crew had been watching him. Once assured he hadn't been observed, he relaxed. What the hell was he doing? Thinking about her and . . . and love?

"Watch yourself," he warned himself. "Cool down and get your mind off *that* little lady right now."

A strong gust of wind whipped through the air. Overhead, the huge canvas sheets filled completely, billowing out like tightly harnessed clouds. The same gust of wind caught Raine's shirt and blouse, flattening them to her body as she looked up, smiling. There was something truly majestic about sailing, she decided. Something just short of awe-inspiring.

"Morning, Miss Sheridan."

Raine turned, spying the first mate behind the helm. "Good morning, Mr. Dennison. Which way are we headed?"

"Southeastwardly, ma'am. Toward Luzon."

Luzon! The northernmost island in the Philippines. The smile on her lips reflected her inner pleasure as she told herself that anywhere they were headed was by far better than Hong Kong had been.

She was about to ask the mate how long the voyage to Luzon would be when Davey came up behind her and greeted her with a pleasant "good morning." His good mood was so infectious, she could not restrain herself from returning his smile.

"You're awfully chipper this morning, I must say," she observed.

"Yes, ma'am, I guess I am."

"It must be all this marvelous sea air. I find it quite exhilarating. But I don't think my companion, Miss Carlisle, is too pleased with it. She was looking a bit under the weather when I peeked in on her a moment ago."

"She's probably just seasick. Some people get that way at first."

"Yes," Raine agreed. "Poor thing. She was positively pea-green. I just hope Adam doesn't take ill, too." Goodness, if both Hetty and Adam came down with *mal de mar*, she would really have her hands full.

"Adam?" Davey queried.

"Yes, my—" Raine broke off her reply as she realized that Davey didn't know about her son. He had been asleep the night before when she had brought the baby aboard. "That's right, you didn't see him last night, did you? Would you like to meet my son now?"

"I guess so." The boy shrugged.

Davey followed her back inside the quarterdeck and on into her cabin, where she found her son just awakening. Sleepy blue eyes swung around, blinking at her in momentary confusion before his bottom lip thrust forward and his face screwed up into a dissatisfied pout.

"There, there, darling," she cooed, hurrying over

to scoop him up in her arms. He was confused and frightened because there was no one around him that he recognized. "Mummy's here now."

"It's a baby!" Davey observed with surprise as he came further into the cabin.

"Yes. I'll bet you were expecting someone older, weren't you?"

"Well, yeah." The boy grinned lopsidedly, blushing. "He sure is cute. You said his name was Adam?"

"Mmm-hmm." She nodded, holding her son fiercely.

"How old is he?"

"About eight and a half months."

"Gosh! I wonder if I was this little when I was his age?"

"You might have been." Turning, she began to search through one of the many bags she'd not yet unpacked and found a dry diaper for her soggy son. "Why don't you ask—"

"Davey." The deep voice boomed from the doorway. "You shouldn't be in here, son. You've still got duties topside."

Slade's curt remark caught them both by surprise. But it was Raine who noticed the stern set of his jaw. "Oh, Captain Slade, I hope I haven't done anything wrong. I merely thought David might want to see the baby."

"There'll be plenty of time for that later," he informed her, guiding his son toward the door. "You finish your chores first, though."

"Yes, sir," Davey replied respectfully before disappearing.

"Please, don't be too hard on him. It was all my fault," Raine stressed, trying to wrestle her wriggling son, the uncooperative diaper and the roll of the ship all at once. "If I'd known—"

"Here!" Slade interjected. "What are you trying to do to that boy? Blindfold him?"

"No, I'm changing his nappy!"

"Well, you're going at it the wrong way." Slade whipped the diaper out of her hand, shaking his head impatiently. "Don't you even know how to change a kid?"

"No, I don't, Captain. I was never given the privilege to learn."

Slade's experienced fingers faltered for a moment when he recalled the story she'd told him last night. Darting a sidelong glance at her, he noted her somber expression and knew a moment of thorough shame at his cruel jibe. Without a word, he slowly finished his task.

"There," he sighed at last, standing back to admire his handiwork. "That's how it's done. Think you can remember how I did it? You see, this way it won't fall off when you pick him up." As if to prove his point, he lifted Adam off the bunk and gently tossed him in the air before hauling him close to his chest. "He's a damn good looking boy. Yeah! You sure are, little one."

The act, so innocently performed, expressed a wealth of affection. Raine was surprised by the knot of emotion which formed in her throat. It was absurd to even think it, but he looked so right, so perfectly at ease holding her son, it was almost as if he were Adam's natural father instead of—

Realizing too late where the conclusion of her thought lay, she stiffened and tried to put it from her mind. It was an insane notion to say the least. Slade wasn't Adam's father, and never would be.

"He favors you, you know," Slade observed, shifting the baby toward her.

"Do you think so?" Raine took her son and smiled, pleased with his compliment.

But Adam's delighted chuckles died when he found himself thrust into his mother's arms. His little fingers maintained a stubborn hold on Slade, pulling at his beard painfully.

"Now, now!" Slade cried. "We can't have that." With the tiny digits pried loose, he rubbed his chin.

"Oh, did he hurt you?" she gasped, reaching up to touch his cheek. The warmth of Slade's skin against her fingertips had the effect of a red-hot iron and she quickly jerked her hand away as if she'd been scorched.

"I'll be all right," he assured her with a strange, half-amused grin. "It's not the first time I've had my whiskers pulled. Davey did it all the time when he was this age." He gave Adam's bottom an affectionate pat then turned toward the door. "You just remember to fold his diaper the way I showed you the next time you go to change him. After a couple of times, you'll be an expert like me."

"It's strange," she murmured. "Even though I saw you, I can't believe that *you*, of all people, can do something as . . . as ordinary as change a nappy."

"Yeah, well, I can." He chuckled. "And have done more times than I care to remember."

"But of course Davey's mother helped too, didn't she?"

Slade's smile vanished in a flash, a cold, brooding look replacing it. "Davey's mother hasn't had a thing to do with him since the day he was born, Miss Sheridan. I raised him alone."

"I—I'm sorry," she stammered. "I didn't know. I just assumed that your wife had recently died and—"

"You can stop right there, lady. I've never been married and probably never will be. But Davey's still *my* son; that much I'm sure of."

"I never doubted it for a moment, Captain," she returned gently. "There's a remarkable likeness between the two of you, even though his features are somewhat Oriental. Is his mother Chinese?"

With a brisk, negative shake of his head, Slade replied, "Filipino."

"He's a very fine boy. You should be proud of him."

"I am." His pride replaced his previous bitterness. "I'm very proud of him."

Adam suddenly stiffened in Raine's arms and let out an angry, bloodcurdling yelp.

"Oh, my word!" she exclaimed, flinching at the sound. "What on earth is the matter with him?"

"He's probably hungry."

"Hungry? Oh, the goats! Where are they? I'll bet they haven't been milked yet, have they?"

"That's" what the goats are for. I wondered."

"You didn't leave them behind. Oh, please say you didn't do that! I don't know what I'll do if—"

"Rest easy, lady. They're down in the hold."

"But they shouldn't be down there," she protested over Adam's loud, persistent cries. "They should be up on deck in the fresh air."

"This is a ship, woman, not a barnyard! I can't let live animals loose on deck."

"But, Captain—"

"Oh, hell!" he spat, stalking out of the cabin. "Cookie!"

"Captain Slade!" Persevering, she followed him. "I really must protest—"

"Aye, Captain?" A short, stocky man piped up.

"Go milk a goat for this hungry kid!"

"Milk a goat?" the bandy-legged cook queried.

"If they don't have adequate sunshine and proper food and water," Raine persisted, "how can they possibly produce milk?"

"Did you say . . . milk a *goat,* sir?" the cook asked again.

"Yes, dammit! Are you deaf?"

"No, sir."

"Then go milk one!"

"Aye-aye, sir." Obviously confused, Cookie scratched his head and wandered off, leaving Raine to deal with the irritated Slade.

"Well, how can they?" she repeated once again.

"What?" Slade whirled around and glared down at her. "What are you yammering about, lady? They're animals, not plants!"

"They still need sunshine."

"Not aboard my ship, they don't."

"Then they'll die, and what will Adam do for food?"

"He's got teeth," Slade asserted, looking into the squalling baby's open mouth. "Let him eat bully beef like the rest of us."

"You're being quite unreasonable, Captain!"

"And you're starting to get on my nerves, lady!"

For a moment, they both stood there, glaring at each other, and neither of them willing to back down. Blue eyes clashed with green and then he hauled her toward him and kissed her soundly before muttering a fertile obscenity as he turned and stalked away.

"Women!" he spat when he reached the solitude of the bridge.

"Did you say something, Captain?" Mr. Dennison inquired behind him.

"What?" he snapped, whirling around to stare at the mate. "No! Just go on with what you were doing, and leave me the hell alone."

"I'm really surprised that Yang didn't see to the goats this morning," Hetty remarked after Cookie brought a warm cup of milk to their quarters. "He was supposed to milk them first thing, you know."

"Did he ever make it aboard last night?" Raine asked. "I haven't seen him around."

"You don't suppose . . ." Hetty began, then shook her iron-gray head. "Oh, no. Yang wouldn't do that."

"Do what?"

"Stay behind," Hetty declared reluctantly. "He was behaving frightfully nervous after we brought the animals aboard. Kept babbling away in that awful dialect of his, and you know I can't understand a single syllable of it. I wonder if he was trying to tell me he wouldn't be coming with us?"

Raine was much too busy filling a bottle for Adam's eager mouth to give the possibility much thought. If Yang wasn't aboard, then he wasn't aboard! It was as simple as that. All the guessing in the world wouldn't change it, either.

Latching onto the bottle with both hands, Adam began to gulp and smack contentedly. Raine smiled and released a long, pleased breath. At last he was quiet, poor darling.

"You know, dear, we really must see to all this unpacking."

"Not now, Hetty. We have months to settle in."

"Months!" the older woman groaned. "Oh, Lord! I'm not sure I can stand it."

"You'll get used to it. After all, you aren't as sick now as you were this morning."

"Well, no, but—"

"You see? I imagine that by tomorrow you'll be even better. We'll just take things a little easy at first and enjoy ourselves.

"Er, Hetty," Raine continued after a slight pause. "Do you know anything about milking goats?"

"Good heavens, no! Whatever possessed you to ask *me* such a thing?"

"Well, one of us is going to have to learn now that Yang is no longer with us."

"That's right," Hetty groaned. "They do need milking daily, don't they? Well, I shall be more than happy to *feed* the hideous little buggers if—"

"Hetty! Do watch your tongue. There are children aboard, remember."

"Me! Watch *my* tongue? Dearest Raine, have you heard that deplorable American? My word, if anyone should guard his tongue, it's him! I haven't heard such colorful, original epithets since . . . well, since Penelope Hampton put lard into Fiona Markhurst's tights backstage at the Drury Lane." A delighted giggle bubbled forth at the remark. "Such a foul mouth that woman had! And poor Penelope did it only because we dared her to. We were such reckless hoydens in those days. But you know, the truly surprising thing is, Fiona went on to marry that younger son, who eventually became the Earl of Oxfordshire, I think it was, and poor old Penny ended up with a broken leg."

Wondering what one thing had to do with the other, Raine merely smiled. Hetty, God bless her, could go for hours at a stretch, recalling little anecdotes which had happened to her during her old board-trodding days. Having already heard most, if not all, of the stories before, she turned her full attention to Adam, who was still busily gulping down the contents of his bottle.

She and Hetty would have to establish some sort of daily routine to follow soon, so that Captain Slade and his crew would not be bothered again. Unpleasant incidents, like the one over the goats this morning, could not be repeated. As strange as it was for her to admit, Slade's anger had somehow ignited her own until they were snapping at each other like quarrelsome children.

In her mind, she could clearly see the angry set of Slade's generous mouth, the flare of his nostrils above his mustache and the narrowing of his devastating green eyes. Lord, but his eyes were deadly! They had seemed to thrust straight through her when he glared at her, penetrating down to the very core of her soul until her blood began to heat to an incandescent glow. And his kiss! Even now, just thinking about it, her palms were growing moist, her pulses were fluttering wildly and her breathing was quite erratic.

What in heaven's name was the matter with her? She shouldn't be behaving like this. She had better stop it and get control of herself. He was nothing to her and never would be, because he was only a means to an end. So it would be better for her and everyone concerned if she put him out of her mind and forgot him.

Occupying her hands and her time with the many chores of unpacking and caring for Adam, Raine did try. Oh, how she tried! But always, in the back of her thoughts, was the memory of Slade and the feel of his mouth on hers. He had already insinuated himself into her mind and would not be dismissed.

Chapter Six

THE *MARY ELLEN*'S DECKS WERE ALIVE WITH ACTIVITY.
Crewmen were busy either lowering the enormous
canvas sails or completing the multitude of orders
which Slade barked out to them in rapid-fire succession. Speed and efficiency were of the essence,
because in a short time they would be dropping
anchor in the port of Manila, the capitol of the
Philippines.

Safely belowdecks with Hetty, Raine sorted
through the last of the unpacked bags as she began to
reflect back over the last two days. Thank heaven,
she'd only chanced upon Slade once since their
heated disagreement over the goats, but that en-
counter had been a most disquieting one to say the
least. Try as she had, she still could not erase the
incident from her mind.

The seas had been rather rough, she recalled, not
glassy smooth as they had been their first day out.
She had intended going topside alone for a breath of
air when she met Slade in the passageway outside
her cabin. Without realizing it, she found herself
sandwiched between his awesome body and the wall

behind her. The ship had rolled suddenly, making matters worse by throwing Slade against her. He had tried to brace himself, bending his parted knees and pressing his hands upon the wall on either side of her, so as not to crush her with his weight, but the move had brought them even more closer together rather than keeping them apart.

Raine had found herself unable to breathe normally, let alone utter a disapproving rebuke. A surge of heat had shot through her, leaving her legs curiously weak. And for a moment, she thought she might end up in a spineless heap on the deck below them if he hadn't been there to support her. In those few moments, with his body so near hers, she had felt the tumultuous thudding of his heart against her breastbone and had been overpowered by the tangy fragrance of his sun-washed skin. She had known by the expression in his hooded green eyes that he was as disturbed as she by the experience.

All too soon, to her dismay, the ship leveled out. They parted, somewhat reluctantly she now had to admit. Each had gone their own separate way and had remained silent about what had happened.

Feeling a shudder ripple through her at the memory, Raine tried again to put the incident out of her mind. It wouldn't do for her to dwell on it, she knew, reaching for Adam's valise and opening it. It wouldn't do at all!

She carefully removed a few of her son's small garments and placed them beside her on the deck where she knelt. "What on earth . . . !" she exclaimed, when she encountered a hard, unfamiliar object at the bottom of the bag. She sat back on her heels and removed an ornately carved box, holding it high for inspection. "Hetty, take a look at this."

"Oh!" the older woman cried delightedly, then in a softer voice so as not to awaken the sleeping baby, she continued, "How lovely! Where ever did you buy it, Raine?"

"I didn't. I just found it here in Adam's bag. Odd, I don't recall putting it there." Reflecting back, she remembered grabbing up his things and tossing them into the valise, but the box hadn't been among them.

"Well, perhaps you didn't, dear. Perhaps it was already there," Hetty speculated, reaching for the box. "We've all left things in our bags and forgotten about them."

"Mmm," Raine conceded, relinquishing the box to Hetty. Roger or Adam's nanny could have left the box in the valise. Shrugging, she turned back to her current chore.

Imagining that she held a music box, Hetty pursed her thin lips into a *moue* as she admired the many delicate carvings. Her fingers searched for and found the latch that opened the lid. But lovely music didn't fill the air; her softly indrawn breath did.

"Raine?"

"Yes, what is—?" Raine pivoted and froze at the sight of the three jewel-encrusted golden statues nestled in the box's crimson velvet bed. Her violet eyes widened as her lower jaw dropped. "My God! Are they real?"

"I don't know. I—I don't think I *care* to know," Hetty professed with alarm. "Here, take them back!"

Raine took the box and carefully lifted the first

statue out, discovering immediately how incredibly heavy it was for such a small object.

"They *are* real! They must be solid gold."

"Well, I don't care if they're real or not, put them away! I'm a good Christian woman, not some uncivilized heathen, but I know a blasphemous idol when I see one!"

"Oh, for heaven's sake, Hetty. Do calm yourself. This little thing couldn't possibly hurt you."

"It couldn't?" Hetty stressed dubiously.

"No! Well . . ." Raine reconsidered thoughtfully, "if you dropped it on your bare foot, I suppose it could break your toe."

Still, Hetty's fear was not relieved. "What do you suppose they are?"

"You mean, you don't recognize them?"

"No! I certainly do not!"

"They're the Hindu Trinity," Raine explained, placing the statue back where she'd found it. "This one is Brahma, the Hindu god of creation." She pointed to the four-armed, four-faced figure. "This is Vishnu, the Hindu god of preservation." That statue also possessed four arms but only one face and one object in each tiny gold hand: a conch shell, a mace, a lotus blossom and a disc. "And this is Shiva, the Hindu god of destruction and reproduction. It's sort of a fertility god, I imagine." By far, it was the least offensive looking of the three, even though it represented something much more provocative.

"How do you know so much about them?" Hetty asked.

"Well, I've not converted to the faith, if that's

what you're thinking." Raine smiled. "I met a missionary's wife on the ship as we were coming out from London. She told me all about the Hindus and what she and her husband were up against in trying to convert them."

Hetty seemed to accept her explanation, but demanded, "What are you going to do with them?"

"Keep them. What else? I'm certainly not going to hurl them overboard," she declared, snapping the box lid closed. "Actually, if you stop and think about it, they're sort of a . . . a gift from the gods." She smiled wanly at her weak pun. "We couldn't have found them at a more propitious time."

"How do you arrive at that conclusion, dear?"

Raine paused, wondering what Hetty's reaction would be to her next remark, then decided to go ahead and jump in feet first. "I promised Captain Slade ten thousand American dollars if he takes us to San Francisco."

"Ten thousand!" Hetty squeaked. "Raine, dearest child, we don't have that much money. We never had! I was under the impression that he'd agreed to take us for the five hundred we possessed between us."

"No. Ten thousand."

"Oh, God! I think I'm going to faint," declared Hetty with a dramatic swoon.

"Don't do that. There's no need. We can pay Slade now that we've found these." Raine motioned to the gold-filled chest.

"You honestly expect that uncultured lout to accept those hideous figures as payment?"

"No, of course I don't. As soon as we dock in

71

Manila, I will go ashore and sell them. They're solid gold, remember. Surely someone there will want them for ten thousand—maybe even more!"

"Lord!" Hetty groaned with a desperate shake of her head. "But suppose you can't find a buyer? Worse than that, suppose that horrid American captain discovers we've deceived him and tosses us off the ship? We're *penniless*, child! We'll be stuck here forever and never see civilized London again."

"We're not totally penniless," Raine disclosed somberly, all previous animation gone from her face. "I still have the *parure* Roger gave me."

Hetty's melodramatic breast-beating stopped abruptly. "Your diamonds?"

Raine nodded. "I didn't sell them."

"But you must have! How else did you pay for our passage from London?" At the sight of her young companion's straight, unwavering stare, she moaned. "Oh, no, Raine. You didn't!"

Raine's pale golden head nodded slowly.

"Who?" Hetty demanded. "Who was it?"

"That elderly duke who wanted to court me before I agreed to marry Roger."

"That old lecher! The one who wanted to set you up as his mistress? Oh, how could you? With *him* of all people."

"Nothing happened! I merely had dinner with him. I certainly didn't go to *bed* with him."

"Well, thanks be for that!" the older woman sighed. "It's good to know that time has finally caught up with the old roue. He was *such* a notorious rake in his day. But, tell me, how did you get the money from him, if you didn't . . ."

"I told him my situation—of Roger's defection, I mean—and he instantly agreed to loan me the money. After the horrors Roger put me through . . ." Her voice trailed off as an uncontrollable shudder passed through her. Slowly she rose from the deck and joined Hetty on the bunk, glancing down at her sleeping son. "There are times, Hetty, when I seriously wonder if I'll ever be able to love a man again."

"In time you will," Hetty soothed solicitously.

"I have my son now. I don't think I'll ever need a man to complicate my life. I don't know if I even *want* one."

"Not now, of course not. You've been hurt and disillusioned by love, but in time you'll recover. You're the kind of woman who needs a man in her life."

Raine silently disagreed with Hetty. She knew that loving a man, *any* man, was a painful ordeal at best.

Manila was not unlike Macao in certain respects, yet it managed to maintain an atmosphere and personality uniquely its own. Where Macao was hilly and its harbor overcrowded, Manila lay like a long, flat crescent, wide open and sprawling for miles into the island.

To his good fortune, Slade found that he had no difficulty in hiring on the crewmen he needed. There was an abundance of sailors, seasoned and green alike, who were looking for work aboard any reputable ship. In this part of the world where piracy still existed and shanghaiing occurred almost regularly, any honest sea captain willing to sign on a crew rather than steal it was looked upon as something of a rarity and a god-send.

Slade ambled through the busy market area of Manila, not far from the harbor, when he had a sudden, unexplainable recollection of the first time he'd dropped anchor here. He had been a cocky lad of twenty-three at the time, serving as second mate aboard a merchant clipper out of Baltimore, Maryland, his hometown. He'd been so young and inexperienced then, he recalled with a chuckle. But he hadn't remained that way for long. Annalise had forced him to grow up fast.

"Quentin?" a soft, surprised voice called out behind him.

Not anticipating the shock he was about to receive, Slade turned and felt his feet suddenly freeze to the spot where he stood. It wasn't possible! Merely thinking about her couldn't bring her to life. Yet, there before him, looking not much older than the last time he'd seen her, stood the specter from his past.

"Annalise?"

"Madre de Dios!" was her soft cry as she closed the distance between them. Her lovely, heart-shaped face reflected her Filipino and Spanish heritage. There was pleasure and sadness in her voice as she said, "It *is* you, Quentin. I saw you from the shop window and thought it could be, so I rushed out to be sure."

"What are you doing here, Annalise?" he asked succinctly, his eyes darting about them. "Where's your husband?"

"He is not with me, Quentin. He is with his troops in the mountains."

"Still playing soldier, is he?"

"He is much more than a soldier. He is a general now." Her voice held no note of pride, merely a matter-of-fact resignation.

"A general, huh? Well then, I guess I'll say good-bye to you now. I sure as hell wouldn't want to get arrested for offending an officer's wife."

"No! Do not go!" she pleaded, placing a hand on his sleeve. "Do not leave yet, Quentin. I must speak to you . . . explain to you how it was."

"No, you don't," he bit out, ungraciously removing her hand. "I *know* how it was."

"How is David?" she asked quickly before he could turn and walk away. "How is . . . our son?"

"You mean *my* son, don't you? He hasn't been yours since the day you left him with those nuns. You wanted no part of him *or* me, remember? So why all the concern now?"

"It is only natural that I would worry about him, Quentin. He was my firstborn, after all. Is . . . is he here in Manila with you?"

Slade didn't answer. He continued to stand there, looking down at the woman who had broken his heart and deserted their child so many years ago. There was not a chance that he was going to give her the satisfaction of knowing their son had grown into a fine, healthy young man. After what she'd done, she didn't deserve to know.

Annalise's black almond eyes suddenly filled with tears and she lowered her head. "I am sorry, Quentin. Of course, you are right not to tell me. I only wanted to know how he is—that is all. It was never my intention to interfere with his life, but he . . . he was such a pretty little baby." Her delicate shoulders began to quake then as a sob tore through her.

Slade muttered an angry oath beneath his breath and dug into his pocket for a handkerchief. He thrust it into Annalise's unsuspecting hands then dragged her into a nearby tavern. Damn these crying women! They'd be the ruin of him yet.

"You want something to drink?" he asked when he'd found them a table in a quiet corner.

Annalise dabbed at her eyes and blinked at the seedy establishment's interior. "A—a glass of wine," she returned tremulously.

"They don't serve wine in places like this, Annalise. How about whiskey?"

"A small one then," she conceded with a nod.

Slade caught the tavernkeeper's attention and held up two fingers.

"I am sorry," Annalise apologized, pushing his handkerchief toward him. "I do not usually cry in public. I have been taught to contain my emotions."

"Yes," he grunted. "I remember."

"You know me so well, Quentin, yet you do not know me at all. I am not the same girl you knew fifteen years ago. I was only a child then."

"We both were," he agreed and motioned for her to be quiet when their drinks arrived.

"You won't be recognized here, will you?" he asked as soon as the tavernkeeper had walked away.

"No. It would not matter even if I were. My husband trusts me implicitly."

"And he's a general?" That didn't seem logical to

Slade. Most of the military men he'd met through the years trusted very few people.

"He . . . he knows about us—you and me. I told him when our first child was born. There was some difficulty, you see, and I felt I had to explain to him . . . about David. About how Mama and Papa took him from me and gave him to the nuns." Her expression held a wealth of appeal. "I had no say, Quentin, no choice. I had to give him up. I was betrothed to Sebastian long before I ever met you. Our families wanted the union and I had to comply. It would have brought much shame and disgrace upon them all if I had not."

"But to give up your own *son*, Annalise!" He could only think of how Raine had killed to get her son back, and yet Annalise had given theirs away without a qualm.

"Do not believe that I did not want him, Quentin. I did! He was *ours*, all that I had of you. But in my country, only the men are permitted to have . . . *bastardos*, not the women."

She paused, taking a deep breath, then continued when he refrained from responding. "I knew one of the good sisters at the orphanage. She would always bring David out into the garden for me to see when I could slip away from home. I would hold him and tell him what a wonderful, loving papa he had, then I would go back to my own papa and become the dutiful daughter I should have been.

"I thought I would die when I went to the orphanage and was told that you had come and taken David. I wept bitter tears when I learned how angry you had been, because I knew what you were thinking and that you would never forgive me. But I had no choice.

"If you had never returned, Quentin, I would have found a way to bring David into my own home after Sebastian and I married. I would have raised him as my son. You must believe me. I *loved* our son. How could I not?"

Slade was more than uncomfortable with her impassioned disclosure. All this time he'd thought she had willingly abandoned their son, put him out of her life as if he were nothing more than an embarrassment to be disposed of. Now that he knew differently, he could feel nothing but sympathy for this woman who'd meant so much to him in his youth. There was no more anger, though, no more resentment or hatred to harbor against her and cloud his memory . . . only sympathy.

Recalling something she'd said earlier, he murmured, "You said you had other children. How many?"

"I have six," she replied, her smile returning faintly. "Four sons and two daughters."

Good Lord! Davey had brothers and sisters he knew nothing about. It was then that Slade began to notice the telltale signs of age about Annalise's lovely black eyes, and the slight thickening of her once-tiny waist. She *had* changed, he thought; not much, but enough.

"Do you have other children?" she queried.

Slade shook his head. "Just Davey."

"You call him Davey?"

"It suits him. David is much too formal."

"And have you never married?"

"Nope. Haven't had time." Or the desire.

"Would you tell me about him . . . please? I have thought about him so often, Quentin."

Slade released a sigh and sat back in his chair, his long legs stretching out beside the small table. "He looks a lot like you," he admitted, "but he's going to be tall like me. He's only fifteen but I can almost look him straight in the eye."

"He is healthy, then!"

"Oh, yeah. Healthy and happy."

More tears glistened in her eyes, but they were happy tears. "Thank you, Quentin. Knowing that means a lot to me." Her unsteady fingers gripped her glass and she took a sip of the watery drink. "Have you told him anything about what happened . . . or about me?"

"No. He thinks you're dead." Immediately, Slade regretted his blunt disclosure. Hearing her soft gasp, he quickly added, "I thought it would be better if he didn't know you were still alive. We don't move in the same circles, Annalise. I didn't want him embarrassing you one of these days by trying to find you."

"I understand," she replied quietly. "How long will you be here in Manila?"

"Just a couple of days. We're here to pick up a crew, then we'll be on our way again." Shifting uncomfortably in his chair, he knew he didn't want to encourage her. After all that she had meant to him at one time, now all he wanted to do was get away from her. "I, uh, I doubt if we'll ever be passing through these waters again."

"Oh, then you are returning to America . . . for good?"

"Yeah," he nodded, noting the disappointment in her tone. "I've still got family back in Baltimore. Haven't seen them in quite a while, but I thought it would be a good idea for Davey to get acquainted with them *and* my part of the world." As soon as he'd said it, he knew it was what he wanted. He no longer felt a compelling need to remain here, not like he used to.

"You have a special girl in Baltimore, waiting for you?"

"Special girl?"

"A woman, I should say. You are far too mature now, Quentin, for a mere girl."

"No," he smiled, the grooves deepening in his cheeks. "There's no special girl, Annalise." But an image of Raine flashed through his mind and his smile quickly vanished. Now why would he think of her?

At precisely the same moment, in another part of the market, Raine had a sudden vision of Slade pop into her head. She froze and quickly glanced around to see if he was following her.

Relax, she told herself. *You're letting your overactive imagination run away again.*

But she couldn't help herself. She had disobeyed Slade by leaving the ship and now her conscience was nagging her. And the fact that she was dressed to look like a man didn't help matters any. Heavens, if he could see her now, he would probably have a fit. But what he didn't know wouldn't hurt him, she concluded and swaggered into the shop she'd been standing before.

At the rear of the long room stood a tall, swarthy-skinned Filipino. "May I help you, *señor?*" he addressed her with exaggerated formality.

"Aye, you might at that, laddie," Raine responded in a gravelly, masculine voice, touching the patch over her left eye. "I'm Angus MacDougal and I've a chest of heathenous idols here I'd like to be rid of."

"Idols?" the Filipino queried.

"Aye, they look like idols to me." She pulled the ornately carved box out of her burlap bag and placed it on the counter that separated them. "I'll be glad to let you have 'em for the right sum."

Giving her a dubious look, the Filipino turned the chest over and around, examining it critically. Only after he had opened the lid did his expression change to one of intense surprise. "Are they authentic, *señor?*"

"Oh, aye! You can take Angus MacDougal's word for that."

"How much do you want for them?"

Raine quoted the price she had to have and watched the Filipino slowly consider the sum.

"That is a lot of money, *señor.* I would have to inspect them more closely under my glass in the back before I could consider buying them." He grasped the box and turned toward the beaded curtain that led into the hidden back room. "I will be only a moment, *señor.*"

He disappeared with a rattle of beads, leaving Raine to wonder if she'd done the right thing in letting the box out of her sight. It wasn't long, though, before she heard hushed voices coming from behind the curtain and knew that the Filipino was confering with someone else. But who?

Just as she began to grow more concerned, the Filipino returned and gave the box back to her. "They are authentic," he assured her with a nod.

"I thought as much," she grumbled. "Well, how 'bout it? You willin' to take them off me hands?"

"Alas, *señor,* I cannot make that decision. At least, not for the price you are asking."

"They're worth ten times the sum I want!" she argued.

"I agree. But without the owner's approval, *señor,* I am unable to buy them."

"The owner, you say. And where would he be?" She pulled uneasily at the vest she wore over her padded middle, feeling a trickle of sweat run down her spine. The heat here in Manila was bad enough, but the thick clothing she wore now was making it quite unbearable. "I've not got a lot of time here, laddie. I must be sailin' with the tide."

"At the present, *señor,* the owner of this shop is away, trading on another part of the island. He should return in a few days, if you would care to wait."

"Ah, that's that then, isn't it?" she replied gruffly, tucking the chest back into the burlap bag. Damn, another rejection; the third one already. "I'll be takin' my business elsewhere."

"You could leave the statues here until—"

"No, no! Heathenous though they are, they go with me. Good day to you, sir."

It was apparent to Raine that the Filipino wanted to detain her, but the longer she stayed, the greater his chances were of discovering her elaborate ruse. She shouldered her way out of the shop door and swaggered on down the street, wondering where she could go next. There didn't seem to be any other reputable-looking establishments around and she had already strayed too far from the *Mary Ellen* to go further afield. From the looks of it, nobody wanted the Hindu figures for the price she was asking, and she couldn't sell them for less. Her only choice now was to sell her diamonds—of all the cursed, rotten luck!

Taking long, masculine steps, she made her way through the crowded market, deciding to go to a jeweler's shop she'd seen earlier. The diamonds wouldn't bring her half what the figures would have, but it was too late to mourn that fact now. She needed the money too badly.

As she passed a pair of modestly gowned ladies, she remembered in the nick of time to tip her cap. Even if she wasn't one, she must not forget to behave like a gentleman.

Her long, golden hair was twisted and tucked beneath the curly red wig she wore, and her smooth, creamy cheeks were covered with a beard and mustache the same bright shade as her wig. How in heaven's name did men stand all this hair on their faces? It was driving her mad, and she'd only been wearing the false covering for an hour.

Resisting the urge to scratch the irritating bristle on her face, Raine ambled past the entrance of a somewhat seedy-looking tavern. She glanced into the cool, dark interior and suddenly found herself with a craving for something cool to drink.

Later, with her pockets fatter by nearly five thousand dollars and her burlap bag lighter by one diamond *parure,* she jauntily returned to the tavern for the drink she'd craved. She propped one foot on the brass railing that ran across the bottom of the bar and loudly demanded a whiskey. A sherry—dry, not sweet—would have suited her tastes more than the whiskey, but she was supposed to be a Scot and they didn't order sherry unless they were begging for a fight.

She slapped the necessary coins down onto the bar when her drink arrived, then, lifting the glass, she casually turned to observe the other patrons seated behind her. With her mouth full of the evil tasting brew, she froze, finding a pair of green eyes narrowly focused on her.

Good Lord, it was Slade! And he wasn't alone. Seated across from him was one of the most exquisite-looking women Raine had ever seen.

Unaware that the tavernkeeper was standing near her, she quickly swallowed the contents of her glass and all but choked as it burned her throat.

"Another one, *señor?*" the tavernkeeper asked.

"No!" Her voice was a thin, ragged croak, and her unpatched blue eye misted as the fire hit her belly. "Er, no, thank you," she restated on a lower, more controlled note. "Angus MacDougal buys but one drink at a time, laddie . . . his own."

With an uncaring shrug, the tavernkeeper sauntered away, wiping the top of the bar and taking her empty glass with him.

Raine didn't panic . . . not at first, anyway. Slade might still be in doubt and panicking would give her away for sure.

She calmly gathered up her burlap bag, checked

84

her pockets to make certain her money was still where she'd put it, then casually started for the tavern's one and only exit, putting much exaggeration into her swagger. It was only when she heard the scrape of chair legs against the bare wooden floor, followed by Slade's angry, "Angus Mac-Dougal, my ass!" that fear overtook her.

She shot out of the tavern like a bullet, holding her wig and cap on with one hand and her burlap bag with the other, and darted into the crowded street. Running as fast as her long legs could carry her, she scooted past pedestrians and carriages alike, nearly colliding with a woman whose arms were laden with parcels. Her only goal at the moment was to get to the ship in one piece before Slade caught up with her. Her life, she knew, was at stake.

Growing winded, she dashed around a corner and thankfully saw the docks loom up ahead. It was only a short distance to safety now. But as she drew even with an alleyway, she suddenly found herself knocked flat to the ground, her head hitting the side of the building there with a painful thud.

A heavy, powerful weight fell atop her slight body, forcing all the air out of her lungs and turning her once clear vision dark and blurry.

They were right, she thought, you really could see stars.

Chapter Seven

SLADE SHIFTED HIS WEIGHT OFF OF RAINE ALMOST
instantly after he'd fallen on her, leaning on his
elbow beside her limp, unresisting body. He hadn't
meant to hurt her, he'd only meant to grab her and
stop her before she could get into trouble. But as he
had chased after her, he'd been forced to dodge a
horse-drawn carriage when they came up to the alley
entrance and it was there that he'd lost his footing.
Finding himself suddenly thrown against her, they'd
both fallen hard against the ground.

With one hand he turned her onto her back and
pushed aside the silly eyepatch she was wearing. Her
deep violet eyes were glassy and somewhat dazed
looking, and he couldn't help but laugh.

"You silly little fool!" He chuckled as her eyes
crossed and uncrossed trying to focus on him.
"Good God, Raine! Whatever possessed you to—?
No, never mind. I'm probably better off not knowing."

His shoulders continued to shake with mirth as he
slowly got to his feet and extended a hand down to
her. She was a strange sight, the little idiot. Looking
this way, all dressed up like some man, she could

have gotten herself into bad trouble. Shanghaiers combed these docks regularly, just waiting for unsuspecting victims like her. She should have stayed aboard the *Mary Ellen* like he'd told her.

Completely oblivious to the hand of assistance he offered, Raine didn't move a muscle. She lay there dazed, her eyes revolving in slow circles as her lids opened and closed.

Slade knew a brief moment of concern when he realized she wouldn't be able to make it back to the ship under her own steam. He would have to take her back himself, he decided with a sigh.

"Well, hell, come on then!" he muttered before bending down to her. He picked her up, gathering her burlap bag in the process, and tossed her over his shoulder as if she weighed no more than a half-grown child.

"You're beginning to be more trouble than you're worth, lady," he grumbled, heading for the docks.

They made a strange-looking pair as they approached the ship moments later. So strange, in fact, that Mr. Dennison, who was chatting with one of the new crewmen on deck, couldn't restrain himself from commenting about them.

"Have you taken to hiring on drunks, Captain?"

"This one's no drunk, Dennison," growled Slade as he stalked past the two men.

"Lord-ee!" the other man—a tall, lanky fellow with a thatch of curly red hair—declared with a decidedly Southern drawl. "He ain't much bigger'n your boy, Cap'n. Whatcha gonna do with him?"

"That's my problem, mister," barked Slade. Colorful visions of lashing Raine to the yardarm and keel-hauling her floated through his head, but he dismissed them. That sort of punishment was a bit too severe but highly suited his current mood. "Dennison, you're in charge until I say otherwise."

"Yes, sir!" the first mate returned with a snappy salute, an impish smile playing about his mouth.

Grumbling to himself, Slade entered the passage-way of the aftquarterdeck, bending his head low so that it wouldn't strike the beams. If he was smart, he'd turn her over to that bossy old companion of hers, Miss Carlisle, and be done with her. Holding her this way was having a very strange effect on him, one he didn't like. That innocent, unplanned en-counter they'd had in this same passageway a few days ago had been bad, but this was decidedly worse.

He quickly approached Miss Carlisle's cabin, wanting only to rid himself of his bothersome burden. But he stopped and swore when he heard the older woman crooning softly to the baby as she urged him to drink all of his bottle.

Damn it! Now he'd have to deal with Raine himself. Muttering another oath, he entered Raine's cabin and shut the door behind him with a backward kick of his foot before dropping her onto the bunk, and tossing the burlap bag to the deck. One hand swept off his cap as he noted her disoriented look then that same hand reached down and removed the cap and red wig on her head, letting his fingers comb through her long, honey-gold locks.

"Blasted woman," he cursed softly, unfastening the buttons on her coat. What the hell was she doing, going out in this sweltering heat in this garb? Well, maybe actresses did that sort of stupid thing.

Raine's body remained as limp and pliant as a rag doll's while Slade pulled off her heavy coat and the muslin shirt beneath it. Tossing them aside, he vaguely noted the heavy chink of coins as the garments dropped, but his attention quickly returned to the padding wound around her waist. That would definitely have to go before she could breathe again.

His fingers slipped beneath the padding, inadvertently going beneath the binding about her breasts as well. Shifting her body into a sitting position, he pulled away the thick stuff and exposed to his gaze the sight of her creamy, pink-tipped breasts. His breath caught and he found himself incapable of further movement.

Seconds ticked past, slowly lengthening into minutes as Slade continued to stare . . . and imagine. She was so beautiful, so unlike any woman he'd ever known he was beside himself with awe. For far too long now, he'd beheld only the tiny, dark nippled breasts Oriental women possessed and they were nothing like Raine's, which were full and firm, jutting out above her ribs like impudent pears. The vision of them was almost more than he could handle.

Without a murmur, Raine quietly lay back against the pillows and Slade swallowed hard as he watched her breasts shift to lay flat and heavy against the outer wall of her ribs, the aureoles like large round circles of the palest pink.

His pulse began to quicken. His breathing became labored. An undeniable need began to throb unmercifully in his loins and he did nothing to restrain it. Just once, he told himself, feeling his ache expand into an outright pain. Just one little touch and no one would ever know. Surely a brief taste of her glorious confections wouldn't hurt.

With no thought at all as to what the outcome of his living fantasy would be, Slade lowered his head, his hands cupping the undersides of her weighty roundness and he pushed the firm flesh upward to meet his opened, hungry lips. In an instant he was lost. Kissing her was like sampling a rare, addictive honey; the sweetness so potent that he couldn't bring himself to pull back. Like a hungry child, he tasted again, and again, drawing into him the flavor, the essence of her skin, as his tongue laved life into her body.

Raine slowly floated upward and out of her disoriented state, the swirling fog which had surrounded her senses vanishing as Slade's erotic ministrations overtook her. Oddly enough, as she became more aware of what was happening to her, she knew no fear. She looked down at the dark curly head which suckled at her breast and knew to whom it belonged.

"Slade," she breathed on a whispered sigh, her hands lifting to cup his bearded face. His head raised away from her for a moment and looked directly into her drowsy violet eyes, his heavy lashes barely exposing the gold-flecked green of his. There was a sad, almost haunted look about him, as if he had battled with his self-control and lost.

He moved, and Raine threw her arms around his

broad shoulders to stop him from leaving. But deserting her had never been his intention. In his frame of mind it would have been an impossible feat. He merely levered himself onto the bunk beside her and began to slowly peel away her false facial hair.

"I've never kissed a woman with a beard and mustache before. I don't intend to start now."

As soon as he had dispatched the sticky appurtenances with a deft flick of his fingers, he placed his lips on the side of her neck and began to slowly nibble his way toward her mouth, muttering between gentle bites, "You're the damnedest woman I've ever met, lady. Stubborn, hard-headed, strong-willed. But I want you. God knows, I want you more than I've ever wanted anyone in my life. I must be crazy."

"If you're crazy, then so am I," she confessed just before his mouth closed forcefully down over hers.

There was no thought of the past, no consideration of the future; there was only here and now, and that was all that mattered. Like two people after the same goal, Raine wanted only to feel, to experience, to take from Slade what he was so willing to give. While he wanted, *needed* the comforting, the release that only she could bring him.

With their mouths joined in an erotic union, her hands roamed the muscled contours of his broad shoulders, the rippling tension beneath her fingertips further electrifying her senses. The need to touch him further became too great to ignore and she slid her hands down the front of his rough shirt to release each button from its confining hole. Pushing the fabric aside, she opened her mouth to allow her tongue the advantage of his lower lip. She traced the slightly salty skin there then went on to outline his mustached upper lip with a slow, provocative lick.

Groaning, Slade sat up with a jerk and stripped away his shirt to fling it aside. His hands returned immediately to her and became exploratory instruments of excruciating delight. With his fingers he discovered uncharted regions of her breasts, touching, fondling and teasing them until she was alive with hunger. And when he had mapped every inch of that land, when he could stand no more, he moved lower and began to remove her trousers. Pulling them off her long, slender legs, he bared other unexplored extremities to his admiring gaze.

"My God! You're beautiful," he praised huskily as he trailed a finger up her inner thigh to just below her pale blonde nest of curls. "So . . . beautiful."

Telling him with actions rather than words what she wanted, Raine reached for the waistband of his trousers and worked the buttons free before sliding her hands down and over his muscled hips. He kicked his legs free from the confining pants and gently moved atop her, kneeling between her parted thighs.

Her breath caught in her throat as she beheld the size of his arousal. He was truly a magnificent, virile male, the proof of his masculinity just as big and strong as the rest of him. As if they possessed a life of their own, her slender fingers grazed over the wiry hairs of his legs upward, closer and closer until they finally encircled and closed over his potent length.

An uncontrollable shudder tore through Slade as he fell forward over her. "I don't want to wait," he groaned into her ear, griding his hips against hers as his manhood searched for her sheltered core. "I know I should, but I want you now, Raine. Let me love you. God, let me love you!"

Her fingers moved to weave through the crisply curling hairs above his ears. She held his face away from hers and looked with longing into his passion-drugged face. "Then love me, Slade. Please, just love me."

She pulled him back to her and hungrily found his mouth with hers, plundering it with her small tongue as he lunged into her body with a sure, accurate thrust.

For Slade it was like coming home after years of being lost. He savored the vibrant sensations she created for him and knew he would not find this kind of security ever again with anyone else.

For Raine, it was a cold, startling slap of reality. The erotic desire she'd felt only moments before was suddenly gone. In its place was the painful memory of what she'd endured with Roger. Though the two men were nothing alike, and could never be compared on a common ground, she could not dispel the mood which assailed her. She could only remember, with total clarity, that other time, that other man, and the agony she had suffered because of it.

Slade's measured thrusts increased, his mind so preoccupied with the joy she was giving him that he failed to detect her sudden lack of response. She was heavenly. She was wonderful. She was his!

Unable to hold onto his control, Slade exploded on a tidal wave of ecstasy. Jets of his fertile seed shot into her velvety warmth, draining him completely. With a shudder he collapsed, his considerable weight crushing her into the thin mattress as his head fell weakly against the curve of her sweet neck.

Long moments passed, moments in which Raine slowly became aware of his breathing returning to normal, of his heartbeat steadying to a regular pace. It was obvious that he was satisfied . . . but she was not.

Overcome with remorse, tears welled up in her eyes and trickled down her pale cheeks. It was her fault. All of it was her fault. She had been tested and found lacking once again, just as she had been tested with Roger.

Eventually Slade lifted his head, his drowsy, sated gaze finally seeing her pitiful, tear-drenched face. "Raine?" he whispered in confusion as he rolled away to lie beside her.

Biting her quivering lips, she sat up and wrapped her arms in front of her, protecting her naked breasts. "Oh, God!" she sobbed, burying her face into her hands. "Don't look at me like that!"

"What the hell . . . ?"

"No, it's not you," she tearfully assured him. "It's me! Can't you see that? *I'm* the one who is cold and unfeeling, not you."

His masculine pride remaining unbruised, Slade relaxed. Poor kid! The experience hadn't been good for her, like it had been for him. Any other man would have brushed it aside and forgotten it . . . but not Slade. Instinctively feeling her pain, her uncertainty, her sadness as strongly as if it were his own, he knew he couldn't let it go. He had to try and heal the hurt.

"Don't cry, sweetheart," he soothed, running his large, callused hand up and down her slender spine, his fingertips feeling the ridges of her backbone. "It'll be okay."

He found her shoulder beneath the heavy fall of silky blond hair and pulled her gently down beside him, wrapping her in an enveloping embrace. God, she was so soft, so feminine, and so damn young.

Between his soft words and tender kisses, her sobs began to diminish. And when at last they ended completely, she found herself incapable of moving from him. It was a wonderful feeling, being this close to someone. Roger had never held her this way after they had made love. He had never seemed to want to.

"My mother used to cry out in the night," she suddenly remarked, feeling a need to share with him some of the things she had held within her for so long. "I was just a little girl at the time, but I remember it so well. I was frightened because I didn't know what was scaring her, what she was afraid of. I know now that she wasn't crying out for fear of something—she was crying because she was happy and complete. She and my father loved each other so very much, and they showed their love for each other as often as they could with their bodies. I've always wanted that kind of love, that kind of happiness."

"You never knew physical pleasure with your husband." Slade's remark was not a question, but a blunt statement.

"No. And in the end, he turned to someone who could give him what I could not."

"That son of a bitch!" Slade spat. "Bastards like him ought to be castrated and put away, instead of being allowed to run loose."

Raine turned bewildered eyes up to face him, his vehemence too pronounced to ignore. "But, Slade, he—"

"Used you, sweetheart," he finished for her angrily. "He never loved you. You even said so yourself."

"Yes, but if I had been more of a woman . . ."

"*More* of a woman! My God, Raine, you're woman enough for any man. Maybe you're too much woman." He chuckled softly. "I don't know. One thing is certain, though, *he* wasn't man enough for you. You're warm, sweet, and you love your son with a passion that I've never seen before. So, for God's sake, don't go thinking you're lacking."

"But, just now, I didn't *feel* anything."

"I told you, don't worry about it. Sometimes it happens that way, but it's all right."

With a resigned sigh, Raine lay her head down on his furry chest and tried to savor the closeness, the intimacy of being near him, but her doubts wouldn't leave her alone.

"Why did you . . . ?" she began, but broke off. "I mean, you were with that other woman then . . ."

A husky chuckle rumbled through his chest and vibrated her ear. "Don't go asking me for answers, sweetheart, because I don't have them." It was a mystery even to him why he had loved her . . . why he *did* love her!

"Who was she?"

"Oh, damn."

"I'm not jealous!" she hastened to assure him, lifting her head off his shoulder to stare at him. "Really, I'm not. But she was so—"

"Why were *you* trying to pass as a man?" he countered bluntly. "That silly beard and mustache you had glued all over your face almost had me fooled when you came into the tavern."

"It did?"

"Yeah, but then you turned around and I recognized your cute little backside in an instant." As if to emphasize his remark, he ran a hand down her bare, lean flank and cupped that round portion of her anatomy with splayed fingers.

"So *that's* what gave me away."

"It sure was. What the devil were you doing, parading around like a man anyway?"

"I . . . I had business to take care of."

"And you had to look like a man to do it, huh? Just what kind of business was it?"

"Oh, er, nothing that would interest you."

"Try me. You never know, sweetheart, I might be more interested than you think."

In as few words as possible, and leaving out a good many details, Raine told him about the diamond *parure* and her desire to be rid of it.

"Looks to me like it would've been easier to sell them as a woman, not as some man."

"Well, it doesn't really matter now. Just forget it."

"But I thought all women liked diamonds and fancy jewelry."

"Now what on earth do *I* need with diamonds?" she paried with a nervous laugh. "I certainly don't have anyplace here to wear them to. And it's not as if we dress for dinner."

At that moment, out in the passageway, a noise caught both their attentions. Realizing how she was dressed—or rather how she *wasn't* dressed—Raine quickly jumped out of the bunk and began pulling clothes out of her cupboard. "We'd better get dressed. Heaven knows what they would think if someone should suddenly decide to pop right in on us."

"I ain't worried," Slade drawled, deliberately stretching to his considerable length on the bunk and folding his arms beneath his head.

With his impressive masculinity so blatantly displayed, Raine could not stop herself from staring at him. The triangular patch of curly hair where his manhood rested so unthreateningly caught her eye. Lord, did he have no modesty at all?

"For goodness sake, Slade," she hissed, nervously tying the strings of her camisole together before bending down to toss him his trousers. "Put something on! Hetty could walk in with the baby any minute."

"Bet she can't blush nearly as pretty as you," he observed with a chuckle, but complied with her request by swinging his legs to the deck and stepping into his pants. "Then again, she might not be as squeamish, either."

"I'm not squeamish! I just happen to think that there is a definite time and place for everything, including nudity, and *now* certainly isn't it."

Still amused at her maidenly discomposure, Slade slowly pulled on the rest of his clothes. But as he started to put on his shoes, his toe came in contact with the sharp corner of the box peeking out of the burlap bag. "What's this?" he queried, bending over to retrieve it.

"Oh! That reminds me. I have something for you."

"I thought I'd had it already," he purred silkily, pulling her against him. Like a man starved for the taste of her, he planted his lips into the curve of her neck, drinking for a moment of her sweetness there.

"I don't mean that, you silly twit!" she admonished giddily. She shrugged out of his embrace and dug down into her discarded coat pocket, finding the bag of gold coins there. "I mean this. It's the money that I owe you."

"Haven't you got that a little backwards, sweetheart? Usually it's the man who pays for the pleasuring, not the woman."

"Oh, here! Take it and hush. It's to pay for our passage—nothing more!"

Arching a thick brow, Slade tossed the ornately carved box onto the bunk and opened the large pouch she had thrust into his hands. "My God, there must be a small fortune here."

"Well, not quite a fortune, but it should be the equivalent of four thousand, seven hundred American dollars."

"Four thousand . . . ?"

"The first half of what I promised to pay you."

"Don't think I'm not grateful, but didn't we agree on five thousand?"

"Yes, we did. But if you'll recall, I paid you two hundred in advance before we left Macao, then there was that bottle of gin you pilfered without my permission."

"Oh, yeah, that." He grinned sheepishly. "But it sure as hell wasn't worth no hundred bucks."

"Maybe not, but it's the principle that counts."

Frowning, Slade emptied the bag of coins out into his hand, letting it drip between his fingers and onto the bunk where he now sat. Slowly the wheels of comprehension began to mesh inside his head and he turned a dubious eye up to her. "Those diamonds you said you sold today . . ."

"Yes?" Raine stiffened. "What about them?"

"You sold them to get this money, didn't you?"

"Yes, as a matter of fact, I . . . I did." Her determination began to slip and she sighed. "Oh, Lord. You may as well know the truth. No, don't get up! You might take it better sitting down." She swallowed with a loud gulp and confessed, "I . . . I didn't have the money that I promised you when I hired you, Slade."

"You . . . didn't have . . . the money," he repeated woodenly.

"No, I didn't. You see, I *did* have the diamonds, and though *I* knew they were worth a good deal, I couldn't give them to you for fear *you* would think they weren't. There are an awful lot of authentic-looking stones about these days, and I couldn't take the risk of making you suspicious. If you had tried to sell them, Roger might have learned about it and would have known where I was. You see, he gave them to me before we were married."

"It makes sense," he finally agreed with a nod. In fact, in her shoes, he might have done the same thing.

She sighed with relief, but then tensed again when he said, "What I don't understand is what you're going to use for the other five thousand you owe me. At a hundred bucks a bottle, you don't have enough gin down in the hold to cover it, and I don't happen to like the taste of champagne."

"It's not mine anyway," she disclosed evenly. "It's Hetty's."

"Hetty's, huh?" He considered this for a moment then looked back at her as a slow grin deepened the grooves in his cheeks. "Now if you were to consider being my mistress for the rest of the journey, I might—"

"No! Definitely not! What happened between us just now was . . . was purely accidental. It certainly wasn't planned. Why, I've never been a man's mistress, nor do I intend to ever be one, either."

"Okay." He shrugged complacently. "Taking it out in trade is out. I guess I can buy that." He gave her an audacious wink at her astonished gasp. "But what are you going to do about the other five thousand?"

"My brother, Rory, is in San Francisco. I'm sure he won't mind loaning me the money when we get there." If he had it, that is. The Sheridans were known for their acting ability, not for their astute handling of money.

At the mention of her brother, a surprised look crossed Slade's face. It was the first he'd heard of a brother. Under other circumstances he would have agreed to the debt, but now he didn't. He was in too playful a mood. After what they had just experienced, he felt like having a repeat performance of it again, and soon. So he strung her along a little.

"That won't do," he remarked with a firm shake of his head. "No, it won't do at all. I'm afraid I'm going to have to insist on some kind of collateral to cover the money you owe me."

"Collateral!" Oh, he was being utterly impossible! If he thought for one moment that she was going to use her body to barter with, he . . .

Then she stopped, her eye catching the ornately carved box on the bunk beside him. Why not? she thought. The figures inside it were worth far more than any paltry five thousand dollars. And using them was the only way she could think of to keep her self-respect intact.

"You don't leave me much choice then, do you?" she sighed, innocently fluttering her gold-tipped lashes.

His mouth spread into a silly, lascivious grin. "Nope, I guess I don't."

Oh, to see that smug look wiped off his face! Slowly she closed the distance between them until she stood directly between his parted knees.

His head was now lower than hers, and he tilted it up to look at her as his large hands moved to settle on her slender waist. With a gentle pull, he arched her even closer.

"It's best not to fight it, sweetheart. I know the

first time wasn't very good for you, but I promise the next time will be a lot different."

"I've never been a man's mistress, Slade," she purred into the thick curls of his head, nearly gasping as his mustache began to tickle the sensitive skin exposed above the ruffles of her camisole.

"I know," he whispered between nibbling bites. "It'll be a new experience for me, too." The idea of having just one woman entirely to himself—especially *this* woman—carried far more appeal than he'd ever imagined. Going to bed with her every night, waking up next to her each morning and making love to her as often as he wished in between —it was almost too good to be true.

As he continued to pay homage to her ever-weakening body, Raine knew a moment of honest regret. It would be a shame to end this heavenly bliss, but she had her pride and her son to think of. Bending slightly to one side so that she could grasp the box on the bunk, Slade's lips captured her up-tilted nipple hidden beneath the thin layer of camisole. Her firm resolve wavered even more.

But gathering up the last remnants of her self-control, Raine deftly maneuvered the ornately carved box between them and pulled away. Already she could see the desire burning in his eyes and it saddened her when it slowly faded as his gaze shifted to the article now separating them.

"What's this?" he queried on a husky note.

"My collateral." Nervous fingers fumbled with the latch and lifted the lid. "As I said before, I've never been a man's mistress, and I don't intend to be. These are worth more than the five thousand I owe you, so they should cover my debt until I can get the money to pay you."

A strange thing happened then. Slade's teak-brown face grew a sickly shade of gray as he glared at the Hindu figures. His mouth twitched open slowly, his green eyes widening, and Raine heard him utter a strangled noise that sounded oddly like, "F-F-Fong!"

Raine then found herself quickly thrust from him as he jumped to his feet.

"Where the hell did you get those?" he demanded.

"It's rather a long story, but—"

"*He* sent you here, didn't he?"

"He, who?" she frowned in confusion.

"Fong!"

"Slade, I don't know any Fong."

"Yeah, I just bet you don't!" he retorted in disbelief. His long legs began to eat up the small amount of cabin space as he nervously paced back and forth. "I *knew* you were up to something no good, but I sure as hell didn't figure Fong was behind it." He glanced back at the figures she still held and groaned audibly. "Oh, my God!"

"What *are* you babbling about?" More confused than ever, she stepped toward him when his pacing ceased.

"No! You keep those damn things away from me. I don't want anything to do with them."

"You honestly aren't afraid of these, are you? Oh, don't be ridiculous, Slade. How could these little things hurt you?"

"You'd be surprised!"

His strange behavior caused her to ask, "Have you seen these statues before?"

"Yeah! They were in Fong's possession when we were hacking our way out of Angkor Wat."

"But if *you*—" she broke off, frowning. "Then how on earth did *they* get them?"

"*Who?*"

"Gerhardt von Koenig and my former husband," she snapped impatiently. "Are you *sure* you don't know them?"

"I'm positive!"

Raine was thoroughly baffled, to say the least. None of this was making any sense. Unless Fong was somehow tied in with von Koenig, and she was certain that it was he and not Roger who was to blame, because Roger wasn't the art expert; von Koenig was. But how did Slade . . . ?

Slade's initial moment of fear passed as he noted the confused look on Raine's face. Maybe she wasn't putting on an act after all. Or if she was, it was a damn convincing one.

"You're telling me that you don't know who Fong is?"

"I never heard of him until you mentioned his name," she declared honestly.

"Then you don't know the story behind those things."

"No! Why, the first time I ever saw them was when I was unpacking Adam's clothes. This box was hidden beneath them at the bottom of his valise. I can only assume that it was there before I packed it in Hong Kong, because *I* certainly didn't put it there." The skeptical look on his face caused her to ask, "You *do* believe me, don't you?"

"Maybe. Maybe not. I haven't decided yet. Has anyone else seen them?"

"Well, Hetty has. Oh, and the shopkeepers when I tried to sell them this morning."

Another strangled groan came from Slade as he stumbled toward the door. "We gotta get outta here!"

"You mean, leave the ship?"

"No, dammit! I mean, leave Manila! Fong's a tricky little bastard. He's got contacts all over— maybe even here. If he gets wind that you've got those damn hideous things, and that you're with me, he'll come looking for us both. God knows, men have died because Fong wanted those little monsters. I wouldn't put it past him to try and kill *us* just to get them back again. But I intend to be long gone from here before he gets the chance."

Disregarding everything, Slade slammed out of Raine's cabin, leaving her more confused than ever.

Chapter Eight

"GET THOSE DAMN DIAPERS OFF MY BOWSPRIT!" Slade yelled.

"Show me a suitable place where I can hang them and I will!" Raine shouted in return. The man was being utterly impossible. "I do have laundry to do, you know! And it *does* have to dry."

"Well, they'll never dry hanging out there." He thrust a thumb over his shoulder at the squares of muslin, dangling out over the blue-green water the *Mary Ellen* was cutting into.

Both were so intent on staring the other down, they failed to hear the approaching footsteps.

"Uh, pardon me, Cap'n," a voice drawled behind them. "I could string up a line here on deck for the little lady, if it's all right with you, that is."

"Tex!" Raine turned slowly, a smile appearing on her lips. "How very *thoughtful* of you. Would you mind terribly?"

"Oh, no, ma'am." The lanky Texan blushed, sweeping off his cap. "I wouldn't mind a'tall." He glanced at Slade for a sign of permission.

"Oh, hell, go ahead," Slade grumbled. "Just keep the damn thing out of the way."

"Yes sir!"

Backing away, the Texan grinned boyishly at Raine. Her face continued to glow like a Botticelli angel's until she turned to look at Slade, then her smile twisted into a sneer. "It's quite refreshing to know that there are *some* men aboard with manners."

Slade's mustache twitched into a snarl as his green eyes narrowed to dangerous slits. Dammit to hell! Having half the crew wrapped around her little finger wasn't good enough—she wanted the other half too! Muttering oaths beneath his breath, he jerked his cap straighter on his head and stalked off toward the stern.

The shake of Raine's golden head was accompanied by a quiet groan as she began to haul in the diapers she'd so painstakingly hung out just moments before. Blast the man! With the way he was behaving, one would think that those few tender moments they'd shared in Manila were mere figments of her imagination rather than a fond reality. There was no sign of his former gentleness, and hadn't been in the week they had been at sea. He had definitely reverted back to his old, surly, caustic self.

"Need a hand with that basket, Miss Sheridan?"

Raine forced aside her anger and turned to smile at Davey. "Yes, thank you. But are you sure it will be all right with your father? I wouldn't want you to get into trouble again because of me."

"Oh, it ought to be okay with Pa. I'm almost caught up with my chores."

She dropped the last wet diaper onto the pile and followed Davey toward the middle of the ship where Tex was stringing up her clothesline. Gusts of wind whipped about her, causing her long white skirts to cling to her shapely legs as her unconfined mane of hair blew wildly about her shoulders. She had just shampooed it that morning and had left it free so that it would dry more rapidly. Oh, to be a man with shorter, easier-to-manage hair. Brushing, combing and braiding it each morning was proving to be a tedious bore.

Davey dropped the basket beside the mizzenmast and ambled away toward the bow.

"That ought to do the trick," the Texan declared, tugging firmly at the rope he'd just secured to the mast.

"Thank you, Tex." Bending over to gather a handful of diapers, Raine chuckled. "I've been wondering—what is a man from Texas doing here in the middle of the Pacific Ocean?"

"Yeah, it's a little hard for me to believe it myself, ma'am," he remarked, scratched the back of his head. "I sure didn't plan it this way, I can tell you that."

"If you don't mind me saying so, you don't look a thing like the typical man of the sea."

"I ain't! By all rights I should be in Waco now, punchin' steers."

"Waco? Is that where you're from originally?"

"Yep. Waco, Texas. The jewel of the Brazos."

"What's the Brazos?"

"Oh, that there's a river, ma'am. Runs just north of town."

Visions of a lush, rolling green countryside, dotted with quaint, thatched-roofed cottages flashed through Raine's mind. "Mmmm, it sounds heavenly." She smiled.

"It's all right, I guess. 'Course it can get mighty hot there in the summertime. But it ain't nothin' like the heat here."

"Tell me, how did you get from there to here?"

As she secured diapers to the rope with carved wooden pegs, Tex relayed to her how he had been shanghaied in San Francisco, after delivering a half dozen bull calves to a wealthy California rancher who had bought them from his father.

"There I was," he said, "as ignorant as a greenhorn, sittin' in that saloon when this real pretty girl sashayed over to me and enticed me up to her room. I thought we was a gonna. . . . Well, you know."

Raine nodded, smiling at the embarrassed blush on his face.

"She poured me a drink from her 'special stock,' she called it, and the next thing I knew, I was a wakin' up in the hold of some blasted ship halfway out to sea."

"That's terrible!"

"You're tellin' me. I put up a pretty good fight at first. Took three of them scrawny little fellers to hold me down, too, but then this right mean-lookin' captain come over to me an' told me if I didn't settle down he'd throw me overboard to the sharks. Well, I've heard about them critters, and I figured I was better off not knowin' 'em intimately, if you get my meanin'. So I developed a fondness for sailin' in a hurry."

"How long ago did that happen?"

"Oh, 'bout a year ago, I guess. I ain't set eyes on the great United States yet. Seen a lot o' other places, though. Japan, Australia, Manila. That's where I decided I'd had enough and wanted to go home. If it weren't for Cap'n Slade, I 'spect I'd still be stuck back yonder with them Filipinos. Uh-oh! I'd best be gettin' on with my duties. Cap'n's comin' this way."

He tipped the bill of his cap and sauntered off.

Raine returned to her laundry, reflecting on the story Tex had just told her. Of course, she'd heard of men being kidnapped by press gangs and forced into sea duty, but she had never met one before. Only now did the importance of it hit her. Good heavens! *She* could have been shanghaied in Manila!

With an imperceptible shudder, she turned to hang out her laundry. Just as she secured the last diaper to the line, Slade appeared beside her. Grabbing her basket with one hand and her arm with the other, Slade pulled her roughly toward the quarter-deck and her cabin.

Slamming the door behind them, he turned her around to face him. "Damn it, lady, if you don't quit flirting with my crew, I'll—"

"*Flirting!*"

"—confine you to this cabin and you'll not set foot out of it until I say so!"

"I was not flirting!"

"I'd like to know what the hell you call it then."

"Why, I was merely being polite," she informed him, her spine stiff with indignation.

"Yeah, *sure* you were. Flashing your big blue eyes and smiling at him like some she-dog in heat."

"That's a *despicable* thing to say!"

"The truth usually is," he countered, dangerously closing the distance between them until only a thin layer of air separated them. "If you've got an itch, honey, *I'm* the one you see to scratch it."

An itch? Oh, the arrogance of this pompous fool! First implying that she was a bitch in heat, and now insinuating that she itched for it!

"You can rest assured, Captain Slade, I have no such itch."

"Not now, you don't," he rasped. "But the time will come."

"That isn't likely!" She continued to stand her ground, staring furiously up at him.

"Just remember what I told you. Stay away from my crew—and that goes double for Davey!"

"Davey!" The sudden mention of the boy caught her off guard. "Why, he's only a boy!"

"That's right, and he's going to stay that way if I have anything to say about it. The day will come when he'll be old enough to learn about the birds and the bees firsthand, but *you're* not going to be the one to teach him."

"That thought has never entered my head!" It was positively indecent, not to mention immoral, to even consider it. Why, David was more like a younger brother to her than a prospective lover.

"Maybe *you* never thought it, but what about him?"

"What!"

"You hear me, lady. He's fifteen years old—just ripe for the plucking. I was his age when I lost my virginity, and the woman who took it was just about your age." Actually, she had been a lot older, but Slade wasn't going to tell her that.

"Oh, Slade, you've got to believe me," she said earnestly. "I would never *ever* dream of . . . of seducing a young boy. Good heavens, what kind of woman would?"

If the truth were known, Slade had never thought her capable of it, but in having raised the subject, he had suddenly gained the upper hand and he wasn't about to let it go. It was too damn hard keeping a step ahead of her as it was.

"Then it's up to the two of us to make sure he never thinks of you as anything more than a friend."

"What are you saying," she asked after a momentary pause.

"Well . . . that offer of being my mistress still stands."

"No!"

"Don't dismiss the idea too quickly. It would keep the rest of the crew in line as well."

"I don't care. No!"

"Evidently, you've never seen two dozen men starved for the feel of a woman."

Slade was speaking from personal experience. Right now he was about as hungry for her as a man could get. The thought of her lying naked and receptive beneath him had plagued him sorely these past few days. She had filled his thoughts both day and night. And unlike the other women he'd bedded so casually in the past, the one taste he'd had of her hadn't been enough.

"They get mean, Raine," he remarked softly, letting his fingers thread their way gently through her long, silken mane of hair until both hands cupped her head. "Mean and vicious. They start out fighting among themselves and sometimes, not often, they even turn on the poor woman herself. I've seen it. I'd hate like hell for anything like that to happen to you."

"If you're trying to scare me, Slade, you're doing a frightfully good job of succeeding."

"Oh, sweetheart, I just don't want you to get hurt. Twenty-four horny men against one delicate little thing like you isn't very even odds in my book."

Raine's thoughts were so full of Slade's warning, she was unaware of his thighs pressing against hers, nor did she have time to deflect the sudden impact of his mouth. But at the moment his lips touched hers and she felt the delightful tickle of his mustache and the delicious probing of his tongue, she knew she had more to fear than just his crew. Lord, they couldn't be half as treacherous as he was!

Her hands began to push ineffectually against his chest, but as the warm power of his kiss stole into her legs, she felt a molten glow begin to radiate in her breasts and loins. Her fingers ceased their pushing and slid over his broad shoulders to curl into the vibrant thickness of his hair. This was sheer madness, giving into him this way, but it was so delightful she didn't have the willpower to stop it.

Her lips parted on a throaty moan and received a welcoming answer when his tongue took possession of her honeyed interior. A large, muscular thigh demanded entrance and she readily complied, allowing it to intrude between her knees. She was only vaguely aware of his callused hands leaving her head to slip down her back, but when he pulled her hips tightly against his, she was left in little doubt as to what his immediate intentions were.

The cabin door squeeked rudely open. "I've mended that ruffle on your petticoat, Raine. . . ."

Raine's lids flew open with a startled shock. She wrenched her lips from Slade's and jerked around to see Hetty in the doorway, looking surprised and embarrassed.

"Don't you ever knock first, woman?" Slade demanded on a furious growl, his entire body tensing.

"I—I—didn't know," came Hetty's petrified response.

Aware of how they must look, Raine tried to step out of his embrace, but Slade's hands tightened about her, refusing to let her leave him. He merely turned a malevolent glare in Hetty's direction.

"Well, now you do. So next time, knock first!"

"Yes, I—I will. Er, I'll . . . I'll wait until—"

"Get out of here!" he shouted.

Hetty flinched and slammed the door behind her.

"Oh, my God," Raine whispered, wilting in Slade's arms.

"That woman's as lethal as a bucket of ice water," he snarled through clenched teeth. Releasing his hold, he stepped away.

Her head bent in shame, Raine couldn't help but notice the way his trousers stretched tautly over his unsightly bulge. Oh, Lord, what had they almost done?

Slade sank weakly onto the bunk, noticing for the first time since he'd entered her cabin that the baby slept there. Hell, even if the old lady hadn't stopped them, the boy certainly would have. There wasn't enough room on the bunk for three. Knowing this forced him to will away the ache between his legs.

"I see now that I'm going to have to put a lock on that damn door," he muttered when the throbbing in his loins was finally under control.

"To protect me from your crew? Or you?"

His head jerked up at her tremulous inquiry and he eyed her with disdain. "It's a little late to be getting virtuous, don't you think? You wanted it as badly as I did."

"I'm not very proud of that fact," she retorted stiffly. Knowing that he wanted the use of her body and nothing more, but capitulating to him anyway was more than her conscience could bare. "I'm thoroughly ashamed of myself."

"Ashamed!"

"Yes. Is it so hard to believe? You were quite blunt about wanting me for your mistress and, Lord knows, you almost had me. But I swear, Slade, that will never happen again."

The proud, erect angle of her head caused his rising indignation to wither and die, and gave way to a deeper understanding. Jesus, it was getting to the point where he could actually read her mind! It was her wounded pride that he was hearing, not her wrath.

"Just how are you going to stop it?" he challenged

on a soft chuckle. At the puzzled glance she shot him, he grinned even wider. "Lady, I've been fighting it myself. But it's a losing battle, believe me."

"I don't know what you're talking about."

"Well, then, I guess that makes us *both* fools." Slowly he got to his feet and crossed to the door, laying his hand lightly on the latch. "We're a well-matched pair, sweetheart. The sooner you realize that, the better off we'll both be."

Raine watched the door close behind him then shook her head in confusion. She had never been able to understand riddles, and his parting remark was about as cryptic as she'd ever heard. Either he was crazy . . . or she was!

Chapter Nine

THE DAY HAD BEEN UNBEARABLY HOT, MUCH LIKE ALL the others had been since their departure from Manila three weeks ago. Only with the arrival of evening and the setting of the fierce sun did the temperatures drop to a point where Raine could risk taking her son topside for a breath of fresh air. It was quite a welcomed change from the stale, humid air they endured all day down below. Her only real regret on this journey was that she couldn't bring her baby outside more often, but being so near the equator, she dared not.

Adam waved his chubby arms excitedly, like a fat baby bird trying to take flight. Wearing only a diaper, he sat on the end of his mother's knees and chortled with delight. Smiling at her son's enthusiasm, Raine turned her attention back to the group on deck.

This was the time of day Raine loved most. In some respects it was not unlike the years she had spent with the touring company in England, where after a performance all the players would sit around until the wee hours of the morning, sharing experiences or just chatting with one another. Tonight, though, was a bit different. Tex had brought out his guitar and was sitting across from her on an overturned keg, strumming the strings.

As Raine guided Adam's fat, starfish hands together, showing him how to "pat a cake," Tex asked, "You sing, don't you, Miss Sheridan?"

"A little," she demurred with a smile.

"A little!" chided Hetty. "You're being far too modest, my dear. Actually, it might interest you all to know that she toured the provinces with a quite prestigious production of *The Mikado*."

"It's not as impressive as you make it sound, Hetty. I was nothing more than an understudy."

"Yes, but you were on your way to becoming the *star*."

Raine was only too aware that this bone of contention still remained between her and Hetty—that she had abandoned her blossoming career in order to marry Roger. Although her companion never said the words, there were times when Raine could see an I-told-you-so look in Hetty's perceptive gray eyes. She saw that look now.

"She has an incredibly beautiful voice," Hetty continued to explain to the crew. "Why, it's almost angelic."

"Hetty!" Raine warned with an embarrassed flush.

"It's true! You know as well as I do that if you had been of a slighter build, you would have gotten the lead as Yum-Yum."

"But I didn't, so let's forget it, shall we?" Her gaze shifted upward as a movement from behind Hetty caught her attention and she felt the impact of

Slade's unwavering green gaze. Oh, Lord, he had heard every word. Blushing, she wondered what he was thinking.

"Do play something else for us, Tex," Raine said nervously.

"I think you ought to sing," came Slade's unexpected suggestion. The tone of his voice clearly indicated that he doubted her ability.

"Yes, why don't you?" Hetty chimed in.

The last thing Raine wanted was to be the center of attention. "Not tonight," she dissented with a shake of her head. "I haven't practiced in months."

"Oh, that's no excuse," the older woman scoffed.

Before Raine had time to know what he was about, Slade pulled her to her feet and maneuvered her across the deck toward Tex, taking the baby away from her before sauntering back to where he'd been standing. He'd heard her many times, humming sweet lullabies to the baby and knew that her reluctance wasn't due to a bad voice—she was just shy. Shifting the little boy into a more comfortable position, he waited for her to begin.

Not having another choice, she turned to Tex and asked, "Do you know 'The Skye Boat Song'?"

"Uh, nope," he answered. "Never heard of it. Here, you're on your own."

Watching Raine take the guitar from the lanky Texan, Slade felt a tingle of awareness crawl up his spine. The way her slender fingers caressed the instrument reminded him only too clearly of the way she had touched him in their far-too-few moments of passion. Seeing the way they floated smoothly over the neck and strings, he could almost feel their featherlike movements on his own body.

He shifted uncomfortably, knowing that it wouldn't do him much good to start thinking in that direction—not now at least, with all these men around. He sliced a quick glance at the faces in the group to see if anyone had witnessed his discomposure, but as it was, only Davey, who stood near him, was looking in his direction. Everyone else was watching Raine. And Davey, thankfully, had his eyes focused on the baby in Slade's arms.

Expelling a quiet sigh of relief, Slade looked down to see Adam's little face staring up at him. An innocent smile stretched the baby's rosebud mouth, giving Slade a delightful view of the pearly nubs in his pink gums. Chuckling, he patted the diapered bottom then looked back at Raine as a haunting melody filled the air.

A slight breeze sang through the rigging above him. With the strumming guitar as accompaniment, Slade could almost hear the whine of bagpipes while Raine's husky voice sang of the plight of Bonnie Prince Charlie and Flora MacDonald. Her voice was so clear, so compelling, he felt a shiver of some unknown emotion spread through him. She wove her sweet, melodious spell about him as expertly as a witch casting a charm. She was the quintessential Lorelei, and he was her unsuspecting victim having fallen to the raw power of her beautiful call.

Just as the last note of the haunting song faded off into the quiet sky, Slade gained the sudden reality that *he* was the only one enticed into her web. All the others—Davey included—were far less affected by the song. Some were applauding quietly, some were nodding and voicing their approval for her unique performance. Only he was forever ensnared.

God, this couldn't be happening to him! Not now! He was above that kind of emotion . . . wasn't he?

Wanting only to escape from the others around him, he gently thrust the baby into Davey's arms. "I—I've got to go relieve Dennison," was all he said before stalking toward the bridge.

Adam started to fret at being held by someone other than Slade. Not knowing what to do, Davey turned in confusion toward Hetty.

"It's getting near his bedtime," Hetty crooned, raising her arms.

"Oh, I'll take him, Hetty," Raine offered, starting to get up.

"No, no! You stay here. I'll just give him a bottle and he'll be nodding off in no time."

In possession of his guitar, Tex began picking out a lively little waltz that Raine recognized. "I know that one," she declared, settling back down beside him.

"You do?"

"Of course. It's 'Green Grow the Lilacs,' isn't it?"

"Sure is." The Texan grinned. "You want to start it off?"

"No, you'd better do that. I'll join you when I feel I'm ready."

Starting out with the cheerful chorus, Tex's deep baritone rumbled out of his chest. Raine soon joined him, her contralto blending pleasantly with his in a duet that was both enjoyable and captivating.

I once had a sweetheart but now I have none,
  He's gone far away and left me to live all alone,
He's gone far and left me contented to be,
  He must love another better than he loves me.

Oh, green grow the lilacs and so does the rue,
  How sad's been the day since I parted from you,
But at our next meeting our love we'll renew,
  We'll change the green lilacs for the Oregon
    blue.

They both laughed as the last note died away. Raine knew a feeling of contentment until she looked around and noticed that everyone had started drifting away. But it was Slade's absence that bothered her the most. Without him nearby, she felt oddly bereft.

"I guess this evening's entertainment is over," she murmured, getting to her feet. "I'd better be going in, too."

"Yeah," Tex agreed, standing up with her. "We got a busy day ahead of us tomorrow."

"Oh? How is that?"

"Well, from what Mr. Dennison was tellin' me earlier, we're gonna be droppin' anchor 'bout noontime to take on fresh supplies."

"But we're nowhere near land," she pointed out.

"We're a lot closer'n you think." He grinned. "By dawn, we oughta be spottin' Anatahan or Sarigan. Who knows, maybe even Saipan."

"I've never heard of those places."

"Comin' from England, ma'am, I don't suppose

you have. But they're out there all right. Well . . ." he dipped his head in a polite nod, ". . . be seein' you in the mornin'. G'night."

"Good night, Tex."

Repeating the odd-sounding island names to herself, she entered her cabin and found Adam on the brink of nodding off to sleep. He roused himself long enough to stretch out his arms toward her, and she gathered him to her, hugging him fiercely.

"By the time you're old enough to remember things, my darling, you will have forgotten all of this. Anatahan and Sarigan will sound foreign to you, too."

Adam's violet-tinted lids were so heavy he no longer fought to keep them open. With a softly expelled sigh, he relaxed his pale, touseled head against her full bosom and fell asleep. Raine sat there and held him for a while longer, cherishing this precious moment with him as she had all the others since she'd found him again. How was it possible to love a child so much?

When his breathing became even, she dropped a loving kiss onto his little cheek then put him down in the corner. He would sleep there undisturbed for the rest of the night, but to insure that he wouldn't roll out of the bunk and hurt himself, she positioned two plump pillows around him then stood and began to remove her clothes.

Sleepiness continued to elude her, though, even as she pulled on her thin cambric nightgown. Perhaps the invigorating night air she'd breathed topside was the cause of her wakefulness. Or perhaps it was the stimulation of the singing she'd done. Whatever the reason, she found herself drawn back outside to the deck.

For modesty's sake, she wrapped a shawl about her shoulders before leaving the cabin. The passageway was empty, but she could hear the faint sounds of the crew, settling down for the night in the quarters below. She stepped out onto the deck and wandered toward the railing to gaze out to sea. Her mind soon filled with a variety of thoughts. Even with the great silvery moon suspended above her in the velvety darkness, and with a thousand twinkling stars to illuminate the night, she could not determine where the horizon met the water. If what Tex had said was true, she knew that out there, somewhere, were the islands he had spoken of. And beyond them were more stretches of ocean, more islands and finally San Francisco, the end of her journey.

With fingers trailing along the smooth wood railing, she slowly glided toward the large sail locker at the bow. Her thoughts distracting her, she was unaware that her movements were being observed by the man behind the helm.

Slade's hands tightened about the great wheel's spokes, his knuckles turning white under the pressure he exerted. Didn't she have any idea what she was doing? Jesus Christ, parading around out here in nothing but her underwear was an open invitation to trouble. So far, the men had behaved themselves, but that was no guarantee that they would continue to do so. Dressed as she was, so provocatively, so beautifully, even a saint would become crazed with lust.

Knowing only that he had to get her back to her

cabin before someone else saw her, Slade secured
the helm with a short length of rope and descended
the short flight of steps to the main deck. His long,
determined stride followed the same route she had
taken until he was but a few feet from her. Hidden
by the shadows near the sail locker he stopped,
frozen, unable to move any closer. The angle of the
moonlight, filtering through the sheerness of her
gown, and the gentle breeze which lifted her un-
bound hair from her shoulders held him transfixed.
She looked like a beautiful, unearthly apparition
standing there. A wraith who had mysteriously
appeared on the deck of his ship to haunt him.

Slade didn't move, but Raine did. Sensing a
presence behind her, she turned and peered into the
darkness.

"Who's there?" she queried softly.

"It's only me . . . this time," Slade jeered, stepping out of the shadows. "Next time you might not
be so lucky." He gripped her shoulders while his
eyes coursed angrily over her body. "Dammit, lady,
what the hell do you mean by coming out here
dressed like this?"

"I—I couldn't sleep. I thought some fresh air
might help."

"That's the lamest excuse I've heard yet."

"It's not an excuse. It's the truth."

"By the looks of it, you're just begging for trouble." His fingers dug into the tender flesh of her
upper arms.

"But I'm not!" she argued weakly, the pain in her
arms nothing to compare with the turmoil churning
in her soul. "You know I'm not, Slade."

His fingers relaxed their hold and his voice dropped to an agonized whisper. "I've warned you before about flirting, Raine. Why don't you listen."

"I'm not flirting. Not now." Her own voice was as soft as his. Guided by an unknown need, her hands lifted and found their way to his broad chest. They rested there, feeling the increasing tempo of his heartbeats.

Was this the reason for her sleeplessness? Oh, dear Lord, was it?

"Raine, do you know what you're doing?" he all but groaned.

As thoroughly confused as he, her head jerked from side to side only to stop as she pressed herself closer to him. She stood on tiptoe and began to place gentle kisses along his bearded jaw.

Tomorrow, a little voice told her, she could plead ignorance, or perhaps temporary insanity. Yes, moon madness! But right now, all she wanted was to hold him in her arms, be held by him and absorb all the love, all the passion that he alone seemed to be able to give her.

Her lips poised for a breathless moment before his as she whispered, "Love me, Slade," and then tenderly took possession of his mouth.

Unable to deny the force of her nearness, Slade groaned and captured her face with his hands, his strong fingers winding through her silken locks as his mouth fought a hungry duel with hers. They nibbled, they sipped, and finally when their appetites had been whetted to life, they drank fully of one another.

Tongues blended, stroking each other through

parted teeth. Bodies strained against the layers of clothing that separated them, pressing, pushing, moving against the other all the while. Soon it became evident that both were aroused and hard with wanting. Her nipples rubbed like small, firm buttons against his chest. His manhood pressed against her thinly clad upper thighs until her legs opened weakly and it thrust hard against her throbbing femininity.

Unlike before, when she had frozen at the rude intrusion, Raine gasped with pleasure and began to move against the bulge. Her hips arched, then drew back, only to arch again as a pleasurable need spread throughout her. She arched toward him once again, wanting more.

Slade allowed his hand to drift away from her head, down the slim column of her throat, over the swell of her ripe, upthrusting breast to tease the taut nipple there with his thumb. Eliciting a whimper from her, his hand slid downward again, his fingers pulling up the fabric of her gown and bunching it about her waist until he gained access to her smooth, bare skin. It played there for a moment over the slight mound of her belly and felt it quiver beneath his touch, then blatantly moved to find the warm, moist nest of curls that sheltered her sex. Searching, his long callused finger soon discovered the hard kernel at the opening of her nether-lips and massaged it slowly, lovingly, relishing in the way her body writhed against his.

Raine had never known such a feeling of wonder. Heat radiated through her, growing, building to such an intense degree that she could not restrain herself from moving against his hand. Her hips undulated and thrust against it over and over again until something within her snapped and she soared with a tiny cry straight into explosive ecstasy.

Their lips still united, Slade heard her cry out an instant before her body shuddered against his. He removed his hand from her nest, sliding it quickly around to her hip where he gripped the firm flesh of her bare buttock. He pressed her to him, trying desperately to ride out the storm within him. The ache in his groin was monumental and he longed to unsheath his aroused need and bury it inside of her, knowing that her velvety warmth would ease away his pain. But his conscience, curse it, wouldn't let him carry through.

In partial control of her senses, Raine began to nibble at his lips. "Oh, Slade," she whispered between tiny kisses. "I love you. I love you so much it frightens me. I've never felt this way before."

One part of Slade wanted to loudly echo her sentiments, but he did not. He found he couldn't. He remained silent as she continued to bathe his face in kisses. It would be so easy to confess his feelings for her, then make beautiful love to her here beneath the stars. But if he did that, they would be bound together forever by the invisible chains that shackled all lovers. *That* was what held him back. *That* was what frightened him. Having her for his mistress was one thing, but this . . . this love he felt was something else. He was not of her world, and she certainly wasn't of his. What possible future could they have together?

Slowly, gently, he pushed away from her. In a tone much colder than he anticipated, he rasped, "Go to bed, Raine. Maybe you can sleep now."

Staring up at him, Raine's expression reflected the shock and confusion she felt. Had her admission meant nothing to him? Overwhelmed by a horrible wave of shame and embarrassment, she felt hot tears sting her eyes. She turned with a whimper and raced toward the quarterdeck, past the small figure that was hidden there in the shadows.

Slade reached out to her, her name silently on his breath as he called to her. Then, gritting his teeth, he turned away and cursed himself for what he had done. God knew he hadn't meant to hurt her! That was the last thing he'd wanted. Hurting her was like hurting himself. But maybe, in time, she would get over it, and in the end she would realize that it had all been for the best.

Turning toward the bow, he glared out into the limitless darkness of the night with unseeing eyes. An agonizing ache tore through his groin and he nearly doubled over from the frustration. *She* would get over it . . . but would *he?*

Chapter Ten

"I DON'T CARE IF HIS SHIP *IS* ONE OF THE FASTEST, I don't like his looks one damn bit!" Gerhardt bit out furtively so that only Roger could hear. His piercing eyes focused on the hulking Cornish seaman who stood across the room at the bar.

"That's odd," Roger rejoined in a bored tone as he gazed into the depths of his half full whiskey glass. "I thought you fancied his type, Hardy."

"My, my! Aren't we feeling touchy tonight! What's the matter? Afraid he might be your replacement?"

Roger snorted derisively. "As the Americans would say, Hardy—you're barking up the wrong tree. From what I've observed, Trehearne is most definitely not of our ilk. So if you've a notion of seducing him, you'd best put it from your mind right now. And you would do well to remember that while *he* may have the ship, *I* have the money."

Gerhardt turned to him and pouted. "You wound me, Roger. Do you honestly think that your wealth is the only thing that has kept me with you all these years?"

Sensing Hardy's anguish, Roger knew he should

131

apologize, but something within him held him back. During these last agonizing weeks, when they'd searched high and low for Raine and his missing son, Roger had come to know a different side to Hardy— one that was decidedly opposite of the gentle, considerate lover he'd known for the past fifteen years. Oh, he knew that Hardy was ambitious, and in the beginning when they'd met at school that had been exciting! But this cruel, ruthless streak that was just making itself known was more than a little frightening.

"As I recall," Roger began carefully, *"you* had all the money and connections when we first met. That didn't change until a few months ago when I acquired my title and inheritance."

"I would *still* have an income if my idiotic father hadn't squandered it all on his loose women and that damn rebellion he so unwisely decided to finance. God, to think that I could now be a baron in Bavaria! But, no, *he* wanted that principality in Africa. Who, I ask you, would want that?"

Choking back a groan, Roger concentrated on the contents of his glass and steeled himself for the dialogue that was about to come. He'd heard it all before, at least a hundred times. But he knew better than to interrupt Hardy before the man had sufficiently vented his spleen. Their relationship was strained as it was; he didn't want to make it worse.

"If only he'd stayed in Bavaria where he belonged instead of wandering off to that hellhole in Africa, we'd have the family estate today. As it is, I was extremely fortunate that Mama was from a good, solid English family and had an income of her own to fall back on, otherwise I would never have gotten my education . . . or met you. I'd have probably ended up as Papa, penniless and a victim of the pox."

"Who's got the pox?" boomed a voice above them.

"An acquaintance of ours," Roger replied easily, looking up at the towering hulk of Trehearne, who had joined them at last. "No one you would know, old boy."

"I should hope not!" the Cornishman snorted, pulling out a chair into which he settled his enormous frame. "I've been fortunate in avoiding *that* particular condition . . . But it's not for the lack of opportunity, eh?" With a hearty chuckle, he slapped Hardy soundly across the back, jarring the smaller man considerably.

"Did you learn anything?" Roger asked, wanting to change the subject before it became embarrassing.

"Ah, that I did! It seems the *Mary Ellen* was here in Manila less than a month ago, and by all indications they were heading east. One of the crewmen mentioned something about San Francisco to my friend behind the bar there."

"San Francisco," Roger mused with a frown. What possible reason could Raine have had in choosing that city?

"When do we sail?" Gerhardt inquired.

"With the morning tide," Trehearne responded.

"And how long will it take us to catch up with the *Mary Ellen?*" Gerhardt asked again.

"Oh . . . two, maybe three weeks, if the weather holds."

"That long?" Gerhardt frowned his disappointment.

"I'm afraid so. My *Sea Gull*'s a swift vessel, but you have to remember that the Pacific is a big ocean. There's only one other ship in these waters I know of that can outdistance mine, and it belongs to a rather colorful little character by the name of Fong Chiang." Failing to detect the sudden rigidity in Gerhardt's frame beside him, Trehearne continued, "But getting him to take you is out of the question. He left Manila early this morning, heading easterly, too, as I understand."

"We're satisfied with you and the *Sea Gull*, Trehearne," Roger remarked, ignoring the wide-eyed look of concern that Gerhardt shot him.

"I've had no complaints yet," the Cornishman replied smugly. "But tell me, why is it so important that you catch up with the *Mary Ellen?* Did the American, Slade, cheat you in some way?"

"Slade? I've never heard of him," Roger admitted with a disinterested shrug. "No, it's one of his passengers that I'm anxious about."

"We'd better return to the ship," Gerhardt inserted bruskly. "It's getting late, and there is that other matter I wanted to discuss with you."

"Oh, all right," Roger relented before downing the rest of his whiskey. "We'll see you back at the ship, Trehearne."

"Yes, I'll be aboard later," the Cornishman assured them smoothly as the two men rose to their feet. "I've a little business to transact with a certain Filipino lady first."

Roger and Gerhardt left the *Sea Gull*'s captain

chuckling softly to himself, both knowing what that "little business" entailed. But as soon as they had stepped out into the hot, muggy night, Gerhardt began to wail.

"Oh, God! Fong's in on it now!"

"How can you be sure, Hardy? For all we know, he may be involved in some other matter."

"I'm not that lucky," Gerhardt moaned. "No, the tyrant is after the Hindu collection just as I am, I'm sure of it."

"Well, I wouldn't worry about it, if I were you."

"Of course you wouldn't! He's not after *your* neck."

He wouldn't be after yours either, Roger thought, *if you hadn't stolen the collection from him.*

"Hardy, let's cross that bridge when we come to it."

"Oh, don't be so damn patronizing! You've no idea what it's like, having your ass in a sling as mine is."

"You're right. I just want my son back, and that's all."

"I just hope we can get to them first, before Fong does, otherwise we'll both be out of luck."

Chapter Eleven

RAINE'S FINGERS TUGGED RHYTHMICALLY AT THE nanny goat's teats, filling the chipped china basin beneath. When she heard a crewman cry out, "Land ho!" she stopped abruptly and felt a surge of excitement race through her. Smiling to herself, she thought what a welcomed change the sight of land would be after looking at nothing but murky green water for the last three weeks.

She quickly emptied the udder then hurried up the gangway and out of the hold, popping into the galley for a moment to deposit the bowl of milk on the worktable there.

"Could you boil this for me, please, Cookie?"

"Sure thing, Miz Sheridan." The grizzled man smiled affably. "You know, it'll do them poor animals a world of good to graze on land for a while. You ask me, it ain't right for 'em to be stuck on this ship all the time."

"I agree! They certainly aren't giving as much milk as they used to."

"Maybe we can work a deal with the islanders. You know, trade your goats for a pair of theirs?"

"Do they *have* goats on the island?"

"Why, sure they do! Goats, cows, pigs, chickens. Just about anything and ever'thing you could ask for. 'Course now, I ain't so sure about horses."

"Chickens, hmm? Well, the egg production has dropped off, too, maybe we could get some fresh laying hens as well."

"I don't know about that. You'd have to speak to the cap'n."

At the mention of Slade, Raine stiffened. It brought back with painful clarity their encounter on deck last night. A rosy blush of shame tinted her cheeks as she recalled her heartfelt confession and his cold rebuke. How could she have been so stupid? All he wanted was a mistress, and when she had offered him her heart, he had repulsed her like a man suddenly confronted with a leper.

"Miz Sheridan? Did you hear what I said, ma'am?"

"Oh, yes, Cookie. I'm sorry. I didn't mean to ignore you like that. Of course, I'll mention it to Captain Slade."

"Uh, you might want to wait a while," the man suggested. "He wasn't in a very good mood this mornin', and with all the business of droppin' anchor an' all, I'd wait till we got settled good before I said anythin'."

Nodding her thanks, Raine left the galley and wandered up to her cabin. She couldn't go to Slade with a problem as minor as chickens and goats. He'd laugh in her face . . . or simply ignore her. No, she couldn't confront him, but maybe Hetty could.

She found her old friend having a rather one-sided conversation with her canary as Adam looked on.

The little boy stood on his bare toes beside Hetty's bunk, pointing and chattering away at the caged bird high above him. At Raine's soft chuckle, they both turned.

"I do believe we have a bird fancier here." Hetty grinned broadly.

"Do we?" Raine came further into the cabin and knelt down beside her son. "He's a pretty bird, isn't he, darling?"

Adam's little mouth worked furiously as unintelligible sounds bubbled out of him. One of his stubby, starfish hands reached out toward the cage.

"I think he's trying to talk, Hetty!"

"Well, of course he is. He's trying to walk, too. The little scamp's been marching up and down beside the bunk all morning."

"My goodness! We're going to have our hands full soon."

"I know," Hetty agreed sagely.

Raine kissed her son's soft cheek then rose to sit on the mattress. "Hetty," she began cautiously. "Would you do something for me?"

"Of course, dear child. What?"

"Well, we need a couple of fresh nanny goats. The two below in the hold are beginning to dry up."

"Yes, I noticed that when I was milking them the other day."

"And the hens aren't laying quite like they should."

"I'm aware of that, too. But what has that got to do with me?"

"Hetty, I wouldn't ask you unless I thought it absolutely necessary, but—" she inhaled a deep breath then said in a rush, "—would you go to Captain Slade and speak to him about replacing our livestock with fresh animals from the island?"

"Why don't *you* do it, Raine? I mean, it's obvious even to me that you're on better terms with him than I."

"No," Raine negated quietly. "I'm not."

"But that day in your cabin, when the two of you were—"

"That was a mistake," Raine interjected. "It never should have happened."

"It didn't look very much like an accident to me," the older woman scoffed.

"Well, it was! Slade and I are barely on speaking terms at the moment." She hoped Hetty wouldn't delve into the matter further, because she wasn't in any mood to elaborate.

"And you think he'll be receptive to me?"

"Yes. You don't mind, do you?"

"No, I suppose not," Hetty relented with a vague movement of her head. "Of course, I've no way of knowing what he'll do. That man has a way of putting one off without trying very hard."

If only Hetty knew how right she was, Raine thought, recalling the coldness in Slade's voice when they had parted the night before. He had dismissed what happened between them as casually as if it were nothing but a bothersome chore to be seen to.

Strange, though, there was that obvious bulge in his trousers; she had felt it against her thigh and had known instantly what it was. That, if nothing else, caused her to believe that he *had* felt something . . . even if it was just a momentary, superficial lust.

Raine was still reflecting on this much later after they had dropped anchor at the island. She stood at the ship's railing, watching Slade and his crew row ashore in the dinghy. Men were definitely strange creatures, she concluded. Strange and, at times, quite unfathomable.

A movement in the corner of her eye caught her attention and she turned to see Davey cautiously approaching her.

"You're not going ashore with your father?" she asked.

"No, ma'am." His eyes seemed unable to meet hers, his tanned cheeks reddening slightly as he shook his head. "He said, that if nothing happened, we might go later on."

Something was bothering him, but what? she wondered, turning to look back at the island. It wasn't at all like him to be this quiet.

Wanting to redirect his thoughts and thereby improve his disposition, she murmured, "It's so beautiful here. It's hard for me to believe that we're actually in the middle of the Pacific and not near England. Why, those trees over on the island are almost as green as the ones back home." When Davey failed to respond, she continued. "Is it my imagination, or is that really a mountain over there?"

"No, ma'am," he remarked at last, chuckling. "It's a mountain, all right."

"Just think of it! A mountain on an *island,* here in the middle of nowhere."

"Well, just about all the islands in this chain have

mountains of some kind, ma'am. They're volcanic, you know."

"Oh, my word! You mean volcanoes with lava and eruptions and things like that?" Her dramatic delivery would have thrilled Hetty.

"Yes, ma'am! But you don't have to worry," he assured her. "We're not in any danger. Pa wouldn't have dropped anchor here if he thought we would be."

"I should hope not!" she proclaimed with a flutter of dark lashes.

An errant breeze ruffled Davey's ebony locks. Her impulses guiding her, she reached up and smoothed the hair back off his wide forehead. For a boy of fifteen, he was already as tall as she, but his stature promised that he would grow even taller. As tall as his father, she ventured to guess.

"You could do with a hair cut, my lad," she scolded gently.

"Yeah, I know." His bare feet shuffled uneasily over the deck.

"If you let it grow too long, you'll have to start tying it in a que, like the Regency bucks wore their hair."

"You mean, like a Chinaman's pigtail?"

"No, not plaited. Just pulled back and tied with a ribbon. I've a book of period costumes with detailed illustrations in one of my trunks—I'll show it to you sometime."

"Were you really an actress like Miss Carlisle said you were?"

Raine could not suppress the chuckle that bubbled

forth. "I'm afraid Hetty puts a bit too much emphasis on my one or two minor successes while totally ignoring my many failures, David, but yes, I was an actress."

"Gosh!"

"It's not so strange really. You see, I come from a family of actors, just like you come from a sailing family. Both my mother and father trod the boards, as they say in the theater, and when my brother and I were born, we just naturally followed in their footsteps.

"I remember the first time I was ever on stage. I couldn't have been more than two or three, but I was so excited, I wet my knickers. My brother, Rory, almost died of shame, but Mother and Father just carried on with their performance as if nothing happened. And when the curtain was lowered they quickly mopped up my little puddle so the actors following on after us wouldn't slip in it."

Davey giggled with delight. "I'll bet that was fun."

"It's a wretched lot of hard work, I can tell you! But it *was* fun. You know, we're a lot alike, you and I. You've only known one way of life—sailing—and I've only known the theater." Her brief bout of being lady of the manor could only be classified as a tragic error; not worth considering.

At that moment, an idea came to her, and she turned to him with a snap of her fingers. "I may not be able to learn all you know about sailing a ship, but I'll bet I could teach you a little about acting."

"What do you mean?" he asked, puzzled.

"Well, we could put on our own little play, right here on the *Mary Ellen*."

"We could!"

"Why, of course."

"You mean . . . with costumes and everything?" His green eyes sparkled with brilliant anticipation.

"Oh, it wouldn't be anything elaborate—we've neither the space nor the props necessary for that sort of production. A brief, one-act melodrama or comedy would be more in order, I think. I must speak to Hetty first and see what she thinks, but I'm sure the two of us can come up with something. Heavens!" She laughed lightly. "I just remembered—there are scads of scripts in our trunks."

As if a light had suddenly been snuffed, the glow left Davey's face. "Would . . . would we have to read?"

"Only at first," she replied. "Just until we'd memorized our parts."

"Oh." His young voice was heavily laced with disappointment.

"David, whatever is the matter?"

"Oh, nothing," he negated, his eyes downcast.

"Don't tell me that." Her finger pressed his chin upward so that he was forced to look at her. "I can see that something is wrong. Now, tell me, what is it?"

The confession did not come easily. Davey's mouth opened and closed, small, incomprehensible sounds coming out as a wide range of emotions played across his face.

"I—I can't read," he admitted finally, pulling away from her touch.

"You can't! Is *that* all? Well, you certainly had me

worried for a moment. I thought something truly dreadful was the matter."

"But . . . but—"

"Now you're sounding like a sputtering steam engine." She giggled. "Don't worry, David. The solution is quite simple, if you'll just think about it. *I'll* teach you to read." Her offhand acceptance of his handicap had the desired effect she'd wanted; he relaxed and began to beam again.

"You'll teach *me?"*

"Of course! You're not an ignorant boy—it shouldn't take you very long to learn." Now, if it had been his father she had to teach . . .

"When?"

"What?" She blinked stupidly at his question.

"When will you teach me?"

"Oh! Why, we can begin now, if you like. But if you think your father might object . . ."

"No, he won't object," Davey guaranteed her, his mouth taking on an angry, almost belligerent line.

"If you're sure . . ."

"Yes, ma'am." He nodded. "I'm sure!"

Slade returned to the *Mary Ellen* sooner than he'd anticipated and with his water casks as empty as they'd been when he left. All but one of the island's freshwater springs had dried up due to the lack of rain and he hadn't replenished his supply from it because he'd discovered the islanders were in need of it more. They were suffering from a fever, one that raced through the populace with almost predictable regularity whenever an unfamiliar ship dropped anchor. This time it had been a Russian whaler and a fever of unknown origin had taken its toll.

When the dinghy was at last secured to the side, Slade issued orders to the crew, telling them to prepare to get underway. They would go to the next island and look for freshwater there. And if they didn't find it there, they would go on until they did find it.

There was no sign of Davey on board. When Slade went in search for him, he found him in Raine's cabin, sitting close beside her on her bunk as Adam played quietly at their feet. Barely taking notice of the slate and chalk between them, he instantly knew a moment of intense anger.

"What the devil are you doing in here when there're still chores to be done, boy?" he barked. "You don't have time to sit here and keep passengers entertained."

"He's not entertaining me, Captain," Raine hurriedly defended the boy. "We are having a lesson."

"Yeah." Slade sneered. "I'll just bet you are."

"Pa . . ."

"Shut up, Davey. I'll take care of this."

"Captain, there is nothing to take care of." Raine rose to her feet and added, "I'm merely trying to fill in the gaping void you've so carelessly left in his education."

"Lady, I've warned you before about—"

"I am *teaching* him to read!" she interjected before he could accuse her of flirting with his son.

"She is, Pa!" Davey was on his feet in a flash. "So don't you be yelling at her."

145

Slade turned a dangerously narrowed gaze on his son, his mouth tight and unyielding. Fearing what he might say to the boy, Raine stepped in once again. "It's all right, David. He's raised his voice to me before. I can handle it."

"It didn't take you long, did it?" Slade asked, directing his cold gaze at her. "Got him wrapped around your little finger just where you've wanted him all along."

"I'm only teaching him to read, Slade. Nothing more!" she reasserted tenaciously.

"Go to my cabin, son. I'll be there in a minute."

The boy looked to Raine for some sign of confirmation. Her pale blond head slowly nodded. "Yes, you'd better do as your father says, David. We can continue with the alphabet some other time."

Flushing beneath his tanned skin, Davey slammed out of the cabin. But before Slade had the chance to open his mouth, Raine knelt down and scooped up her son, deliberately putting him between her and Slade.

"I take it, Captain, you don't *want* me to teach David," she remarked evenly so as not to alarm the baby.

"You got it, lady! If you're so hot to teach somebody, why don't you start with your own kid there?"

"Adam is far too young for one thing. Even a blind idiot like you could see that." Her voice almost dripped honey. "More important, though, your son *needs* to learn. He needs to learn now! Good Lord, Slade, he's fifteen years old and doesn't even know how to write his own name. How do you think that makes him feel? Very inadequate, I assure you! You've done him a great disservice by not teaching him."

Slade shifted uneasily. Like most men, he didn't like having his shortcomings and deficiencies pointed out to him so bluntly. *He* knew he wasn't perfect—knew it probably better than *she* did—but that didn't mean he had to stand here and listen to her scold him about it. Jesus, she wouldn't understand that there just hadn't been enough time, that he *had* intended to teach Davey, but just hadn't got around to it yet. After all, it wasn't easy, raising a boy and running a ship at the same time.

"If you don't want *me* to teach him, I won't," she replied benevolently. "But someone should. I can speak to Hetty—"

"No, don't bother her," Slade grumbled, all his anger gone. "I guess it's all right for you to teach him, but you've got to let him get his chores done first. This is still a ship, you know, not a floating schoolhouse."

"I'll leave it to you to decide when he has his lessons," she agreed, successfully suppressing the smile in her voice.

It was only after Slade had closed her cabin door behind him that it dawned on him; he owed her an apology. Turning back, he frowned at the panel for a moment then shook his head and headed for his own cabin instead. No, he would quit while he was ahead. One more confrontation with her and God only knew what would happen.

Davey was angrily pacing up and down the small space in front of Slade's desk when he entered.

Stopping midstride, he glared at his father, who was more than a little surprised by cold reception.

"You got some nerve, Pa, being mean to Miss Sheridan like that!"

"I wasn't being mean, son, I—"

"Yes, you were! You're always mean to her and she's the nicest lady I've ever met. Why, she even told you she loved you and you had to throw it back at her."

Slade sank weakly onto the bunk at the remark, his ability to stand suddenly gone. God, what was Davey saying?

"She's a nice lady, Pa. But what she sees in a man like you is something I can't understand. But then, I'm just a kid, so what do I know?"

"Davey," he began with a painful wince. "Son, when did you hear her say she loved me?" It was the hardest thing he'd ever had to ask, but his tone held no anger, only calm regret.

"Last night."

Slade visibly crumbled at the answer, knowing that he and Raine had been observed the night before.

"I went topside to relieve myself," the boy went on to explain. "But when I saw you two kissing and . . . and touching each other, I decided to wait. I didn't mean to watch, honest I didn't. But when you pushed her away and told her to go away, it made me mad. She said she loved you, Pa! Don't that mean nothing to you?"

"Yes, Davey, it means a lot. But she . . . she . . . Well, what I'm trying to say, son, is, when you get my age . . . and a woman says she loves you . . . under *those* circumstances, it doesn't really mean a lot."

"She was lying?"

"No. Now I didn't say that."

"Then she was telling the truth."

"I didn't say that, either."

"Well, either she was or she wasn't, Pa. Which is it?"

"Oh, hell!" Slade groaned, dropping his head into his hands. A gale force wind was easier to face than this boy. How did he go about explaining to a fifteen year old about lust and carnal urges?

"You know what I think, Pa?" Davey asked after a lengthy pause. "I think she really does love you. What's more, I think you love her, too, but you're just too hardheaded to admit it."

"Now, look here, Davey, I—"

"After all, you wouldn't look at her the way you do if you didn't," the boy observed. "And don't say you don't, because I've seen you!"

"Just how do I look at her?" Slade inquired cautiously.

"Well, I don't know how to describe it, but—but I know it's not like the rest of the crew looks at her. It's just different, that's all. Even Mr. Dennison and Tex have seen you. I heard them laughing about it one day."

"Oh, damn!" Slade moaned. It was worse than he'd thought.

"They weren't making fun of you, though. Honest they weren't," Davey assured him. "They were just betting each other as to when you'd surrender to old Dan Cupid." He frowned thoughtfully and asked, "I don't know him, do I, Pa?"

A strange, forced sound that was half laughter, half groan erupted from Slade. He rose to his full height and ambled toward the porthole. "Dan Cupid? No, he's one scallywag you're better off not knowing, son. You'd best be about your chores now—we weigh anchor soon."

The door closed quietly behind him and he muttered. "I knew I should have left that woman in Macao."

scoffed. "I've called it a floor all my life and I'll continue to do so until the day I die. Being on a ship is not a valid reason for altering my entire vocabulary."

Raine sighed and decided to change the subject. "Did you get a chance to speak to Captain Slade about exchanging the animals?"

"Yes. Oh, do be careful, baby," Hetty chided Adam, having to step back out of the water's line of fire. "You're getting my and your mummy's skirts all wet."

Adam, intent on hitting the water, simply ignored her.

"What did he say?" Raine urged.

"Who? The captain? Oh, well, he said he would ask around in the village and see what he could do."

"That's a relief."

"Yes, isn't it? I must say, though, I liked the looks of the other island much better than I like this one. I'll wager that the natives there were more modest than the ones here. Did you see how those men were dressed as they rowed out to us? It was scandalous, my dear, simply scandalous!"

There must have been a Puritan among Hetty's ancestors, Raine thought before replying. "You've got to remember, dear, the islanders have been dressing that way for ages. They don't think it's scandalous at all."

"I know, but it's still a shock to see all those young men wearing nothing but those little scraps of cloth about their . . . their loins! And the women! Why their arms and limbs were exposed."

Personally, Raine thought the natives' costumes

were quite colorful and comfortable looking. A part of her longed to wear something as brief and unconfining as what she'd seen the island women wearing; she would certainly be a lot cooler than she was now. But, alas, she wasn't a native. She was instead a proper young Englishwoman, and as such would just have to suffer through this stifling, tropical heat in her long skirts and layers of petticoats.

"Did the captain say if we were going to be allowed ashore?" she queried, wiping away beads of perspiration from her upper lip.

"No, he didn't," Hetty sighed. "It was all I could do to get him to listen to my request about those poor animals in the hold. He seemed very preoccupied. I say, Raine, don't you think you should take your son out of his bath now? I mean, he's beginning to get all wrinkled."

Raine smiled down at her little boy. "You're probably right, but he's having such a good time." Adam's pale blond locks were plastered against his small head and runnels of water dribbled off his dimpled chin.

"I imagine he is, but too much water is not good for him, dear."

It was Raine's turn to scoff. "Stuff and nonsense, Hetty. Water is good for him." But she complied and extracted her wriggling son from the tub, wrapping him in a soft towel. "Did you see all those island children? They probably spend an enormous amount of time in the water and they certainly looked healthy to me."

"Yes, but they're island children, dear. They're accustomed to this wretched climate and casual way of life. Adam, there, is not. He's English, the same as you and me."

"I don't see what that has to do with it," Raine countered, a puzzled frown marring her brow.

"You will," Hetty rejoined, opening the door as she prepared to leave. "If and when we ever get back to England, that is."

Alone in the cabin with her son, Raine diapered Adam as she heard Slade bark out an order to his men on deck. With her thoughts still centered on the subject of children, she wondered what sort of childhood Slade had had. Had it been a happy one, as hers had been? Or had it been filled with sadness and tragedy?

"I'll probably never know," she murmured introspectively.

"Da," Adam jabbered, sitting up to reach for a stuffed toy near him.

Raine barely took notice of what the baby said. Of late he had been jibbering quite a bit, his limited vocabulary consisting mainly of one-syllabled baby sounds. It was only after she took him topside with her for a breath of fresh air and they spotted Slade that she realized Adam was actually talking.

"Da-da!" he squealed, extending his fat little arms toward the tall American.

Raine froze, her blue eyes widening with surprise.

"Da-da!" Adam cried out once more.

"Oh, no!" she moaned softly when Slade pivoted around to stare at them. Oh, surely he wouldn't think that *she* had taught Adam to . . . But he must, because he was coming straight toward them, his blank expression giving her no outward indication of what he was thinking.

Adam began to squirm furiously in his mother's arms. His sturdy little body twisted and turned so sharply that Raine almost lost her tenuous hold of him. Slade stopped before them, and as if it was the most natural thing for him to do, he gently took hold of Adam and gathered him close to his broad chest.

"Settle down, boy, before you hurt yourself," he scolded gently, giving the diapered bottom a tender pat.

"Da-da. Da-da." The baby chortled happily, pulling at Slade's shirt.

"I hope you don't think *I* taught Adam to say that," she challenged.

"Of course I don't." He chuckled. "He's just a baby; he doesn't know what he's saying." But it pleased him to hear it.

Adam decided, at that moment, to grab Slade's beard and he pulled it hard. When he heard the man cry "Ouch!" in pain, he giggled merrily, as if it were some kind of treat and pulled the beard once again.

Sharply inhaling an alarmed breath, Raine reached up to remove her son's clenched fist from Slade's face, not realizing that Slade did the same. Their fingers reached his jaw at the same moment, and his instinctively covered hers. With a need he could not explain, Slade pressed her hand to his cheek and held it captive there as an electric charge surged through him. It was like being hit with a lightning bolt from out of the clear blue.

Gazing down into her lovely, upturned face, he

experienced an emotion he'd felt only once before, fifteen years ago, and had thought never to feel again. Had she felt it too? She must have, because he heard her slight gasp and noted the odd, almost startled look on her face.

God, she was beautiful. More beautiful now, perhaps, than she had been the first time he'd seen her in that unconvincing dark wig and mourning cheongsam. Her pale blond hair, now bleached lighter by the sun, glinted like newly minted silver and gold in the late afternoon light. Her once fair complexion was now the color of rich honey, a faint line of freckles dusted the bridge of her short, straight nose. But it was her mouth, inviting and provocative as ever, which beckoned to him the loudest. He was sorely pressed not to answer its call.

Raine saw the tender look in his dark green eyes and thought her heart would leap out of her breast. It was not the look of a man bent on lust; it was something far more precious. He cared. He really cared for her!

In an instant, the fragile spell which held them was shattered as the sounds about them penetrated their senses.

Slade's eyes jerked away, as if he had suddenly remembered where they were. His head turned and she let her hand drop down to her side again. Inhaling deeply, she wondered if the moment they'd just shared had been real or merely imagined. She started to turn away, too, but his soft, imploring voice stopped her.

"Raine? About last night . . ."

She swallowed nervously. "Yes?"

156

"I—I'm sorry."

Sorry for what? she wondered. That he had rejected her so callously? Or that he had ever kissed her at all? Whichever it was, she could tell by his expression that his apology was a sincere one.

"It's all right," she murmured, lowering her gaze to the tanned column of his throat. "I understand."

"No, I don't think you do. I—"

"Captain?" Mr. Dennison called to him from the bow.

"Oh, hell!" Slade spat through gritted teeth. "I've got to go. Duty calls. Here, you'd better take the boy."

But as Adam was returned to her and their hands briefly touched again, he added softly, "We'll talk about this later, when there's time."

"There's really nothing to talk about," she heard her prideful self announce.

"Yes, there is. But we'll go into it later."

Adam began to squirm and fret in her arms.

"Settle down, young man," Slade ordered the baby. He gave Raine one last, unreadable look then turned and strode toward the bow where his crew waited.

Raine couldn't help from marveling at the play of muscles beneath Slade's clothes. For someone as big as he was, he moved with effortless grace. She could detect nothing clumsy or awkward about him, and he certainly didn't lack for physical beauty either. Oh, he was rough and unpolished in drawing-room manners, but he was still an incredibly handsome man.

The gentle, early evening breeze which had

sprung up ruffled his collar-length hair, the low angle of the sun clearly defining the curls that brushed his nape. Even as she fought to retain a secure hold on her still-wriggling son, a part of her longed to go over to Slade and comb through his unruly curls with her fingers, to feel again their strong, vibrant texture. She longed to rediscover those muscles shaping his broad shoulders, to caress the smoothness of his bare back, to feel the wiry crispness of the hairs on his chest that tapered down to his. . . .

"I see you and the good captain are on speaking terms once again."

Rudely jolted out of her indecent perusal, Raine turned a startled glance at Hetty, who had suddenly appeared beside her. Her heart fluttered wildly and she felt her cheeks flame with color. "What? What did you say?"

"Good heavens, Raine! You were positively drooling over the man. Can't you control yourself better than that?"

"Drooling? Me? Oh, come now, Hetty."

"Don't 'come now, Hetty' me, young lady. I know that look when I see it. You're in love with him, aren't you?"

Raine released a laugh that sounded oddly like a strangled sob. "I don't have to stand here and listen to such nonsense. I'm going below."

But Hetty stayed close behind her as she descended the passageway steps. "You can't run away from it, you know."

"I'm not running from anything!" Raine announced as she entered her cabin. "And will you please keep your voice down? You've no idea how it carries."

"Well, of course, my voice carries. Any well-trained actress's voice should!"

"Not here, it shouldn't."

"What's the matter? Don't you want the others to hear what they've already seen? I wasn't the only one up there watching the two of you. The entire crew witnessed that little scene."

"Oh, God, Hetty!" Raine sat the baby down on the deck before sinking weakly onto the bunk. "I've fought it as best I know how, and I've lost. I promised myself I wouldn't feel anything for *any* man because of what Roger put me through, and now I . . ." She shook her head in defeat. "What am I going to do?"

"Dear child, I wish I could help you. I wish there was something I could say to make it easier, but I can't. This is a problem you have to solve yourself."

"Yes, it's a problem all right." If Hetty only knew how big the problem was.

"It'll never work, you know." Hetty's voice was laced heavily with sympathy. "I've been where you are now, so I do know what I'm talking about. The two of you are poles apart when it comes to background and breeding. You'll only find yourself with a broken heart if you let this . . . this thing between you get out of hand."

Raine blinked at her friend questioningly.

"I was about your age," Hetty continued, her gray eyes drifting past Raine to focus on a long forgotten past. "Perhaps I was a bit younger when I fell in love. He was older, I do remember that . . . and married. But even if he hadn't had a wife, there was still his mother and his position to think of. I was merely an actress, a nobody, but he made me feel special as if I were a queen.

"My friends tried to caution me, but I wouldn't listen. Young women in love often don't, you know. Their hearts are much more influential than their common sense.

"So, I had my affair with Ted. It ran its course and ended, just like my friends told me it would. I've never loved anyone else since, Raine. I—I can't."

"Oh, Hetty!" Raine could feel the older woman's pain.

"No, don't feel sorry for me. The one thing I don't want or need is your pity. I chose my life, so I've only myself to blame for its outcome. You see, I've had plenty of proposals before and since Ted, but I've preferred to remain independent and unattached."

"That's all well and good for you, perhaps, but I don't think it's right for me. I'm not a great actress, Hetty. I never will be."

"Now, *that* is nonsense."

"No, it's the truth. I haven't the drive or the ambition it takes to become great. Mother and Father did. Rory does. But I do not."

"Raine—"

"No, hear me out. I know we've been over this same ground before, but I want to impress upon you how utterly ridiculous it is for me. Even before I met Roger and married him, I was getting tired of the theater. All those rehearsals, all of that endless traveling from one place to another. I had done it all

Chapter Twelve

ADAM SAT IN THE CHINA HIP-BATH, HIS SKIN AS PINK and rosy as the flowers that were painted on the outside. Just moments before, Raine had finished giving him his bath—his first in fresh spring water and not boiled sea water—and now he was playing. Or rather he was fighting, Raine thought, dodging the spray that flew out of the tub in her direction. His splayed starfish hands slapped furiously on the water's surface as he screamed angrily at it. One drop succeeded in hitting his little face, startling him, but he screamed again and slapped at the water with even more determination.

Raine held a towel in front of her, giggling delightedly. "You're not supposed to get me wet, too, you little scamp. I've already had my bath."

"Cheeky little blighter, look what he's done," Hetty exclaimed from the doorway. "The floor's all wet."

"Deck, Hetty," Raine corrected, getting to her feet. "You must remember to call it a deck, not a floor."

"Oh, stuff and nonsense," the older woman

my life and I simply wanted to settle down in one place and establish some . . . some sense of permanence." Being lady of the manor hadn't been quite as important to her as she had once thought; but putting down roots had been. Maybe if Roger had been a bit more . . .

But, no! She wasn't going to start thinking about him. Not now. He was dead, a part of her past, and she would be better off letting him stay that way.

"But you have talent, my girl!" Hetty insisted.

"Maybe I do. But it doesn't really matter now, does it? I'm exactly where I want to be—with my little boy. I'll tell you something, Hetty. I've had more pleasure this last month being just his mother than I did the entire time I was in the theater. No amount of applause can match the simple smile he gives me each morning."

When Hetty left her moments later, Raine's thought returned once more to Slade. His instantly recognizable voice drifted through her open porthole, assuring her that he was on the bridge just above her cabin. Something told her that he would have liked her mother and father, and that they, in turn, would have adored him. He was unconventional enough to appeal to their eccentric tastes, for they had always surrounded themselves with colorful scoundrels; and Slade was certainly that.

Rory, however, was another matter. She wasn't sure if he would take to Slade or not. Always the wariest of the four, he hadn't made friends as easily as she and their parents had. But, given the time, he would come around. She was almost certain of it.

Chapter Thirteen

A STRANGE RESTLESSNESS AWAKENED RAINE EARLY the next morning. Leaving Adam asleep in their bunk, she donned a simple skirt and blouse then wandered topside to the deserted deck. Gasping with awed wonder, she gazed at the quiet serenity of the island in the distance. In a few more hours she and Hetty, and maybe the baby, would be going ashore.

Looking up, Raine thought the dawn sky was more like a beautiful canvas painted by the Almighty than just a mere morning heaven. Red streaks slashed across the horizon and intermingled there with the fiery golds and deep purples. As she wandered over to stand at the ship's railing, she thought it one of the most religiously inspiring sights she'd ever seen.

"Good morning, Miss Sheridan."

She turned and spied Mr. Dennison, descending the steps from the bridge.

"Oh, good morning!" She smiled. "It's beautiful, isn't it? Almost like a rainbow."

"It's pretty, all right." Coming to stand beside her, the mate's voice held a note of discrepancy.

162

"Is something the matter?"

"Yes, ma'am, there sure is." He frowned down at her. "Haven't you heard the old saying, 'Red sky at morning, sailor take warning. Red sky at night, sailor's delight'?"

"No, I don't believe I have. But then I haven't done much sailing, either. What does it mean?"

"Well, ma'am, it means we're in for some bad weather. Captain Slade's not going to like it, either. He was hoping to avoid the storms if he could."

"But we should be all right, shouldn't we? I mean, we're here at the island and not out on the open sea."

"We are now," the mate agreed. "But we're weighing anchor this morning. Didn't you know?"

"No! I was under the impression that we would be here for a few more days. Miss Carlisle and I haven't been allowed to go ashore yet."

"I'm sorry about that, ma'am, but from the looks of it, you'll have to wait until we hit the Raliks to stand on dry land again. With the fever here and all—"

"Fever!"

Mr. Dennison shifted his large frame uncomfortably under her probing glance, his swarthy skin reddening even more. "Er, I think you'd better see the captain, Miss Sheridan. I've said too much already."

"Mr. Dennison!" she called to him as he started to turn and walk away. "Is there a fever on this island? Please, tell me. I think I have a right to know." Her concern continued to climb as he delayed in answering.

Reluctantly, he finally responded, "Yes, ma'am, there is."

"Oh, my God!" Visions of her healthy little boy becoming gravely ill flashed through her mind.

"But there's no need to get worried, Miss Sheridan. Chances are we won't get it. Only the islanders seem to be susceptible to it."

"They didn't look the least bit ill when we arrived yesterday," she hastened to point out, recalling the friendly faces she'd seen. "Just what kind of fever is it? Typhoid? Bubonic plague? What?"

"Well, we don't really know, ma'am. You see, a whaler was through here a few weeks back, and it appears that the crew infected the islanders. It's hit the other islands pretty bad, too."

"Were there any deaths?"

"A few." He nodded gravely. "But they seem to be mostly old folks and . . . and sickly little ones."

Raine felt the blood drain from her face. She clenched her fists and compressed her lips into a thin, angry line before turning on her heel to stalk toward the quarterdeck hatchway.

"Miss Sheridan?" the mate called out to her. "Where are you going?"

"To see Captain Slade, as you suggested I do," she tossed over her shoulder.

"But, ma'am, he's not up yet. He's—"

Mr. Dennison's voice trailed off as she descended the steps. Her only thought now was to confront Slade and find out for herself just what was going on. If they were in any danger, if there was the slightest chance that Adam might contract the illness, she wanted to know about it. Without bothering to knock first, she entered Slade's quarters, letting the door swing wide so that it banged against the cabinet behind it.

Startled out of a very pleasant dream in which she was one of the featured players, Slade bolted upright in his bunk. He glared at her for a moment in total confusion.

"I want to know just what the hell is going on?" she demanded, stalking over to where he sat.

"I—I—uh, you what?" he babbled incoherently.

"Mr. Dennison has just informed me that we're in danger of becoming infected by that island's plague."

"Plague! I don't know anything about any plague." Scowling, he raked a hand through his touseled hair. "Good God Almighty, lady! I thought we'd been attacked by pirates or something." His long legs bent beneath the white sheet which covered him, and he propped his elbows onto his upraised knees, his head falling wearily into his hands.

"You might *wish* we had been if my son gets sick," she declared vehemently.

"Oh, get the hell out of here and let me get some sleep. He's not going to get sick."

"How can you be so sure of that when you don't even know what kind of fever it is?"

"I just do, all right?" he returned sleepily, his lids slowly closing.

"No, it is *not* all right! My little boy's health is in jeopardy because of your carelessness and I *demand* to know the reason why!"

Slade opened one eye and shot her an icy glare.

But Raine didn't quail beneath his gaze. Instead, her spine stiffened and her chin lifted a notch higher.

"Let me tell you something, lady," he snarled. "I had the late watch last night and only got to bed an hour ago. I'm not in any mood to be having this little chat with you. Two more hours sleep and I *might* be civil, but right now you're really pressing your luck. I'm just going to say one thing more—Don't worry about the damn fever; it's harmless. Now close the door behind you on your way out."

And with that, he stretched out again on his bunk turning his back to her as he drew the sheet up over his head.

It was tantamount to waving a red flag before an irate bull.

Raine gnashed her teeth together as an angry, frustrated sound formed deep in her throat. He wasn't going to dismiss her this easily and get away with it!

She reached out for the corner of the sheet and, with a dramatic sweep of her arm, ripped it back. Then she jerked to a halt, nearly toppling over onto him in the process.

"Oh, my God!" she whimpered, staring in stunned amazement at the six feet four inches of naked skin before her. He slept in the nude!

A deep, masculine growl of rage came from the direction of Slade's pillow. Before Raine could step back to a safe distance, he flipped over and grabbed her, his face contorting into a snarl as he pulled her down on top of him.

"You've gone too damn far this time, lady!"

"Slade, I—"

"I told you I wasn't in any mood to be civil, but you wouldn't listen."

"But, I just—"

"You've had this coming to you for a long time now."

"No, Slade!" she cried out. "Don't—*Ohhh!*" The mattress met her face with a slap and she found herself staring at his bare waist. An iron band of muscle and bone clamped across her shoulder blades, holding her tightly in place as her skirt and petticoats were tossed over her head.

"Stop it!" she shrieked, tensing for the paddling she never received.

Slade's hand was lifted in midair, prepared to strike her curvaceous bottom. But the sight of it caused him to smile instead. She deserved a sound thrashing, but instead he lowered his arm and gently pinched one rounded buttock. It would be a sin to beat something this pretty, even though she did deserve it.

Assured that he had given her what she had coming, Slade released his tight hold on her, and pulled down her petticoats and skirt.

That, he realized later, was where he made his mistake.

Raine turned on him in a towering rage. More than just her posterior had been pinched. Her pride had suffered as well!

She slapped him as hard as she could, and was about to hit him again when her wrist was shackled in a viselike grip. She suddenly found herself thrust beneath him, his nose a mere inch from hers.

"Just what the hell do you think you're *doing?*"

"You pinched me!" she accused shrilly. "Nobody does that and gets away with it. I've got every right to fight back!"

"You picked the wrong man to tangle with, lady! I'm a helluva lot bigger than you, or hadn't you noticed?"

Squirming futilely beneath him, she found his considerable weight too heavy to budge. "I noticed, all right," came her seething growl. "Now get off me!"

"So you can slap me around some more?" he yelled back. "Not on your life!"

"You—you're the most barbaric son of a bitch I've ever had the misfortune to meet, Quentin Slade!" she screamed. "You deserve to be slapped and a whole lot more!"

"Not by the likes of you!"

"If you don't move your arrogant carcass off me, I'll—"

From out of nowhere, cold water suddenly chilled their heated flesh. The back of Slade's head was completely drenched, as was one side of Raine's startled face. The bed upon which they lay was a wet, sodden mess.

Both heads turned at once toward the door to see Hetty standing there with an empty, but still dripping, wash basin in her hands. She resembled an avenging Valkyrie with her fat gray braids dangling in front of her shapeless cotton nightgown.

"Thank God. *That* shut you up. Don't the two of you realize that there are people aboard still trying to sleep?" A heavy, disgusted sigh escaped her as she shook her head. "I think we were all better off when you *weren't* on speaking terms. It was certainly much quieter!"

Hetty turned then, only her profile visible to the two still entwined on the bunk.

"Oh, *do* step aside!" they saw her demand impatiently, and heard a noticeable shuffling of many pairs of bare feet in the passageway. But as she started to move, she stopped and directed her next question to an unseen party. "What's the matter? Haven't you ever seen a woman in her *dishabillé* before?" Her chin then lifted to a regal angle before she finally disappeared from the doorway.

Two wet heads slowly turned toward each other. Raine felt a smile tug at her lips and noted the nervous twitching of Slade's mustache. Discovering the ridiculousness of the situation, they soon filled the cabin with the sound of their combined laughter.

"Didn't I once say she was like a bucket of ice water?" Slade remarked, moving to lie beside Raine.

"Yes, but I didn't think you meant it so literally," she rejoined between giggles.

Their amusement continued for a few moments longer until it began to diminish, slowly dying a natural death as another, more potent emotion began to overtake them. Green eyes softened into twin pools of emerald fire. Violet eyes warmed under their gaze.

Before Slade had wanted to punish her for having interrupted his well-earned sleep, but now he longed to reward her for being here beside him. An all-too-familiar ache began to throb in his loins. He inhaled deeply, absorbing into his lungs her rare, sweet fragrance and found himself oddly light-headed from the scent. Oh, how he wanted her! It was taking every ounce of self-control he could muster just to keep his hands off of her.

Raine, however, knew no discipline. She brushed the damp strands of dark hair away from his forehead, feeling his rapid pulse beating in his temple. Her fingers combed through the thick locks again and again until it lay smoothly against his well-shaped skull. Then they trailed down his cheek to lightly mark a path through his beard. She wanted to tell him so much, but she dared not! The memory of her previous confession held her back.

"Raine."

Her name was expelled on a masculine whisper, but she covered his lips with two slender fingertips and muttered, "Shhh," so softly it almost went unheard.

Her fingers drifted aside and were replaced with her soft, yielding mouth. The kiss was so sweetly compelling, Slade felt his restraint shatter about him like shards of broken crystal and knew he had to give in to this coersive hunger which drove him. He started to press her more closely to him, but she moved, leaving his side and his bed.

"We can't," she professed with remorse, her slender body quivering like a leaf in the center of his cabin floor. "Not here—not now."

Knowing she was right didn't lessen the ache he felt. "Then you'd better go before I earn your title of barbarian," he groaned.

"It's my turn to say I'm sorry," she intoned quietly

as he adjusted the sheet over his aroused masculinity. "And I *am* sorry, Slade."

"Don't be. I'm not."

"I didn't mean for this to happen."

"I know."

"I only—"

"No, I don't want to hear it. Just get out of here and let me get dressed. We'll talk later." When we've both had a chance to cool off, he thought.

"But you need your rest."

"You think I can go back to sleep *now?*" he challenged dryly, the grooves deepening in his cheeks.

A maidenly blush stained her lovely features as she realized what he meant. With a shy smile, she turned into the passageway and left him to deal with his uncomfortable condition.

They would talk later, he'd said. Oh, yes, she agreed with a secretive smile, they most certainly would do that!

But "later" took a lot longer than either of them anticipated.

The storm that had been only a colorful promise on the dawn's horizon became a frightening reality shortly after they sailed away from the tiny, nameless island. At least, to Raine it was frightening. The experienced crew members took to the tossing and rolling waves as if the storm was nothing more than a minor inconvenience. With the sky almost black and the winds howling, the water churned violently, hitting the side of the *Mary Ellen* so hard that it rocked the ship back and forth upon the waves.

Hetty escaped to her bunk the moment the first of the swells began to rock the barkentine. She vowed, with a sickly green expression, that she would surely die before the day was out.

Of the three of them, Adam seemed the most unaffected. The movement of the ship lulled him into an early nap, and he slept through most of the storm.

"There ain't nothin' to really get worried about," Tex assured Raine with a dismissive shrug. Streams of water dripped off his bare head and slicker-covered shoulders into a puddle on the galley deck where they stood. "It's only a little-bitty squall."

"A *little* squall?" Raine repeated, bracing herself between the cupboard and the galley bulkhead behind her as the deck tilted to an extremely uncomfortable angle. "I would certainly hate to see what a *big* one is like."

"Well, 'fore we get to Frisco, you just might get to, ma'am."

"Why—why do you say that?" Her voice was a slender thread of fear.

Chuckling at her horrified expression, Tex explained, "'Cause we're in the part of the ocean where most of the really big storms start."

"You mean . . ." she gulped, " . . . *hurricanes?*"

"Yes, ma'am. Worse than that, though, if one of these little specks of land out here decides to have itself an earthquake or volcanic eruption, we could find ourselves in the middle of a tidal wave. Now *them's* the ones you gotta fear."

"I think I'm going to be sick," she moaned,

pressing a hand to her churning stomach. The deck, which had been higher than her head at one point, leveled out for a moment and she tried to make her way out of the galley and into the passageway. But just as suddenly as it had leveled out, it tilted again and she found herself rudely thrust back against Tex's whipcord-lean frame.

"You gotta watch your step in this kind of weather, Miss Sheridan," he warned softly, wrapping her in a brotherly embrace until the boat righted itself once again. "You know, it might not be a bad idea to wait out the rest of this here little blow in your cabin."

"My thoughts exactly," she agreed with a weak nod. In fact, she thoroughly intended to copy Hetty; crawl into bed and pull the covers over her head.

Slade chose that precise moment to enter the galley. But if he was at all bothered by Tex holding Raine, or that the other man was smiling down at her, he didn't show it.

"Any hot coffee left?" he asked amiably, glancing over at the cold, unlit stove.

"No, sir," Tex replied. "I came in a lookin' for a cup myself, but all I found was Miss Sheridan here, tryin' to stand up. How's it lookin' topside?"

"The wind's beginning to die down some," Slade responded. In one, economical movement, he pulled the rain-drenched slicker over his head, splattering water over Raine's cool, clammy skin. "We should be out of the worst of it fairly soon now."

Raine struggled to free herself from Tex's arm, but the constant pitch and roll of the deck made that feat impossible. What must Slade be thinking of her? She was allowing Tex to hold her as if it were the most natural thing to do. Telling herself that she should put up some show of resistance, she mumbled thinly, "You can let me go now."

"Are you sure?" Tex frowned down at her. "I need to get back up on deck, but I wouldn't want you to get hurt or nothin'."

"I'll take her," Slade injected easily, winding his arm about her waist. "Go on up and help with the sails."

"Yes, sir," Tex complied, ambling out of the galley. "See y'all later."

Though Slade's nearness had some degree of comfort, Raine's stomach continued its sick churning. "I wasn't flirting," she confessed on a reedy whisper. "I was only trying to . . . to survive this little blow."

"Now did you hear me accuse you of flirting?" Amusement laced his query.

"No, but I wouldn't put it past you. Oh, Slade! I'm going to be sick!"

Perceiving her greenish pallor, Slade adroitly maneuvered her toward the big pail in the corner where Cookie tossed his leftover food scraps. One strong arm held her firmly about the waist while his free hand cupped her moist forehead. Bending her forward, he ordered, "Go ahead. Let her rip."

And Raine did.

Spasm after violent spasm wracked her slender frame until her stomach was completely empty. Only twice before, that she could recall, had she ever been this ill, and both of those times had been in her childhood. Her mother had held her head then. Oddly enough, Slade's touch was just as gentle, just as loving as her mother's had been.

When the last spasm had subsided, she straightened and leaned her head back weakly against Slade's broad chest.

"Feel better now?" His soft query was like a feather's touch above her ear.

Breathing deeply, she nodded.

"Good. Let's get you back to your cabin."

Utterly drained and quite exhausted, she didn't protest when he casually lifted her off the deck and held her close to him, one arm braced beneath the bend of her legs as the other supported her back. Like a trusting child, she wound her arms around his neck and rested her cheek against the strong column of his throat.

He was being so wonderful now, she thought, so kind and considerate, it was hard to believe that within him there lurked a stern, almost cruel, obstinate streak. But perhaps, being the captain of his own ship, he needed to be unyielding. Heavens, the crew didn't seem to mind his harsh outbursts. In fact, they showed definite signs of respecting it. Just as she was beginning to admire it herself?

Carrying Raine up the narrow passageway while the ship tossed and rolled was not an easy task, but Slade managed to do just that with only a minor amount of effort. When at last they entered her cabin, he gently placed her onto her bunk, being careful not to disturb the sleeping baby there.

With a smile, he brushed aside a tendril of pale honey-gold hair from her face, then straightened and started to move away.

"Thank you," she murmured. "I don't think I could have made it back here on my own."

"What were you doing down in the galley anyway?" He leaned one hip against her cupboard, his feet spread to brace him, and crossed his arms in front of his chest.

"I had the silly notion that someone might want fresh coffee. But when I got down there, the fire was out in that monstrosity Cookie calls a stove and I didn't know how to get it started. Tex came in just in time to save me from falling headlong into the coal skuttle."

"Hey! You're not embarrassed about it, are you?"

Feeling her cheeks flame, she admitted, "Well, yes, a little."

"There's no need to be."

"Yes, there is. Women—I mean, *ladies* prefer to be ill in private."

A chuckle rumbled through Slade's chest. "Honey, you're not the first to get seasick, and you're sure as hell not the last. Why, I've seen sailors with years of experience heave it over the side during a storm. There's nothing you can do about it now, so just forget it ever happened."

That was easy for *him* to say. He hadn't disgraced himself as she had done.

"Slade?" she called, when it looked as if he might leave.

"Yeah?" he turned back.

"Are we in any danger?" It had been preying on her mind for some time now, and she had to ask him.

"No, like I told Tex, we're through the worst of the storm."

"I don't mean that. I mean the fever. Are we in danger of getting it?"

His chin dropped to his chest and he smiled, shaking his head. "No, sweetheart, no danger at all."

"But you left the island so suddenly, I—"

"Because I was worried about the islanders. It's real strange, you know, but we can catch a little cold or something and it doesn't bother us, but if the islanders catch it . . . it can sometimes kill them." At her dubious look, he stressed, "It's a fact, sweetheart. I wouldn't lie to you."

"I hope not, but—" she broke off abruptly as she saw Slade's brows pull together in a preoccupied frown. "Oh, no! What is it?"

"Oh, nothing." He shook his head briskly. "Well, nothing important anyway. I was just wondering if you knew how to shoot a gun."

"Shoot a gun!" Startled, she jackknifed into an upright position. "Are you anticipating an insurrection, a—a mutiny?"

"No, nothing like that! It's just that in these waters, it never hurts to be prepared." Pausing for a moment, he then asked, "Well, can you? Handle a gun, I mean."

"I'm an *actress*, Slade."

He released a disappointed grunt. "I guess that means you can't, huh? Well," he sighed. "I guess I'll just have to teach you how."

"Whatever on earth for?"

"In these waters—"

"Yes, I know, we should be prepared," she finished for him.

She lay back down as he left her cabin, and turned to look at her sleeping son. "Well, my innocent little darling, it looks as if your mummy is about to become a gunslinger."

Chapter Fourteen

"JUST IMAGINE THAT IT'S YOUR WORST ENEMY," SLADE murmured, his gaze indicating the empty bottle sitting on the stern railing. "If you don't kill it first, it'll kill you. Understand?"

Raine didn't, but nodded her head anyway. "Do I have to kill it? I mean, couldn't I just injure it a little bit?"

"No! Never aim a gun unless you intend to kill, otherwise you don't aim it at all. Now. Hold out your arm. Keep your elbow bent just a little. That's it. Now look straight down the barrel and center it on the bottle."

She did just as he instructed, but the weight of the weapon caused her hand to wobble slightly. "Aren't I supposed to cock it first, or something?"

"No, not unless you want to. Stop shaking, dammit!"

"Well, I can't help it—it's heavy!"

"Damn!" he spat. "Then use both hands."

Her left hand came up and curled around the knuckles of her right. With an impatient groan, Slade repositioned it so that both of her arms supported the weighty weapon instead of just one.

"Now then," he sighed, moving to stand behind her, his knees bent so that he could look over her shoulder. "Center the barrel again and *squeeze* the trigger."

Anticipating the loud explosion that was sure to come, Raine winced, closing her eyes as her right hand tightened about the trigger.

BANG! the weapon fired, and the recoil thrust her back into Slade.

She opened her eyes and, through the acrid smoke, saw the champagne bottle sitting intact on the railing.

"Oh, damn. I *missed* it."

"By a mile," Slade agreed, his attention focused on the new hole splintering his deck.

"Do you want me to try it again?"

"Once more," he replied hesitantly. "But this time, hit the *bottle,* okay?"

Again Raine aimed the gun and fired, putting a hole through one of the mizzenmast sails.

She turned and saw Slade shaking his head in utter disgust.

"Well, I told you I was an actress!"

"You're nearsighted, too. Let's try it one more time, and this time don't take your eyes off the bottle!"

For Raine, the third time was the charm. She left her eyes opened and shattered the champagne bottle into a million tiny fragments.

"I hit it!" she cried jubilantly. "I actually hit it!"

"Finally," he conceded with an ungracious groan.

"Do you want me to shoot another bottle?"

"No, one's enough for today." He took the gun from her and emptied the unfired cartridges into the palm of his hand. Hell, at the rate she was going, she would destroy his whole damn ship before she became a crackshot.

"But I was just getting the hang of it, Slade."

"Yeah, I know, but I've got a much better idea."

"Oh? What's that?"

"If we run into trouble—and I hope to God we don't—my double-ought shotgun will suit you much better."

"A double-ought shotgun?"

"Yeah. You don't even have to aim it. You just point it in the general direction of the target and pull the trigger."

"Do you want me to try it now?"

"No! I mean, no," he replied more calmly. "There's no need. We'll save it for when we really need it."

"Well, if you're sure . . ."

"Trust me. I'm sure." One eye closed in a condescending wink.

"Oh, well, all right then. I'll go below and . . . and mend something."

Glancing back at his torn sail, he banished the thought of asking her to mend it. He'd see to it himself, later. She would probably try to sew it up with pink thread or something.

"What was all that noise?" Hetty inquired when Raine went below.

"Captain Slade was teaching me to fire his revolver," Raine announced with pride. "It makes quite a loud noise but it's not quite so bad when you get used to it. I must say, you're looking better this morning, Hetty."

Her companion made a disparaging sound and gave her a weak smile. "I'll not be completely well again until we get off this bloody ship. I've discovered, my dear, that my constitution is not suited to this form of travel. My feet want to be on dry land again."

"Oh, I rather like it," Raine countered. Once her bout with seasickness had abated, she felt like a new woman. "This sea air is quite invigorating."

"Yes, you do have a healthy bloom in your cheeks."

Raine giggled, feeling thoroughly at peace with her lot in life. She lifted Adam off the deck and hugged him fiercely. "I'm more than just blooming, Hetty. I'm happier than I've ever been."

The older woman sighed and shook her head. "Would the good captain have anything to do with it?"

"Oh, Hetty, is it so obvious?"

"Even a blind man would see that you're in love."

"Oh, I am, Hetty, I am! I feel so complete when I'm near him, and I feel so desolate when I'm not. Right this moment, when I know I need to be here with Adam, I want to be up there on deck with him, too."

"Does that . . . *American* share your feelings?"

"I don't know," Raine responded with a soft sigh. "I pray to God that he does, but as yet he's not said anything." Only his gentle tenderness toward her told her that he felt something more than fondness for her.

"Raine," Hetty began, sitting down on the bunk to look at her earnestly. "Dear, you must not let your hopes build up so on this man. He's used to taking his pleasure where he can find it. His boy, David, is proof of that."

"No, you're wrong, Hetty. I know about David, but Slade loved the boy's mother, truly he did. He didn't toy with her and then desert her."

"That's what *he's* told you."

"And I believe him." She placed a hand on Hetty's and gave it a tight squeeze. "When we were in Manila, I saw the two of them together; Slade and David's mother. She was a beautiful woman, but she looked so sad. I've not heard the whole tale, but I'm sure she regrets what happened."

"What *did* happen?"

"All I know is, she gave up her son and Slade raised him alone."

"Well, before you get in too deeply with him, I would demand to know the whole story."

Raine opened her mouth, but then closed it again. How could she tell her old friend and companion that she was "in too deeply" already?

The following weeks became something of a learning experience for Raine as they sailed toward their next port of call. She had never known frustrations of a sensual nature before, but after feeling what physical pleasure could be like at Slade's hand, she itched to know it again. However, with the duties they were all responsible for, she could only think and dream, but could not experience.

Her nights were hard to endure. She would sleep soundly for a while, then would begin to dream about Slade holding her, touching her, caressing her breasts until they ached terribly. A tingle would begin in her loins and then would throb unmercifully until she was forced to press her thighs tightly together, the pressure she exerted there finally easing her desires somewhat.

But if the nights were hard, the days were agonizing. She forced herself to silently stand by and watch Slade, giving no outward indication that she wanted him. And it was hell, pure hell! He would climb onto the rigging and up to the top of the masts as she stood below. His buttocks and thigh muscles were so clearly defined beneath his taut trousers that it caused her heart to pound erratically. And when he would turn, she would see in her mind's eye, that part of him which was so blatantly male.

Never once did Slade tell her what his true feelings for her were. But she knew, mainly by his actions toward her, that they were more than mere fondness. He was kind and pleasant toward her, paternally playful with little Adam, and he even became mildly tolerant of Hetty, whom Raine sensed he disliked. As she tutored David in his lessons, he would stand by and watch her. Then at night, when the rest of the crew had gone to bed, she would hear him across the passageway, reviewing with the boy what she had taught him that day. But in all that time, he never once tried to compromise her or even come near her when he knew she was alone. He kept his distance and held his passions in check while she was left to wrestle with hers.

The Raliks, where they next dropped anchor to replenish their dwindling supplies, were nothing like their last port of call. There were no towering mountains to preannounce the islands while the *Mary Ellen* was still miles away. They were merely small patches of lush green land in the middle of an endless expanse of ocean.

"That's because they're coral atolls," Davey explained to her as she gazed at them from the deck.

The ship crept closer and closer, all of the giant sails lowered except for the foresails, which were raised to catch the gentle wind.

"You mean, there are no volcanoes on the island?" Raine queried, bouncing her squirming son on her hip.

"No, ma'am. None at all."

"But why are we going so slowly? I would think, if there were more sails raised, we could get there much quicker."

"It's too risky with all the reefs around. See down there?"

Raine peered over the side and down into the blue water below the hull where Davey pointed. Large masses of what looked to her like land were there just below the surface.

"That's a coral reef," he explained. "It can tear a hole in a ship and rip the hull to pieces if you tried to sail over it."

"Then why *are* we?"

"We're not." He grinned. "Well, not *over* it anyway. We're going through one of the gaps in it.

There's a lot of them just wide enough for us to get through. But you got to watch for them and take your time. That's why Pa is going so slow and being so cautious." His teak-brown face looked skyward and his green almond-shaped eyes squinted into the glare of the brilliant sun. "We're lucky we got here in good weather, 'cause if we were in a storm and the sea was the least bit rough, then we'd really be in a mess of trouble."

"Yes, I can imagine we would be," Raine agreed.

Adam arched his back at that moment and almost slipped out of Raine's arms. She released an impatient groan and settled him back on her hip.

"He's getting too big for me to handle," she grumbled as he wriggled again.

Without preamble, Davey took the baby from her, lifting him high over his head to settle him on his shoulders. Adam squealed loud with delight, his two little fists clenching clumps of Davey's black hair.

"Oh, do be careful!" she warned.

"He's not going to get hurt," Davey assured her.

"It's not him I'm worried about—it's you. He could leave you baldheaded."

"Aw, there ain't much chance of that." Davey laughed, then sobered. "I mean, there *isn't* much chance of that."

Raine smiled and watched him slowly jog toward the bow, Adam bouncing happily on his shoulders. When Davey turned and started back toward her, her breath caught in a shocked gasp. With Davey's arms raised high above his head to hold Adam, his shirt had pulled free of his trousers' waistband. It was there on his flat brown belly that she saw the dark patterns of hair. Her eyes flew up his torso back to his laughing face and there she perceived the faint bristles of what would soon be a beard on his jaw.

Lord, why hadn't she seen it sooner? Had she been too busy, too preoccupied with just teaching Davey not to recognize and know the signs? Davey was fifteen, nearly sixteen, and by all outward accounts, well on his way to becoming a man. Slade had seen it. Naturally he had; he was the boy's father. *That* was why he had warned her not to get too close.

"They get on good together, don't they?" came a deep voice beside her.

She jerked her head around and felt her face burn as her heart beat rapidly. Slade had seen her, watching Davey and Adam.

"I just realized," she confessed with quiet awe. "David is almost a man."

"Yeah." He smiled wistfully. "They do grow up fast, don't they? One day you're bouncing them around on your shoulders like that and the next day you're showing them how to shave."

Glancing back at the boys, she felt an unexplainable twinge tug her heart. Who would be around to teach Adam to shave? She desperately wanted Slade to have that honor, but until he said something, or made the first move, she would just have to stand by and continue to wish.

"Are we past the reef now?" she asked, redirecting her thoughts.

"Mmm-hmm." He nodded. "You'd better get ready if you're going ashore with the rest of us."

"Ashore!" Her violet eyes sparkled. "Oh, yes, I

will!" She turned to go below to her cabin, but stopped and looked back at him, a hand pressed to her throat. "I don't know what to wear."

"Well, don't ask me." He chuckled.

"No, what I mean is, are we going to be meeting only the islanders or . . . or someone of importance?" She certainly didn't want to make a bad impression on whoever met them; it would reflect badly on Slade.

"The most important person on that island is a fifty-year-old lady, and believe me, she won't *care* what you're wearing."

Raine nodded and dashed below, calling for Hetty as she entered her cabin.

"What's the matter, dear?" Hetty asked, coming in after her.

"Slade just told me we were going ashore! You've got to help me out of this dress and into another one."

"Heaven be praised!" Hetty held a dramatic prayerlike pose and addressed the ceiling. "Dry land at last!"

As rapidly as their nervous fingers and the small confines of their cabins would allow, the two of them changed into their best, most suitable frocks for this much long awaited occasion. Raine wore a pale blue muslin with high lace collar, long tapering sleeves and a modest bustle in the back, while Hetty wore her simple dove gray, which highlighted the silver in her hair.

Just as they were putting the finishing touches to their toilet, Davey entered with a fretful Adam on his hip. A large, wet stain covered the older boy's shirt, and Raine knew in an instant what had happened. She took the complaining baby from Davey and whipped off the damp diaper.

"He's crying because he didn't want to come inside," Davey explained.

"Yes, I guessed as much. Oh, before you go. Just who is this important woman on the island? Is she their queen?"

"I don't really know, to tell you the truth, Miss Sheridan. All I do know is everybody over there respects her a lot and they give her things. I guess, if she's anybody, she's their high priestess, or something."

"High priestess!" Hetty snorted. "That sounds rather pagan, doesn't it, Raine?"

Raine tossed her companion a baleful glance when Davey had gone and warned, "Don't start being critical, Hetty."

"I wasn't, Raine. I was merely stating my opinion."

"Yes, and rather a faultfinding one at that." Grabbing a damp cloth, she began washing Adam's face and hands. "If Slade so much as suspects we're going to embarrass him, he will leave us behind. And I, for one, have waited too long to go ashore to let you endanger this chance for me."

Hetty was clearly astonished at Raine's outburst. "I'll have you know, dear girl, that *I've* never embarrassed anyone, much less some surly upstart of an American."

"Good! Let's keep it that way." She tugged a

clean, ivory linen baby dress over Adam's head and ran a brush through his touseled gold curls. Standing, she said, "We'd better not forget our hats. The sun's awfully bright today."

The population of the island numbered about fifty, Raine discovered as they stepped out on the deck. And by the looks of it, all of them had come out to greet the ship. Men in odd-looking canoes were paddling their way out to where the *Mary Ellen* had dropped anchor, while the women and children remained on shore, waving to them as they shouted out their welcomes.

"Oh, my word!" Hetty groaned quietly. "They're all naked here, too. Don't these people know *anything* about clothes?"

Raine shifted her gaze from the small brown figures in the distance to Hetty, narrowing her eyes in warning.

"You ladies look mighty nice." Slade grinned as he stepped up beside them. "Out to impress the locals, are you?"

"We're not out to impress anyone, Captain Slade," Hetty proclaimed disparagingly before Raine could open her mouth.

The grin Slade wore took on a mischievous twitch and he gave Raine a sly wink before helping her into the dinghy, which was still suspended in midair beside the main deck. What on earth was he up to? she wondered. That glimmer in his eye was there for some reason, and she had a most uncomfortable feeling because of it.

Once she and Hetty had settled themselves into the little boat, two of the crewmen slowly lowered it with a hand crank down to the water. Then Tex, who was manning the oars, began rowing to shore.

"Isn't Captain Slade coming with us?" Raine asked him, holding Adam in her lap with one hand while her other maintained a secure grip on the wide brim of her straw bonnet.

"Oh, yes, ma'am. But seein' as how he's the captain an' all, he's gonna be given the honor of goin' in the outrigger."

"Is that what that little canoe is called?"

"Yes, ma'am."

Glancing surreptitiously over her shoulder, she saw Slade descend the rope ladder dangling down the side of the ship. Stripped of his shirt, his sun-bronzed torso glistened like polished teak as he held onto the rope-rung for the lead outrigger to reach him. Lord, she thought, if it weren't for his beard and mustache and long trousers, he would look exactly like the island men—exotic and decidedly uncivilized.

"Uh, Miss Sheridan?" Tex began hesitantly, drawing her attention back to him. "There's somethin' I think you and Miss Carlisle ought to know before we reach shore."

"What would that be, Tex?" Her wide violet eyes blinked at him in polite inquiry.

"Well, ma'am, these people—the women, I mean —they're real innocent."

"We're not about to corrupt them, young man," Hetty chided.

"No, ma'am! I didn't think y'all were. But . . . but they're not like you all are. That is, they don't set any great store in the same things y'all do. I guess what I'm tryin' to say is, they're a lot like a bunch of kids; just happy and playful and . . . and kinda ignorant about certain things."

"I'm not sure I understand what you're saying, Tex," Raine confessed with a frown.

"You will," he mumbled prophetically and began rowing with more determination.

Wincing against the glare of the sun reflected on the surface of the water, Raine admired the fertile greenness of the island. Tall palms swayed gracefully in the breeze, their trunks bending ever so slightly. She smiled at the peaceful beauty of it all and thought that this was truly a paradise.

Only when they drew closer to the wide expanse of white sandy beach did she let her gaze shift from the treetops to the figures waiting for them on shore. She blinked, not at first believing what she saw, then she stiffened indignantly.

"The cad!" she hissed through clenched teeth. "He knew all along and didn't say a word." *That* was what his sly little grin had been about. He *knew* the women here went about bare-breasted and he hadn't said a word of warning.

"Hetty dear," she addressed her companion, who was facing her and not the island. "Prepare yourself for a little shock."

"What?" The older woman started to turn, but Raine's hand on her knee stalled her.

"No, don't look yet. Just listen to what I have to say."

In quiet tones that Tex barely heard, she informed her friend of what they were about to encounter. Pulling at the oars, the lanky Texan saw the older woman stiffen with a jerk and heard a strangled cry erupt from her stout, gray-clad figure. If either one of them was going to cause trouble or make a scene, he thought, it would be the old lady. He knew they should have told them before they left the ship. He knew it, but the captain had other ideas.

When his oars dug into sand beneath the waves, Tex stopped rowing and hopped agilely out of the dinghy to find himself standing knee-deep in water. With the help of two strong island boys, they pulled the little vessel further up onto the beach and there he proceeded to assist his passengers ashore.

Both Raine and Hetty held onto their composure quite admirably. They smiled and spoke politely to the bare-breasted maidens and matrons who greeted them with giggles and stares. And with no hesitation whatsoever, Raine relinquished her son to one of the women who reached for him. Odd sounds of what seemed to be awed admiration came from them as the women began to touch and stroke Adam's corn-silk blond hair. But rather than balk at all of the fondling, Adam chortled with delight.

A hush descended over the assembled throng about the same moment Slade's outrigger reached shore. But the islanders weren't looking at him. Their stares were directed instead toward the dense growth of palm trees and Raine saw two sturdy island men appear there, supporting a litter between them. Seated upon the structure that reminded her of an Indian sedan-chair of interwoven vines, tree limbs and palm branches was a regal-looking woman about Hetty's age. The high priestess, she told herself, lifting her chin to a proud angle.

Slade jumped free of the outrigger and waded through the pounding surf as well as the press of islanders, his dark head towering high over the shorter ones about him. He reached the litter at the same moment the bearers deposited their important burden onto the white sand. Extending a hand to the woman in the sedan-chair, he assisted her to her feet before bending to kiss her fingers.

"Not only is he a surly upstart, he's a cad as well," Hetty hissed. "Look at him, fawning over that woman!"

"Hetty, watch your tongue," Raine warned softly.

"Well, it's galling to see him behave that way over a heathen."

"Shhh!"

Raine waited patiently and watched as Slade conversed with the small, dark-skinned woman. From the way they behaved toward one another, this wasn't the first time they'd met. There was an easiness about the two of them that acquaintances of long standing shared.

But then Slade said something, and the woman turned and looked directly at Raine, then allowed him to take her arm to escort her to where she and Hetty stood.

Slade's expression could only be described as roguish. Raine had the uncomfortable impression that he was just waiting for one of them to make a fool of herself. But did she have a surprise for him!

"Ladies," he announced grandly. "Ruaita wishes to welcome you to her island."

Without blushing at Ruaita's lack of dress, and without batting a lash, Raine dipped into a deep curtsy and inclined her head. "We are very honored to be here," she proclaimed humbly, and yanked at Hetty's skirt until she, too, curtsied.

"You stand!" the noblewoman ordered. "We not do that here."

"You speak English!" Raine declared in surprise as she rose.

"Yes! My father big-kind English doctor. He teach me good!"

"Do your subjects speak English as well?" Raine queried.

"Sub-jects?" Ruaita chuckled at that, her full, weighty breasts jiggling with the effort.

"She means your children, Ruaita," Slade informed her.

"Yes!" The island woman nodded. "Not so good like me, but some. Come! We no stay in sun here. We see you long way off and make welcome for you."

Raine didn't so much as look at Slade as he led the other woman back to her litter. What she had to say to him would be best said in private, when no one else was around to hear. Then she would tell him what she thought of his sneaky underhandedness.

She waited for a moment, then began to follow him.

"If she's so bloody well-educated," Hetty hissed beneath her breath, "why in heaven's name doesn't she put some clothes on? She's positively disgusting."

"She's also the head of her people, Hetty dear, and she's been gracious enough to allow us to come here. Now *do* keep that in mind."

The young island girl who was now holding Adam fell in step beside Raine. An engaging, innocent smile parted her full lips, giving Raine a glimpse of perfect, even white teeth. She couldn't help but return the smile, then her gaze fell to the budlike breasts, jutting proudly through the girl's long swath of black hair. She gulped in dismay. Lord, this was going to be difficult; pretending to one and all that she wasn't bothered by their lack of dress.

Not only were the women unclad above the waist, but the brightly colored tapa cloth wound about their hips left most of their legs exposed as well. And the men's garbs, she noticed, were not much better. In fact, in her opinion, they left a lot less to the imagination than they might have.

After treking down a well-worn path for some minutes, through a dense growth of vines, exotic flowers and tangled shrubs, they reached the village near the center of the island. Raine was surprised at how sturdy-looking the collection of huts were. Built on stilts high above the ground, each building appeared large enough to house a family of four or more. The thatched roofs were supported by poles above grassmat-covered floors, and there were no walls to hinder the flow of air. Before each of the huts' entrances was a smoking fire and a wooden frame where fish were hung to dry.

"It's amazing," Hetty remarked, gazing about the village. "Utterly amazing!"

"Yes, they *are* civilized, Hetty," Raine agreed quietly. "Just not in the same way we are."

"So it would seem."

"You two will stay in the unmarried women's hut," Slade said, coming up beside them.

"You mean, we're going to stay here?" Raine turned to stare at him. "We aren't returning to the ship?"

"Not tonight." He grinned, his heavy brows lifting as his handsome head cocked to one side. "And probably not tomorrow either. We're in for a celebration, remember?"

"But, Slade—" she started.

"I can't talk now. Ruaita wants to see me alone in her hut. Go with who'sits, here." He nodded to the young girl holding Adam. "She'll show you what you need to do." He turned and started to walk away, but stopped and looked back at them. "Oh, one other thing. Ruaita's going to expect a gift of some kind from you."

"A gift!" Raine cried.

"Don't worry about it. She'll let you know what she wants." And with that, he turned and walked away.

"What can I possibly give her?" Raine wondered aloud.

"I'd dearly love to give her one of my gowns," Hetty intoned as they climbed the makeshift ladder into the hut the young girl had entered. "Lord knows, she could use it. In fact, we have enough costumes in our trunks to clothe the entire population here."

"Oh, Hetty, do shut up. It's not half as bad as you're making it appear."

"It isn't?"

"No, it isn't!"

"Do you mean to tell me that you aren't shocked by the sight of all those . . . those flabby teats out there?"

"Keep your voice down!" Raine spit out, nodding toward the young girl. "And no, I'm not shocked. Only the older women are flabby, as you so graphically put it. All the others seem to be robustly healthy. You must try and be a little more open-minded about this whole thing. Just look on it as—as sort of an adventure in the Garden of Eden."

"The Garden of Eden, hmmm? All right, I will." Hetty nodded. "And we can cast that wretched American in the role of the serpent."

Raine smiled at the analogy and laughed. He *was* rather like a snake in some respects. He had probably enticed more than one young maiden into sampling his forbidden fruits—of that she could attest to personally.

Her first order of business, as it happened, was to take care of Adam. He had wet his diaper, soaking his pretty little baby dress as well. But when she looked around for something dry in which to change him, the young girl shook her head and pointed a finger toward one of the island children, a little boy about Adam's age, toddling about naked in the clearing below.

"He no need this," the girl said, tossing the sodden baby dress aside with a shake of her head. "He be mo' better like Kai."

Looking first at Hetty, who sniffed with disgust, Raine managed an uncaring shrug. "Well, why not? Little Kai seems to be comfortable enough." And it would save her from having to worry about an endless succession of clean nappies.

As it was, Adam took to being nude like a baby duck did to water. With his dimpled bare bottom exposed to the warm island air, he crawled happily across the grassmat floor and began playing with a mound of woven baskets. Laughing at her son's exuberant curiosity, Raine began to remove her straw hat.

"Why you no stay with your man?" the girl asked her.

"Oh, he's not my—"

"You no belong here with Lani when you got him. He look plenty good, give you mo' fine babies like boy there."

"But—Lani? Is that your name?" At the girl's nod, she continued. "What I'm trying to tell you is, I'm not Captain Slade's . . . er, woman."

"He say you are," the girl argued. "He tell Ruaita."

"He did *what*?"

"It no be bad, have man like Slade. It be good! Lani want man like him."

Raine would gladly give him to her, too, at this point in time, if he was hers to give, that is. How dare he tell Ruaita that she was his woman! How dare he, when he hadn't as yet told her!

"I'm not taking *his* side, mind you," Hetty remarked cautiously. "Heaven knows, I'd be mad to do that, but maybe he had a good reason for saying such an outrageous thing."

"Well, I for one would certainly like to know what it could be!" Raine snapped.

She was still fuming when the celebration began later that evening. Everyone was seated on the ground, around long grassmats piled high with the food the island women had spent hours preparing. With such a wide array of dishes to choose from, Raine didn't know where to begin. But as she began to eat—a little bite from one dish, a little taste from another—she knew one thing for certain, it was a decidedly pleasant change from the salted beef and beans they'd been eating aboard the *Mary Ellen*. In fact, she was so caught up in the experience, she felt her anger at Slade abate somewhat.

Clean, hollowed-out coconut shells served as their glasses, while roughly carved wooden bowls served as their plates. Their fingers, much to Hetty's horror and Adam's delight, made a worthy substitute for knives and forks.

At the head of the long arrangement of mats sat Ruaita. She ate very little that Raine could see, but did drink excessively of the highly potent beverage some of the women passed around in enormous gourds. Slade, who sat on Ruaita's right, drank only two shells full before he stopped, covering the top of it with his hand when a comely islander tried to pour him more.

A very wise move on his part, Raine concluded, taking a sip of the fruity brew. She didn't know what the drink contained, but it certainly tasted good. Though she hadn't finished her first shell of it, her toes were already numb and her skin felt hot and moist.

"What you give me, Slade?" Ruaita suddenly asked in a loud slurred voice.

He hurriedly swallowed the bite he'd been chewing and stated, "I thought you could choose your own gift, Ruaita."

"Ah!" she nodded, obviously approving of his decision.

Raine nibbled on a piece of tasty, dried fish as she watched the noblewoman shift her gaze slowly from herself to Hetty, who sat beside her.

Ruaita's glassy-eyed scrutiny returned to Raine. "I decide I want your woman's behind."

"My what?" Raine choked.

Grinning, Slade said, "You'd better give it to her."

"My—my *behind?*" she sputtered.

"I think she means your bustle," he interpreted dryly. "She's had her eye on it ever since we landed."

"But I *can't* give it to her," Raine argued. "It's attached to my dress."

"Then give her the dress," he stressed with maddening calm.

"I will not!"

"And I want the old woman's headpiece," Ruaita announced as her final choice.

"You'd better," Slade whispered to Raine. "I've seen what she gets like when she doesn't get her way."

"But I didn't bring any other clothes with me!" Raine pointed out.

"Who's she calling an old woman?" Hetty demanded.

"No offense, Miss Carlisle, but I think she means you," Tex spoke up from across the mat.

"Did she say she wanted my *hat?*" Hetty asked.

"Yes, she did." Slade nodded, then looked back at Raine. "You'd better hurry."

"I cannot—I *will* not just strip down to my . . . my unmentionables and give her my clothes!"

"If you don't want all hell to break loose you will," he remarked doggedly.

"What on earth does she want with my hat?"

"Hetty, shut up!" Raine snapped, getting stiffly to her feet. "At least you've still got your clothes."

"Oh, well," Hetty grumbled, untying the ribbons that held the hat in place. "I didn't like it very much, anyway."

"Need some help?" Slade leered up at Raine as he passed Hetty's straw hat to Ruaita.

"No, I do not! Not from you, at least. Ruaita, I will be honored to give you your gift . . . *after* I have removed it in private." And with that, she turned on her heel and stalked toward the hut she was to share with Lani and Hetty.

Minutes later, she returned with the garment draped over her arm. Her pale, blond head was held at a regal tilt as she presented the bustled-gown to Ruaita. And as she settled herself back down next to Slade, she tried not to chafe under all the crewmen's stares. Her *broiderie anglaise* camisole and petticoat still adequately covered her body, even though it did leave her arms and a good portion of her chest bare.

"What are you gawking at?" she bit out between clenched teeth when she felt Slade's inquisitive perusal.

"Nothing," he denied with a shake of his head, his mouth twisting into a silly grin. "Nothing at all!"

When she was sure that the others had returned their attention back to their food, Raine could contain her fury no longer. "You are the most despicable man I've ever met, Quentin Slade!"

"Who, *me?*"

"Yes, you! Not only are you despicable, but you're a liar as well."

"Liar! Now when did I lie?" he challenged with feigned indignation.

"When you told Ruaita that I was your woman!"

"Oh, that." He chuckled and shook his head. "I didn't think you'd mind it much . . . considering."

"Well, of course, I mind!"

"Why?"

"Well—well, because I just do, that's all. *You* know I'm not your woman, and *I* know I'm not, so why tell *her* that I am?"

"Are you going to eat anymore?"

His sudden change of topic was so unexpected she merely sat there, gaping in confusion at him for a moment. But when she at last regained her ability to think, her wrath increased even more. "Slade! I demand—"

"Come on," he interjected, hopping to his feet. "We need to take a walk. Lani," he addressed the young girl, holding Adam. "You watch our boy for us."

"Our boy!"

"Ruaita," he then turned to the now quite tipsy island woman. "I wish to show my woman your lovely island."

Gulping down her shell of brew, Ruaita merely motioned them away with a wave of her hand.

"What do you think you're doing?" Raine demanded as he pulled her away from the firelit clearing.

"Keep your voice down, sweetheart. I wouldn't want to have to show all the island men how I'm forced to keep you in line."

"As if you could!"

"Then don't tempt me."

When they had gone far enough away from the assembled diners, he loosened his hold on her arm. Smoldering, she refused to take another step and stood rooted in her tracks.

"You are the most despicable man—"

"Yeah, I know. You've said that already," he groaned, turning to look at her over his shoulder. "But you wanted to know why I told Ruaita you were my woman, didn't you? I thought it would be better . . . *safer* to tell you in private than with an audience eavesdropping."

It made sense, of a sort, she thought. "But why did you tell her such a preposterous thing?"

"I had to." He began walking again, and she slowly followed him. "You've got to understand, Raine, these islanders are very simple people. They have customs that are unconventional to say the least."

Glancing down at her partially clothed body, she replied, "I already know that."

"Yes, but what you don't know is they have a very good reason for being the way they are. There aren't very many of them—you saw that for yourself—but

I'm sure that you did notice how healthy and happy they are."

"Just what exactly are you trying to tell me, Slade?"

Slade stopped, sighing heavily, and turned to face her. The moonlight, filtering through the overhang of trees, threw his features into a mask of craggy shadows that twisted oddly when he said, "They share their women with visitors, Raine."

"They *what?*"

"Now I know you think it's pagan and barbaric. . . ."

"How right you are!"

"But they do it for a very good reason. There's no evidence of inbreeding here and it's because of their custom. Lord, I've been some places and seen some people that would curl your beautiful hair. Little children with deformities are a sad sight to behold and they're that way only because of their isolation. These people, Ruaita's children, aren't deformed in any way. They're healthy, and very happy."

She digested this for a moment then murmured, "Still, it doesn't seem right."

"Not to you, maybe. Well, not to me, either," he admitted as an afterthought. "But that's the reason I told Ruaita that you were my woman."

His woman. The thought rolled pleasantly around in her head and she almost smiled. His woman, yet he condoned the islanders' custom of—

"Oh, my God!" she gasped, her eyes widening with horror. "You don't honestly expect *me* to—"

"No!" He all but roared. "I damn sure don't! Good God, Raine, don't you know that being my woman entitles you to my protection? It disqualifies you from any participation in the . . . er, ah, activities that'll be taking place tonight."

"And you honestly approve of your crew committing adultery with those women?"

"It's not my place to object or judge. They're grown men, answerable to their own consciences, not mine. They've been without a woman's solace for nearly two months now. You don't know what that does to a man, Raine. If they don't find release soon, they're liable to get dangerous." He peered down at her lovely face, softly illuminated by the glow of the moon. "They can have the island women, but I won't let them have you."

Her spirits soared and she asked, "Why?" *Oh, say it, Slade,* her heart cried out in silent longing. *Say it aloud so we can both finally admit it.*

"Because, I just can't, that's all." He closed the scant inches that separated them and cupped her face with his hands. "I can share you with Adam, and Davey, too, I guess, but not with anyone else."

"Why?" she persisted, her eyes blinking saucily as her hands came up to rest on his shoulders.

"Dammit," he blustered. "Don't you know?"

Her pert nose wrinkled with a ghost of a smile. "Tell me anyway."

"I . . . You . . . Oh, the hell with it!" He grabbed her face, pulled it close to his and kissed her soundly.

It was a hard kiss, driven by his pent-up frustrations, but soon it began to soften, and he let his lips blend tenderly with hers. He drank of her sweetness like a man long starved for the taste and when he felt the shy probing of her small tongue, he groaned and allowed her entrance. Moving his hands down the slope of her neck, over the curve of her back to her hips, he gripped her buttocks with both of his large hands and hauled her tight against him.

Overwhelmed by the feel of his hot, hard body on hers, Raine's blood sang through her veins. Her pulse beat so loudly, she was deaf to all the other sounds around them. No longer able to hear the rustle of the trees overhead or the pounding of the surf in the distance, she gave herself over to the heady sensation. This was what she wanted. This was where she wanted to be: with Slade, in his arms, forever.

"I love you, lady," he murmured at long last, sliding his mouth away from her to worship the tender skin along her neck.

"I know," she breathed. "I love you, too."

He pulled back a scant space to look down at her, his astonishment mirrored in his eyes. "You do?"

"Is it so hard to believe?"

"Yeah! It sure is."

"I told you once before that I loved you. I haven't changed my mind."

"My God, I don't deserve a woman like you."

"Nonsense. Of course you do."

"But how? I mean, why? I can't give you the kind of life you should have."

"Slade," she interjected, catching his bearded cheeks with her hands. "Think of me as . . . as a two-legged chameleon; I fit in where I have to, and right now, I fit very well with you. Now shut up and kiss me."

Standing on tiptoe, she silenced any further remark he might have made. With her body and her hands, she showed him just how well they suited one another. And when he lifted her into his arms, cradling her against him as he carried her to a more comfortable patch of ground, she did not protest, but instead gloried in the experience.

He lovingly placed her down on the sand and stretched his long length out beside her, all the while his mouth continued to express his feelings for her where his simple words could not. He pulled the pins from her loosely coiled hair until it fell about her like a pale, gold nimbus. She was the most beautiful woman in the world to him at that moment. No other on earth could come close to matching her special qualities. She was his, he thought proudly, all his, and she would be forever if he had his way.

"I want to love you, Raine," he whispered on an aching groan.

"Then do, Slade. Do!"

But he continued to hesitate, holding her fiercely to him, rather than embark them on that final, blissful journey they both longed for.

"What's the matter?" she queried, sensing his uncertainty.

"I guess I'm afraid."

"Whatever of?"

"You. Us. Oh hell, *me*. Lady, I want to give you so much, but I don't want it to be like the last time. I want it to be the very best for you."

"Oh, darling," she murmured tenderly, her fingers outlining his lips. "I wasn't ready then, but I am now."

"Are you sure?"

"Yes! Yes, I'm sure!" In the bright moonlight, she could see the desire and love written in his eyes.

"Oh, God, lady, I love you!" Then his mouth found hers and they began their earthbound climb into the heavenly realms of ecstasy.

Each was so enraptured with the other, neither of them noticed the small, dark form that joined them on the quiet stretch of beach.

"Ah, Slade!" the intruder spoke. "Just as I thought. You're with a woman."

Chapter Fifteen

SLADE WRENCHED HIMSELF AWAY FROM RAINE AND jumped to his feet with the suddenness of a man who had been stabbed with a red-hot poker. The one man he had tried to avoid these last ten years was standing not a dozen feet away from him.

"What the hell are you doing here, Fong?" he bit out, vaguely noting that Raine was standing behind him.

"Looking for you, old man, what else?" Cocking his bald head to one side, Fong scrutinized Raine thoroughly. "I did not startle you, did I, fair lady?"

"Slade?" she queried cautiously. "Who is this man?"

"Fong, sweetheart."

"Fong?" The name sounded familiar to her, but she couldn't quite place it.

"Fong Chiang," the Oriental announced with a nod of his head. "And you would be . . . ?"

"Who she is isn't important," Slade interceded, snaking an arm behind him to hold Raine where she stood. "If you've got a beef about something, you take it up with me. She's got no part in this, you hear?"

"Oh, but I think she does." Fong dug down into his loose-fitting trousers and produced a handful of glittering stones. "These, I suspect, belong to you, fair lady."

Raine gasped, her hand flying over her mouth. Even with the distance separating them, she could clearly see what the Oriental held. "My *parure!*"

"You see, my old friend." Fong all but preened. "She is a part of this after all."

"H-how did you get them?" Raine asked hesitantly, fearing what Fong's answer would be.

"Let us just say I acquired them through an equitable transaction. Do you wish to have them, fair lady?"

Raine didn't know what to say, how to answer. She stuttered for a moment, looking first at the *parure* and then at Fong, who was slowly closing the distance between them.

"I would be willing to make a trade with you," he proposed.

Slade could remain silent no longer. "Just what do you want, Fong?"

"Only what is rightfully mine, old man."

"We haven't got them with us," Slade acknowledged, knowing exactly what his old adversary wanted. "They're aboard the *Mary Ellen.*"

"What is he talking about?" Raine asked, looking up at Slade, who stood so ominously protective in front of her.

"Those damn Hindu figures—that's what!"

"The Hindu . . . ? *Oh!*" Of course. Now she remembered. Slade had told her about Fong when they had been docked in Manila. But with that recollection came another, more unpleasant one. "Mr. Fong, Slade didn't steal those figures from you. But I think I know who did."

"Oh, *I* know who took my sacred relics, fair lady."

"Gerhardt von Koenig?" she intoned cautiously, praying that her guess was right.

"Ah! You know von Koenig?"

"I *knew* him, yes, but he—"

"Hush, sweetheart," Slade ordered. "You've said enough."

"Oh, do let the fair lady continue; old man. I would be interested to hear just how well she knows the thief who stole my property."

"How she knows is none of your business, Fong."

"I think it is." The Oriental's tone held a sharp edge. "If she is in any way connected with that human vermin, I want to know about it. Well, fair lady, are you?"

"I know von Koenig, Mr. Fong, because my late husband was his . . . his lover."

"You speak of him as if he no longer exists."

"He doesn't," she admitted, feeling a pain tear through her. "I—I killed him."

"You . . . *killed* him?"

"For God's sake, Fong," Slade snapped, wrapping a protective arm around Raine's quivering shoulders. "Can't you see she's in no condition to talk about it now? Show a little mercy, for God's sake."

"I will show mercy when I have my property again," Fong snarled, slicing his gaze to Raine. "You said you killed him. Was this before or after you took the figures?"

"But I *didn't* take them," Raine cried. "Well . . . not intentionally anyway. I found them. Oh, God! I only wanted my son. I didn't intend for anyone to die. You believe me, don't you, Slade?"

He peered down into her tearful face then crushed her close against him. "Shhh. It'll be all right, sweetheart. Don't cry. You didn't do anything wrong. If anyone's at fault, it's your lousy husband and that lover of his." Then, to Fong, who continued to glower at them, he added, "She killed the man, trying to get her son away from them. She didn't know a damn thing about your precious figures until she was aboard my ship."

"If what you say is true," Fong stressed, "why was she trying to get rid of them?"

"For money, what else?" Slade countered. "She has no use for the figures."

Fong seemed to ponder this for a long moment, then slowly he nodded his shiny bald pate. "And when no one would buy them, she sold her jewels instead. It makes a very convincing tale."

"That's because it's the truth," Slade insisted.

"Not quite," Fong dissented, "but we will speak of that in the light of the day. I think you should both return to the village now. And you would do well to remain apart for the rest of the night."

The little bastard hadn't changed a bit, Slade thought as he and Raine preceded the Oriental through the tangle of vines back to the village. His rule of thumb was still divide and conquer. Not that it would do him, Slade, any good to try and seduce Raine now. No, that particular urge had been squelched the moment Fong reared his conniving little head.

Only a few familiar faces still remained in the clearing when they returned. Most of his crew had departed with the women to their huts, leaving only the island men, Ruaita and some of the group from the *Mary Ellen* seated around the mat. But in the background, standing like silent watchdogs, were a number of gun-toting strangers. Fong's men, Slade concluded.

"It wouldn't harm you at all, my dear," Hetty was saying to Ruaita with a measured primness of a woman well into her cups. "In fact, it might do you a world of good to cover those bosoms of yours for a change. Why, even our *own* beloved queen has lived to her great age and she wears clothes all the time."

Ruaita's head seemed to nod in acceptance of this news, but then it fell forward to rest on her bare chest as she began to snore softly. As if taking their cue from her, one by one the island men collapsed on the spot where they sat, falling soundly asleep.

Slade snorted in amused disbelief. "They're all drunk as skunks. Cookie!" he called to his bandy-legged crewman who was about to doze off. "You'd better help Miss Carlisle get settled for the night."

At the mention of her name, Hetty turned and scowled at Slade, but then gasped as she noticed Raine, being held so close to him. "My word! What have you done to her?"

"He's done nothing, Hetty. I'm all right." Raine smiled wanly.

"Who is that with you?" Hetty slurred when Cookie started to help her to her feet. "Another one of your disreputable crewmen, Captain? I must say, you do seem to have a lot of them. Bounders, the lot of them. Watch where you're grabbing me!" she snapped at Cookie, who was having a difficult time supporting her stout frame with his considerably lesser one. "You could get your face slapped for that, you know."

Slade thought it wise not to linger, and led Raine back to her hut. "Try and get some sleep, if you can," he whispered.

"Will *you* be all right?" She peered around his broad width at Fong, who stood near the clearing, watching them.

"Yeah, I'll be okay. There's no need for you to worry. I'm almost certain he won't try anything until he has his damn figures back."

"Slade, I—"

"Shhh! Don't say it. Just kiss me good night and go take care of our boy."

"Speaking of our *boys*—where's David?"

"Already asleep, I imagine. He'll be all right, too, so don't worry about either of us."

That was easy for him to say, she thought, lifting her lips to his. It wasn't the fieriest kiss they'd ever shared, but under the circumstances, it still possessed a wealth of warmth.

Slade watched her ascend the short ladder then, steeling himself for what lay ahead, turned and faced Fong.

"You aren't to harm her, or the boys," he growled as they stalked toward another of the huts.

"I wouldn't dream of it, old boy. Women and children are out of my league altogether."

"And you can just cut the 'old boy' shit, too. I've seen you in action, so that English education of yours doesn't carry any weight with me."

"Ah, Slade," Fong sighed sadly. "Always the skeptic. We could have made such a great pair, you and I, if you hadn't left Cambodia in such a hurry."

"I'd have been dead by now if I hadn't."

"Skeptical *and* cautious. Not a very good mix for a great man. Whatever happened to your sense of adventure?"

"I left it behind with those dead men in Angkor." Even now, he could clearly remember waking up in that jungle encampment surrounded by corpses. A shudder rippled through him as he reached the ladder to his hut.

"They were warned about the snakes," Fong declared. "I told them, but they wouldn't listen. Can I help it if they were bitten during the night?"

"The snake that poisoned those men was a lot bigger than the *hanuman,* Fong."

"You do me a great disservice, Slade, by thinking that I killed those men. They were bitten by the green *hanuman,* not I."

"Uh-huh." Slade nodded and placed a foot on the bottom ladder rung. "And I suppose if I wake up tomorrow morning and find half of my crew dead, I'm to blame the *hanuman* for that too?"

"Are there snakes on this island? That's odd. I thought it was reptile-free."

Slade growled at Fong's display of innocence. "I'll see you in the morning, Fong."

"To be sure, old boy, to be sure."

Slade crawled into the hut, feeling his way in the darkness for an empty mat. As in most bachelor quarters, there was a lot of snoring going on.

"Pa? Is that you?" Davey whispered from nearby.

"Yeah, son. Go back to sleep."

"Some strangers came into camp after you and Miss Sheridan left."

"I know, Davey. We'll talk about it in the morning."

"Okay," the boy agreed with a yawn. "'Night."

"Good night, son."

But for Slade, it was anything but a good night. His mind continued to click and grind at a rapid pace throughout the long, dark hours. Not knowing what Fong would do after he got his figures had him worried. The sneaky little bastard had a way of getting at you when your back was turned or when you least expected him to attack. He would have to be twice as cautious as he had been before.

Morning did not arrive gently on the heels of night. It arrived rudely with a loud, frightening scream.

Jerked out of his worried musings, Slade leaped to his feet and nearly fell down the hut ladder in his haste to get outside. Close behind him, from the other huts, his crew were making their appearances too. Some were pulling on pants, while others were already fastening theirs.

"What the hell's going on?" he demanded of Mr. Dennison, who was stuffing his shirt into his trousers.

"I don't know," the first mate frowned sleepily. "Sounds to me like somebody's dying."

The shrieking and cursing continued as Slade made his way to Raine's hut. But seeing her emerge all touseled and sleepily concerned, he knew she was not the one whose life was in peril.

"Slade?" she queried, running to him. "Oh, thank God! You're all right."

"I was just wondering the same about you."

"But who—?"

Her question was never finished. They both turned at a loud noise behind them and saw Cookie come flying out of the hut across from them. Directly behind him appeared Hetty, trying ineffectually to pull her bodice together.

"You odious little man!" she screamed. "How *dare* you take such liberties with me."

"I—I—" Stunned and confused, Cookie turned to Slade. "Cap'n, I only—"

"He *only* tried to molest me! And this isn't the first time it's happened, either. But those two little kisses I allowed you in my one rare moment of weakness does not give you any right to seduce me! Do you understand that, Eugene?"

"I wasn't tryin' to molest you, Henrietta!" Cookie managed to muster as much indignation as he could under the circumstances. "Fact is, you were doin' a pretty good job of molestin' *me* until I woke up."

"I never! Don't believe a word this man says, Captain Slade. Why . . . why I wouldn't touch him with a barge pole!"

"Barge pole, no," Cookie persisted, "but your *hand* had a hold of my—"

"*Oh*, you filthy little swine, shut up!" Hetty tore down out of the hut, gray braids flapping and claws bared, ready for a fight.

Slade intervened at that moment, stepping between her and the rightfully frightened Cookie to stop it.

"This has gone far enough," he growled, trying his damnedest to keep a straight face. "Now, before it gets out of hand again, I think you both owe each other an apology."

Hetty and Cookie, of course, didn't agree. They both began to bluster effusively, each loudly voicing their reasons why they should not apologize to the other. But Slade, being the biggest of the three, shut them up again and calmed them down before sending them off in separate directions.

"I don't need this," he grumbled a moment later to Raine. "A lovers' spat this early in the morning is the last thing I planned on refereeing."

"Is his name really Eugene?" Raine giggled.

"Hell, I guess. In the ten years I've known him, though, he's never gone by anything other than Cookie."

"Strange, he doesn't look like a Eugene." An Ernest or a Willard maybe, but not a Eugene, she thought, looking at the bandy-legged cook in the distance.

"You don't look much like a Raine, either," came Slade's soft remark, bringing her gaze back to him. "Not this morning, anyway." With her hair all touseled and her features still soft from sleep, she looked more like an Aphrodite.

His sudden absence of humor brought back to

Raine all the seriousness of their dilemma. Regarding his red-rimmed, fatigue-etched eyes, she felt a flood of love pour out to him. "Oh, my darling, you didn't get any rest at all, did you?"

"I got enough," he murmured, catching her hand before it could reach his face. He brought it to his lips and planted a kiss on the opened palm before giving it a gentle, reassuring squeeze. "Stick with me today."

"I will. I'll be right beside you every step of the way."

"That's what I was hoping you'd say. God knows what Fong's got in store for us, because I sure as hell don't."

"Darling, I may be presuming too much, but I don't think Mr. Fong intends to harm us. I think he only wants his figures back, and when he gets them, he'll leave us alone."

Slade issued a mirthless snort. "You don't know him like I do, sweetheart."

"Well, no," she conceded. "I don't."

"I've seen that little bastard take on a half dozen men at one time—no gun, no knife, nothing but his bare hands, and *he* was the only one still standing when the dust settled."

"Slade!" Her tone held a wealth of disbelief. Not only could she not envision what he'd just told her, she couldn't fathom Slade being afraid of Fong. Well, not *this* afraid.

"I'm not lying, sweetheart. He's a little demon when it comes to taking care of himself. He does things with his hands and feet no normal man would ever dream of doing. God knows, I'm twice his size, and I'll be the first to confess to being in a fight or two, but I've got better sense than to tangle with him."

"A very wise decision, old man," came a voice behind them.

Slade pivoted sharply and glared at Fong. "But that doesn't mean I *won't* if I have to."

Fong merely looked at him, his Oriental expression inscrutable as always. "You do me a grave injustice, Slade. But then you always have." He turned his glance to Raine, his almond eyes narrowing slightly with a touch of amusement. "Fair lady, I am not as terrible as he makes me out to be."

"I know." She nodded with a grim little smile.

Slade looked at both of them, not fully comprehending or believing what was taking place.

"I thought you might," Fong remarked and dug down into his loose-fitting trousers. "Here, I believe these are yours. In all the confusion of last night, you forgot to take them."

Raine blinked stupidly at the diamonds he held out to her. "But wouldn't you rather keep them until you have your figures?"

"No, that isn't necessary . . . now."

Slade just stood there, growing more baffled by the minute. He couldn't believe this newest side to Fong's multifaceted personality. He was actually *trusting* somebody? No, that couldn't be right. "Just what are you up to?" he challenged with a scowl. But when Fong merely shrugged and released the diamonds into Raine's cupped hands, he added, "You wouldn't be doing this unless you had some other trick up your sleeve."

"I am not a magician, old man," Fong scoffed. "Call it a gesture of good will, if you must label it. I have discovered that we have come to a point in our lives when we must learn to trust each other."

"I don't understand," Slade remarked.

"You will . . . in time."

And Slade did.

But what he discovered as they boarded the *Mary Ellen* later that day was more unsettling than he'd ever imagined.

"Where's the rest of my crew?" he demanded of Fong, looking around at the number of unfamiliar faces on deck. "What the hell have you done with them?"

"I have done nothing with them," the Oriental stated matter-of-factly. "They have kindly consented to work aboard my vessel for a time, while my men will work aboard yours."

"They *what*?" Slade shot a look at the sleek clipper ship in the distance, picking its way cautiously through the reefs. "You sneaky little son of a—"

"Darling!" Raine interjected hurriedly, coming to his side. "Don't get so excited. No harm has been done."

"But—but he *stole* the biggest part of my crew!"

"No, he didn't," she rejoined calmly. "He merely traded with you."

"Traded hell!" Slade barked, his chest heaving with agitation. "Dammit, we didn't even get the fresh supplies loaded."

"All of that was taken care of before we boarded this morning, old man." Fong's remark was cool and unconcerned. "Freshwater, food and even a pair of healthy goats have been brought aboard. All you need concern yourself with now is weighing anchor and setting sail."

Slade's lips narrowed to an angry line beneath his mustache. He would have voiced his thoughts had Raine not place a hand on his arm.

"Don't say anything you could be sorry for later," she whispered softly, her violet eyes pleading.

His narrowed lips curled back into a snarl before a frustrated growl rumbled out of his throat. It was hell, holding onto his temper. But she was right.

"Mr. Dennison!" he roared. "Prepare to get underway!"

"Aye-aye, Captain!" came the first mate's response from the bridge.

With a naked Adam resting on her hip, Raine descended the gangway steps. Slade wasn't the only one who was confused by this sudden turn of events instigated by Fong; she was confused, too. No matter how hard she tried, though, she just could not feel alarmed by it. Fong apparently had a very good reason for doing what he had. Only time would tell what that reason was.

She nearly dropped Adam, entering her cabin a moment later, so stricken was she by the sight which greeted her. All of her clothes had been removed from the cupboard and drawers, and they now gaped emptily back at her. In fact, there was nothing of hers in the cabin that she could see. All traces of her occupancy had been thoroughly and effectively removed.

"It was that Chinaman's man that did it," Hetty announced behind her. "I saw him taking your things out as I was going to my cabin."

"Where are they?" Raine demanded. Would she now have to share quarters with Hetty?

A slightly malicious sneer appeared on the older woman's tired-looking face. "They're in *his* cabin."

"Slade's?"

"Yes, you poor darling. He's given that little Oriental your room."

"Cabin," Raine corrected vaguely, knowing that Slade was not to blame. This move, like the others, had Fong's obvious stamp of ownership on it.

"And Adam's things," she continued. "Where are they?"

"With yours, I should imagine," Hetty professed before pressing a hand to her stomach. "Oh, Lord, not again."

"Mal de mar?" Raine queried.

"No. At least, not yet." A loud gurgling sound erupted from the area of Hetty's belly. Raine watched her companion bend forward, clutching her skirt tightly in front. "That damnable fruit punch we had last night . . . I think there were fermented prunes in it." And with a whimper, she spun on her heel and raced to her cabin.

Raine wisely chose not to follow. At a time like this, it was best to leave Hetty alone. However, she did wander across the passageway into Slade's cabin and found her things there neatly paired with his. Another time she would have thought it very apropos, maybe even a bit romantic, but now all she could think of was why Fong had done it.

"I just hope he doesn't mind having us as his cabinmates," she muttered to Adam, who rested on her hip.

The next few minutes were busy ones for Raine. Not knowing where her and Adam's things were located, she had to search through the cupboards and drawers until she found his nappies, then she had to wrestle her son to put them on him. He had obviously enjoyed romping about *au naturel* and didn't want to be put in clothes again.

She had just finished fastening the diaper when Slade stormed in and threw his hat angrily across the cabin.

"Da-da!" Adam cried excitedly, holding out his little arms.

"Shhh," Raine cautioned, picking up her son. Slade was in no mood to play daddy now, and she knew it. "What's happened, darling?"

"That sneaky little son of a bitch, *he's* what's happened!" Slade snarled.

"Well, I can easily move in with Hetty. I didn't know Fong had put my things in here with yours."

"What?" He cast her a confused look, then realized what she was talking about and shook his head. "No, don't even give that a second thought. I was planning on moving you in here anyway."

He was? But her pleasure gave way to concern as she asked, "Then what are you so angry about?"

"Fong, I told you! The conniving little bastard's acting mighty strange if you ask me. He told me to carry on as if he wasn't aboard. As if that's supposed to make me feel more at ease!" He muttered a fertile expletive. "I mean, he takes over my *ship,* replaces my *crew,* then expects me to act like nothing's happened."

"But why?"

"I wish the hell I knew, sweetheart." Slade wearily sank down onto his bunk and ran a hand through his burnished brown hair. "Dammit! I know he's got some scam going, but for the life of me, I can't figure out what it is."

"Could he, perhaps, be testing you?" Raine offered softly after a short, thoughtful pause.

"He knows I don't want **any** part of him. After what happened on that expedition to Angkor Wat ten years back, he ought to know better."

"Just what did happen?" she asked, sitting beside him. She had heard bits and pieces from him, but nothing that could explain his apprehension toward Fong.

For a moment, it looked as if Slade might tell her, but he suddenly decided against it and just shook his head. "It's better if you don't know. Hell, I don't even like remembering it, much less recounting it all over again to you."

It must have been a horrifying experience, she thought, whatever had happened. "I'm not quite as squeamish as some are, darling," she tried to assure him.

"I know," he sighed tiredly. "In some ways, Raine, you're a helluva lot stronger than I am."

"Now that's nonsense." She smiled. "You're just about the strongest man I've ever known." She lifted a hand to stroke his lean, hairy cheek. "Although your features clearly imply the opposite. A dimpled pirate," she ended with an amused toss of her head.

Something flashed in the depths of his green eyes as he turned to gaze lovingly at her. It was desire blended with respect. "I'm no pirate, sweetheart; not anymore. I'm just an ordinary man." Then his gaze shifted downward to graze the contours of her camisole-covered breasts before it slowly returned to her face. "Don't you think you ought to put something on?"

"Why?" she twinkled. "I'll just have to take it off again."

His green eyes darkened. "Are you flirting with me?"

Raine merely looked at him then gently lowered Adam to the deck. Instantly intrigued with his new surroundings, the baby began to explore on all fours, forgetting about the two people still seated on the bunk.

"I take it you've changed your mind about being my mistress."

"Oh, I've got something a lot more permanent in mind than that, darling," she declared, brazenly winding her arms about his neck.

Unprepared for her sudden direct move, Slade was helpless to defend himself when she began to nibble the lobe of his ear. Feeling an overwhelming surge of heat flare in his loins, all notions of fighting her off fled his mind. He drew in a ragged breath and held it as her small tongue slowly circled the shape of his ear over and over again.

"You—you're begging for trouble, lady," he groaned.

"Mmm-hmm," was her purred reply as she shifted her slight weight into his lap.

She began placing tantalizing little kisses about his face, tasting the slight saltiness of his eyes, the bridge of his straight nose, the curve of his cheekbone. It was when she reached the outer corner of his mouth that he made his move. His hands came up and cupped her face, stilling any further movement she might have made. He held her gaze for a moment, drowning in the depths of her deep blue eyes, then hauled her face up to his. Their mouths met and fused, and both became lost in the heat of the moment.

Maneuvering her slowly onto her back, her head resting on the pillows, Slade's only thought at the moment was to relieve the unbearable tension that he could feel they both shared. This was what she wanted. Hell, it was what he needed! And it was so right, so perfect, holding and loving her this way, he nearly lost all control.

But reality, as it was bound to happen, returned with the sharp rap on his cabin door.

"Mr. Dennison wants you topside, Cap'n," came Tex's familiar voice.

"God Almighty!" With a disgusted grunt, Slade fell to one side.

"Ignore him." Raine turned to him, trying to find his mouth again with hers through the haze of passion which blinded her.

"I can't." He sat up and raked his hair with a very shaky hand. "I shouldn't have stayed down here this long. You have a way of making me forget my duty, lady."

Smiling, she placed a hand on his muscled thigh and let it play toward his groin. "Is that so terrible?"

"Until we get through that damned reef it is. I'd like nothing better than to stay here with you, but . . ."

"Go ahead, then," she demurred. "I'll be here when you come back."

"You'd better be."

It was as he stood to retrieve his hat that she noticed the unmistakable bulge in his trousers. A look of pure satisfaction crossed her lips, knowing she had aroused him so.

Slade looked down at himself and gave a harsh chuckle. "See what you do to me?"

"You mean, *I* did that?" she queried, her violet eyes wide with innocence.

"You know damn well you did. You've been doing it for quite some time, too."

"Well, hurry and get us through the reef and I'll . . . fix it." Rising, she joined him at the cabin door and wound her arms around his neck then kissed him with all the love she possessed.

"Cap'n?" Tex called once again.

Slade wrenched his mouth away from hers with reluctance. "Coming!" Then he donned his hat and was gone.

Leaning against the closed door, Raine smiled. Her devious little mind began to plan just how she would greet him when he returned.

Chapter Sixteen

THREE HOURS HAD PASSED BEFORE RAINE DECIDED to venture topside. The easy rolling movement of the ship told her that they were now safely through the dangerous reefs, yet Slade still hadn't returned. When she spotted him, standing on the bridge with Mr. Dennison and Fong, she could tell by his tight-lipped expression that he had forgotten about her.

So intent was he on hearing what Fong had to say, Slade didn't notice the flaxen-haired woman's brief appearance just below him. Nor did he see her resigned slump before she disappeared belowdecks. He could only gaze out to sea as Fong repeated his earlier instructions.

"Keep to the course you have set. I find no need to change it."

"We're bound for the Hawaiians, you know," Slade all but snarled. "It'll be weeks before we sight land again."

Fong's hairless pate bobbed like a newly polished copper coin in the late afternoon sunlight. "It suits me."

Slade couldn't stop the sneer that appeared on his

face. But Fong merely looked at him, his expression unreadable as always, then turned and descended the short flight of stairs to the main deck.

Alone with his first mate, Slade muttered a disgusted oath before hitting the helm with his fist. "He's got me right where he wants me, dammit, and I can't do a thing about it."

"Captain, the men and I have had a long talk and we're prepared to back you in whatever you decide to do," Mr. Dennison assured him in a low, quiet voice.

"That's just it . . . until he makes a move, I don't know what to do."

"There are still enough of us left. We could try and overpower him and his men."

"Yeah, and then what?" Slade challenged, realizing how futile a move like that would be. "It's going to take more than the ten men we would have left to man the sails. And even if we *did* succeed in getting Fong in chains, his men wouldn't cooperate with us; they'd refuse to work. No, he's in control now. We're better off letting things stand as they are. But spread the word to the rest of the crew that they're to be ready to take action if it's necessary."

"Aye-aye, sir."

Slade remained on the bridge long after Mr. Dennison departed, his weary, unrested brain a turmoil of confused thoughts. But out of that turmoil, there came one, clear undeniable impression: Fong was here for something a lot more important than just the statues. But what? That was what Slade couldn't figure out.

"Pa?"

He turned at the sound of his son's voice, but it took him a moment to notice the plate of food in his hand.

"Cookie thought you might want something to eat."

"Yeah," he replied wearily, taking the plate. "I'd forgotten it was time for supper. When you go below, tell him I said thanks."

"You want some company for a while? I've had my supper already."

Shoveling a forkful of food into his mouth, Slade nodded. Maybe the boy would take his mind off Fong for a while.

Davey settled himself against the bridge railing and stuck his hands in his pockets as he'd seen his father often do. "Miss Sheridan let me feed the baby," he said with a grin. "He sure is a cute little fellah. 'Course, he can't eat too good yet. He gets more in his hair than he does his mouth."

Slade chuckled. "You were like that."

"I was?" Davey's almond-shaped green eyes widened with surprise.

"Sure, all babies are. But, after a while, they grow out of it and become humans like the rest of us."

There was a moment of silence in which Slade managed to finish his plate of beans. When he placed the empty plate on the helm platform, Davey asked, "Pa? What's gonna happen to us after we get Miss Sheridan to San Francisco?"

"I don't know, son." Hell, he wasn't sure what was going to happen tomorrow or in the next ten minutes. Fong had made sure of that. "What do you want to happen?"

"Well," the boy dropped his chin and perused his long bare feet. "Well, I like Miss Sheridan. I mean, she's such a nice lady and all, couldn't we maybe stay with her for a while? I ain't . . . haven't seen San Francisco."

Slade's next question brought Davey's head up with a jerk. "What would you think about us living with her? Legally, I mean?"

"You mean . . . marry her?"

"Yeah."

"Both of us?"

"Well, no." Slade chuckled, realizing how misleading his question had been. "Only one of us can actually marry her, son. Since you're still too young to be her husband, that leaves me as the one."

"Yeah!" the boy beamed. "I like that idea a lot, Pa. We'd be like a real family then, wouldn't we?"

"Just about," Slade nodded. "She'd be your stepmother, and little Adam would be your stepbrother."

Davey's face held an enthralled look as he digested this idea. Only then did it occur to Slade just what his son had missed in his short life. Oh, he'd seen numerous exotic ports and had met a wide assortment of colorful characters, something few lads of fifteen could boast, but he hadn't had the security that a loving family could give.

"What would the others be?" Davey queried.

"Well, Raine's got a brother—Rory, I think she said his name was—he'd be your uncle."

"No, I mean the other kids you and Miss Sheridan might have. Would they be my stepbrothers and stepsisters, too?"

That possibility hadn't crossed Slade's mind. But it wasn't as unlikely as he might have imagined. In time, certainly there would be other children. With his attraction to her, how could there not be? "No," he answered. "They would be your half brothers and half sisters."

"Ohh!" Davey nodded, his expression remaining even. "Well, when are you getting married?"

"I don't know. I haven't asked her yet."

"You gotta *ask* her? She don't already know?"

"That's right." Slade could not suppress the yawn that suddenly forced its way out. The lack of sleep and too much worry had finally caught up with him. "I don't think we have to worry about her turning me down, though, when I pop the question."

"Great!" Davey cried, bounding for the stairs. "I'll go down and tell her—"

"No! That is," Slade began in a calmer voice. "You've got to let me do the asking, Davey. If it comes from anyone else, she just might say 'no.' Women are very picky when it comes to matters like this."

"Okay," the boy agreed with a laconic shrug.

Amused, Slade watched his lanky offspring stumble down the steps and end up on both feet at the bottom instead of his scrawny rear before disappearing belowdecks. Lord, had he been that clumsy and exuberant at fifteen? Yeah, most likely he had been. But one thing was certain now, he thought with a wide yawn, his exuberance was overshadowed by his exhaustion. He could feel each one of his thirty-eight years as if they were linked in a heavy chain and weighted about his neck.

"You're getting old," he muttered to himself. Old and decidedly run down. There had been a time, not too long ago, when he could have gone for forty-eight hours or more without sleep and it wouldn't have bothered him in the least. But now, having gone for a mere day and a half without rest, he was almost done in.

Hard pressed to keep his eyes opened, he leaned his muscled forearms over the helm and let his weariness rapidly claim him. If Mr. Dennison hadn't come up to relieve him at that moment he would probably have fallen asleep, standing up.

Raine was a welcomed sight when he entered the cabin a moment later.

"Oh, darling," she soothed. "You look so tired."

"Just need a short nap," he confessed, dropping onto his bunk. "I'll be fit as a fiddle in no time."

"Here, let me help you with your shirt." She began undoing the buttons, most of them unmatched and crudely stitched into place by his hand, before pulling it off his unresisting arms. "You rest a while."

In no mood to protest, Slade unfastened the two top buttons on his trousers and stretched out his long body on the bunk. For a moment, he allowed his weary gaze to follow Raine's graceful movements as she folded his shirt. Then his lids grew too heavy for him to keep them open any longer. He heard her say, "There's something I've been meaning to tell you, darling," before his fatigue finally overtook him and he slept.

As she placed his shirt on a nearby shelf, Raine heard soft snores come from his slack mouth. Turning, she sighed. "But I guess it can wait." It would have to. He was certainly in no shape now to listen to what she had to say.

She scooped Adam up off the deck before he could object, then quietly let herself out of the cabin. There would be time enough for conversation later, she thought, heading for Hetty's cabin. Right now, he needed to rest.

But when she returned some hours later, he was still fast asleep. He had turned onto his side and was hugging the edge of the bunk. One of his long legs was bent at the knee while the other remained straight, and his bare foot dangled over the end like an odd-shaped flag.

Raine smiled at the sight and decided that there was just enough room for her to slide in beside him, but there wasn't enough room for Adam, too, who was already dozing in her arms.

She carefully arranged a blanket and pillows on the deck in a quiet corner, and after placing the baby onto his makeshift bed, she slipped out of her clothes and into her nightgown. Crawling into the bunk beside Slade, he didn't move a muscle. Only the tempo of his breathing changed for a moment before it returned to the deep, steady cadance it had been before.

Sleeping with a man was a new experience for her. She had never done it before, not even when she had been married to Roger. They'd had separate bedrooms at his big house in London, with an adjoining dressing room in between. After he had "done his duty" on those few occasions he'd been intimate with her, he had left her to sleep the remainder of the night alone. She hadn't particularly liked it, but she hadn't objected, either. It had all been a part of being lady of the manor.

But Slade was a different matter altogether, she decided, turning on her side and wrapping an arm over his brawny chest. There would be no sleeping alone with him in another room. They would share a bed together.

It was the violent pitching of the ship that aroused Slade the next morning. His eyes flew open and he would have rolled out of bed if it hadn't been for the slender body curled tightly against his. How did *she* get here? he wondered, frowning down at the top of Raine's head. Then his expression softened as he remembered the events of the day before.

"Don't move," Raine purred sleepily, cuddling closer to him. "You're so comfortable."

He tilted her face up with a crooked finger and lightly kissed her parted lips. "I'm afraid I've got to," he confessed a moment later. "We've hit some rough water."

"How?" she asked, rolling over onto her back as her arms stretched wide. The movement gave him a lovely, unobstructed view of her full breasts barely hidden beneath the sheer fabric of her gown. "It wasn't rough yesterday."

"It's hard to tell in these parts," he admitted, sitting up and swinging his legs around to the deck. "This time of year, you never know from one day to the next what'll happen. We could be on the outer edge of a big storm that's building up, or we could be catching the tail end of a little squall. Whichever one it is, though, I've got to get topside and see after things."

"Slade, you will be careful, won't you?"

"You better believe it, sweetheart." His eyes darkened with desire as he leaned over to kiss her long and deeply one last time before wrenching himself away. He found his shirt and pulled it on, leaving half the buttons undone, then grabbed his slicker and headed for the door.

"It might be a good idea," he said, turning to look back at her, "if you and the baby don't move around too much. And for God's sake, don't wander up on deck. You're liable to get washed overboard."

"Don't worry about us. We'll be all right," she assured him. After what happened to her the last time they sailed through rough waters, she knew she wouldn't be straying too far from their chamber pot.

When the door closed behind Slade, she threw aside the sheet and tried to stand. The rolling deck made it a bit difficult for her to walk without holding onto something, but she managed to cross over to where the baby still slept and carefully lifted him off the floor. After placing him in the bunk, she gathered an armful of fresh diapers and put them near the bed. From the looks of things, it was going to be a long day.

Only twice did she leave the security of the bunk; once to change out of her nightgown and into a skirt and blouse, and again to open the cabin door when Fong knocked. He stood on the other side, holding onto a bowl of dried biscuits and a bottle filled with white liquid—Adam's milk, she learned a moment later.

"We must all fend for ourselves today," he said, weaving into the cabin. "Even the cook is topside."

"I hope everyone is all right up there. It sounds very nasty, doesn't it?"

The wind roared at an ominous pitch and whenever a wave washed across the top deck, it could be heard below.

Fong thrust the bowl of biscuits toward her, but she shook her head. "I don't think I'm interested in eating at the moment, thank you."

"Your companion, Miss Carlisle, said the same thing when I looked in on her. I have discovered that if you eat something, it will settle your stomach."

"You're a veteran of storms such as this, I take it."

"I've been through a few," he admitted. "For the most part, though, I prefer to remain on dry land."

Raine splashed a little of the milk into one of Slade's clean whiskey glasses and held it while Adam drank his breakfast. Surprisingly enough, most of it went into his mouth rather than on his clothes.

"You're a most unusual man, Mr. Fong," Raine observed, wiping Adam's mouth before handing him a biscuit crumb. "But then I suppose you already know that."

"Unusual?" he countered. "I've always thought I was quite ordinary."

"There aren't many ordinary Oriental gentlemen who speak English the way you do, without a trace of an accent, or who lead the sort of life you lead."

"I suppose that's true," he concurred with a nod. "As to the subject of my speech, I can only say that most of my fellow countrymen were raised by their families, whereas I was brought up among a group of highly intelligent English missionaries. You see, I lost both my father and mother when I was just a baby—not much older than your son there. A very violent uprising occurred in our province shortly after I was born, or so I was told. If it hadn't been for the generosity of the missionaries who sheltered me, I suppose I would have died as well."

"That explains your flawless English," Raine professed, "but it doesn't begin to tell me about your . . . shall we say, somewhat unsavory occupation?"

"I'm a businessman, fair lady. What could be unsavory about that?"

"A good number of things, and you know it. Take the Hindu figures, for example. I know how you got them. Slade told me about that place called Angkor Wat. No reputable businessman that I know would ever dream of undertaking a dangerous journey through miles of snake-infested jungle just for the sake of the company he works for."

"Ah, but he might, if that company were his own."

"*Touché*. I stand corrected. But where do the Hindu figures come into all of this? I mean, why risk life and limb for a few little statues?"

"Because they are the only proof left of an ancient civilization that once flourished in my corner of the world, and I wanted to be the one to protect it." His voice had lost its bantering quality and had suddenly become very serious. "For many years men from your country have been coming to my country, stealing our precious artifacts and taking them back with them. They've robbed graves without giving a second thought to what they were doing. Little by little my homeland is being stripped of its heritage and I intend to put a stop to it.

"When von Koenig saw my Hindu statues, he never considered their religious or historical value, he only saw the money they would bring him."

Raine was about to point out to Fong that von Koenig was now dead, and therefore no longer a threat to him, but a loud noise above the roar of the wind penetrated through to the cabin.

She flinched. "What was *that?* It sounded like an explosion."

"It couldn't have been," Fong negated. "There aren't any explosives aboard. I made sure of that while we were at the island."

"Then what was it?"

If Fong had any ideas, he kept them to himself. His silence caused Raine's concern to increase drastically. Had they struck something in the water and damaged the ship? And if they had, were they in danger of sinking?

The silence seemed to stretch tautly between them, broken only by the creaking of the timbers and the howling of the wind outside. Raine felt her stomach churn even more violently than the roll of the ship. The brilliant flashes of lightning didn't help matters any, and when there was a deafening crash of thunder, she shivered even more.

So caught up in the tension of the moment, she nearly jumped out of the bunk when the cabin door suddenly flew open. A water-sodden Tex entered first, carrying an equally drenched Slade. Mr. Dennison, supporting the other half of Slade's body, came in last, the water from his slicker joining the puddles already on the deck.

"My God!" Raine cried, seeing Slade's limp form between the two men. "Is he dead?"

"Naw, just hurt," Tex replied, hooking the leg of Slade's chair with his foot and pulling it out.

"He was holding onto the rigging when the mast broke and he burned his hands," the first mate added.

"Burned his hands!" She was beside Slade the instant the two men deposited him into the chair. It was then that she saw the mangled condition of his hands. The skin had been literally ripped away from the palms, leaving them a horrible, bloody mess.

"Get back up on deck," Slade ordered, his voice trembling noticeably. "And for God's sake, don't forget to tie yourselves onto a safety line. The last thing I need now is for someone to get washed overboard. I'll be back up as soon as I get these taken care of." He lifted his injured hands, wincing as the pain shot through him.

"You're not going anyplace," Raine stated firmly, stumbling over to his side with a handful of clean diapers. She became so involved in cleaning his wounds, she failed to notice the gradual departure of the other three men.

"We're in the middle of a storm, Raine. I haven't got time to stay down here. I've got to get back up there and help the crew!"

"And then what will you do?" she challenged. "Good Lord, Slade, you can't even tie a safety line around yourself now. If anyone were going to be washed overboard, it would be you!"

"Well, I can't stay down here."

"You're going to have to."

"This is my ship, dammit! Don't you understand that?"

"Yes, I do! And there's no need to yell. I can hear you perfectly without you raising your voice. Let your men handle the ship for a while. It's what they're trained for, isn't it? You'll be next to useless to them in this condition." She wiped the last of the water and blood away and shuddered with a noticeable grimace. "They look horrible."

"Yeah, they don't feel too good, either," was his shaky reply. He cocked his wet head in the direction of his seaman's chest. "You'll find some salve in the top drawer over there."

Raine had to brace herself against the pitch and roll of the deck, but she made her way over to the chest and found the salve along with some rolls of clean bandages and Slade's half-empty bottle of gin.

"Here, drink this," she said, uncapping the bottle. "It might take away some of the pain." She placed the mouth of the bottle to his lips and tilted it until the liquid flowed down his throat. Jerking his head away, some of it dribbled down his bearded chin, but she ordered, "Drink some more. That's not enough."

"No! What are you trying to do? Get me drunk?"

"Of course not. I merely want to dull your senses before I start work on your hands."

"Well, this stuff'll do it."

Raine glanced down at his wounded hands, then back at the liquid in the bottle. Knowing what she had to do now caused a shiver to ripple through her. It was going to hurt like the very devil, but it had to be done. The whiskey was the closest thing to an antiseptic they had on board.

She shot a quick glance over her shoulder to see what Adam was doing—he was still safely perched in the corner of the bunk, watching the two of them with curious blue eyes—then gathered up her courage and turned back to Slade. "Do you want to bite down on something?"

"Hell, no!" he growled. "Just hurry up and get it over with."

Taking a deep breath, Raine splashed the whiskey onto both of his mangled palms then quickly moved aside as his long body jerked into a rigid stiffness caused by the shocking sting of the alcohol. His face, mirroring the pain he felt, turned a mottled shade of red, only to become pale, almost ashen in color seconds later.

"I wouldn't have minded it at all if you'd cried out, you know," she murmured soothingly as she spread the salve over his palms and wrapped them with the bandages. "In a situation such as this, I know *I* would have."

"Yeah, well you're a woman. Grown men aren't supposed to cry over a little scratch like this." But his voice quivered with the effort.

Men! she thought, screwing the cap back onto the salve jar. Why did they have to be so stubborn?

"Let me have another swig of that whiskey before

you put it away." And when she tilted the bottle to his lips, he drank the remainder in two long gulps.

All of the fight was drained from him, all of his stubborn defiance gone. He no longer insisted on going back up on deck to assist his crew, and he didn't raise a fuss when she helped him out of his slicker and wet clothes.

"I always knew you were a bossy woman," he confessed on a thick tongue when she helped him into the bunk.

"Not bossy, darling. Just determined."

His gaze continued to follow her as she lifted Adam off the bunk so he could have more room. "I knew you were going to be trouble even from the first moment we met."

"Oh, did you now?" But her tone held no note of censure, only slight amusement. It was the whiskey talking, not him.

"Yeah. Of course, I didn't realize then just how much trouble you really are."

"You'll get used to it," she replied, leaning over him to drop a kiss on his parted lips. "Mmmm, we're going to have to do something about that beard."

"Why? Whassa matter with it?" he slurred.

"It's getting a bit scraggy, don't you think? And with your hands all bandaged, you're not going to be able to trim it properly."

"You just leave my beard alone, lady. I'll take care of it when these come off." He waved his hands for emphasis. "Where do you think you're going?"

"To Hetty's cabin. I thought I'd pop in and see how she's faring. She suffers from *mal de mar*, you know." Slade merely grunted at that. "Shall I give her your love?"

"No! You won't be gone long, will you?"

He was already behaving like a little boy confined to his bed, she thought, shaking her head. "I'll be back shortly. Oh, you will promise not to get into trouble while I'm gone, won't you?"

"What kind of trouble could I get into? You've taken my pants."

But as the door closed behind her, Slade smiled. He could think of a lot of things to do where he didn't need his pants, and most of them involved Raine. Well, maybe when his hands got better. Until then, though, he'd just have to let his imagination entertain him.

Chapter Seventeen

"WITHOUT THE MAIN SKYSAIL AND THE MAIN ROYAL, it's going to take us at least two weeks longer to make it to Hawaii, maybe even more." Slade was looking up at the ravaged, splintered mainmast that had once been the pinnacle of his ship. There was no way on God's green earth he could repair it here in the middle of the ocean, either. From where he stood, it looked as if the entire mast would have to be replaced, and that would take time and a lot of money.

"You are fortunate," a familiar voice said behind him.

Slade turned slowly and glared down into Fong's unreadable face. "Fortunate!"

"We came through the storm with only minor damage," Fong replied. "And there were no lives lost."

"Not only that," the first mate spoke up. "We've enough supplies to last us the extra weeks at sea. I had Cookie check out the stores early this morning."

"Well, I sure am glad that the two of you seem to think we're so well off." Slade sneered, pushing back the bill of his cap with his bandaged hand. "We got only half a mainmast, but what the hell! We'll probably just sail right on through the next storm we hit."

Mr. Dennison lowered his head, looking properly chastised. Fong, on the other hand, was unruffled by Slade's sarcastic outburst. Swearing an angry oath under his breath, Slade turned on his heel and went below. Let the two of them handle it for a while, he thought, slamming into his cabin.

"What's the matter now?" Raine inquired as he fell into his chair.

"Not a damn thing," he barked. "Everything's just dandy!"

"Yes, I can see that it is. You always snap people's heads off when everything's going right, don't you?"

Slade looked up at her and then slumped dejectedly. "Oh, hell! I shouldn't be taking it out on you. I'm sorry, sweetheart. It's just that I feel so damn helpless, and that sneaky little bastard doesn't help my disposition any."

"Oh, Fong!" she nodded, finally understanding. "What has he done now?"

"Nothing. Oh, hell, everything! He's got a way about him that just sets my teeth on edge."

With a sigh, Raine turned to gather together the salve and fresh bandages for his wounded hands. Now was definitely not the time to point out Fong's more admirable qualities to Slade. She would only gain his wrath by doing that.

"Where's the baby?" he asked when she returned to his side.

"Oh, he's with Hetty. She has some trinkets in her cabin that he enjoys playing with."

Kneeling before him with her attention focused on his hands, she missed the warm look Slade bestowed on her. With the bright sunlight streaming through the open porthole, her hair looked like a golden halo surrounding her lovely face.

"How did you get to be so beautiful?" he asked softly.

Violet eyes flashed up at him in surprise and her cheeks bloomed with color as a smile found its way to her lips. "Just lucky, I guess."

"It takes a lot more than luck, sweetheart. You're beautiful inside, too."

"Have you been at Hetty's supply of gin again?" she asked impishly.

He leaned forward to quickly brush his lips against hers, then he sat back, his face full of a familiar emotion. "Does it taste like it?"

Unable to answer, Raine merely shook her head. That one, brief kiss was all it took for a need to begin growing inside of her, a need that directed all her further movements. She carefully, cautiously removed the old bandages then applied the soothing balm onto his injured palms before rewrapping them again. Without giving him the opportunity to voice an objection, she rose from the deck and sat down in his lap, winding her arms about his neck and tenderly kissing his bearded face.

"Raine?"

"Mmmm?"

"Do you know what you're doing?" His challenge came out on a husky moan.

"Mmm-hmmm!" Her moist lips grazed his closed lids, heating the fire in his blood even more.

"You're taking advantage of a defenseless man."

"That's right!" She smiled and began to nibble the strong curve of his cheekbone as her hands slipped down the front of his shirt, undoing the buttons they encountered there.

"*Un*fair advantage, lady. I can't even fight you off." And the loud roaring in his ears even made it difficult for him to think clearly.

"Do you really want to?" she purred, briefly pulling away from him. But as he opened his mouth to reply, her lips hungrily covered his, melting away any resistance he might have had.

God, he had known that beneath her very proper exterior there lurked an untapped core of passion, but her taking command of the situation this way came as a total surprise. Still, he did not fight it. He welcomed it as any man in his shoes would do, wishing with all his heart that he could touch and caress her as she was him. As it was, his hands remained useless and limp at his side, as he felt the fire continue to blaze out of control in his loins. Only when she moved, to stand before him, did he reach out to her, his bandaged palms looking oddly out of place at this moment in time.

"I can't even—" he began woefully.

"Then let me," she injected huskily, her fingers beginning to fumble with the buttons on her blouse and the fastening of her skirt.

The gentle rolling and swaying of the deck added to the sensual excitement Slade felt. In rapt amazement, he sat there, watching as her slender body emerged bit by bit from the many layers of clothing she wore. His breathing became noticeably labored when she was at last fully undressed, and on a softly expelled moan of pure joy, he drank in the sight of her pale loveliness. The slender curve of her hips, the inviting golden triangle of curls at the juncture of her thighs, the generous fullness of her deep-rose crested breasts elicited a louder, huskier groan of pleasure from the depths of his soul.

Stepping back toward the bunk, she extended a hand out to him, wordlessly beckoning him to join her. In answer, he stood and began to follow. All of the pent-up frustrations they had suffered would soon come to an end. They both knew it, and they both welcomed the fact without remorse.

At last, standing beside the bunk where she now sat, Slade started to join her, but she stopped him by placing both hands on his hips. Her fingers then began to unfasten and remove the last of his clothes, pushing down his trousers with slow unhurried movements over his lean, muscular hips.

His desire for her was plainly evident. It sprouted out from his loins with blatant pride and he did nothing to hide it from her eager gaze. Only when her hand reached up to touch it did he find his ability to stand sorely tested.

"Move over," he growled, bending a knee onto the thin mattress. She readily complied by scooting into the corner and he joined her, wrapping her in an embrace that was long overdue. Their mouths fused in a kiss so fiery both felt beads of perspiration break out onto their already heated flesh.

As Raine's untrained hands began to run over his shoulders and down his back, and as he felt the brush of her breasts against the hair on his chest, he knew a hunger so intense, it was difficult for him to remain unappeased. Taking his lips from hers, he murmured sweet, erotic love-words down the slender column of her neck. Her breasts were pale mounds pillowed in his bandaged hands so that his lips could capture one ripe tip. There he savored its rare taste with his tongue before opening his mouth wide and consuming it fully.

Raine gasped as the electric thrill of his action shot through her, sending her thoughts into oblivion. This was the heaven she had longed for and needed so desperately. Slade, loving her this way, was giving her more courage and strength than she'd ever hoped to have. There was no past for her at this moment, no pain, no regret, only the present and a promise of the future to come.

While his mouth continued to pay silent tribute to her breasts, loving first one tip and then the other until they were both hard points of desire, she thrashed wildly beside him. A whimper formed deep in her throat and her legs opened with a jerky movement, allowing his thigh entrance between. The moment she felt its hairy presence there, she arched herself wantonly upon its muscled hardness and felt the ache pulsating within her spread throughout her entire body until she glowed with desire.

Knowing the time for consummation was at hand, Slade tried in vain to push her onto her back and climb between her parted thighs. But a pain shot through his hands, stilling his movements instantly. With a frustrated growl of anger, he fell to one side and gulped in deep breaths of air in order to calm his raging need.

"I can't do it," he confessed at long last, waving his bandaged hands for explanation.

"Well, then, *I* will!" And with that, she slowly moved to sit atop him, her legs straddling his hips while her hands were bracing her on either side of his head. "I love you, Quentin Slade. Let me show you just how much." Then she bent forward to claim his mouth with hers as her nipples grazed the hairy roughness of his chest.

Slade was more than a little surprised by her sudden spurt of ingenuity, but he welcomed it eagerly. In all the years he'd been bedding women, never once had he been on the receiving end of their passions. He'd always been the one to do the mounting. But then again, he thought dazedly, none of the others had been Raine, either.

Slowly sliding her body against his, she rode him until the need within her threatened to explode. Some latent instinct, though, told her that now would be much too soon for either of them to find fulfillment, and she maneuvered herself more cautiously until she was at last impaled upon his turgid staff.

"Oh, God!" he growled on a throaty sigh, his lids closing to shield his lustful gaze. "Take it easy, honey . . . Nice and slow so we can make it last."

"Tell me what to do," she whispered against the moist skin of his neck, the pressure within her beginning to build.

"Try and sit up," he murmured, placing his hands on her hips.

It wasn't easy, getting her long legs to cooperate, but with his help, she finally managed to sit upright. The movement caused his member to go even deeper into her core. She gasped at the pleasurable agony it created.

"Now move nice and slowly . . . Yeah, that's it. . . . It doesn't hurt, does it?"

Unable to form a coherent answer, Raine's head could only fall from side to side, her lids barely opened. The world was spinning crazily about her as the feel of him inside her pushed her onto an even higher plain.

"You feel so good!" he groaned, looking up at her passion-drowsed face.

"You, too," she agreed breathlessly.

"Now stop a minute. . . . That's it. Catch your breath and just feel me." Her muscle instantly tightened about him, causing him to gasp sharply. "No! Don't do that yet. I'll come before you do."

Lifting his hands, the coarse fabric of his bandages became an exciting, stimulating irritant to her sensitive skin as he touched and fondled her breasts. It heightened the pressure that still continued to build within her, forming a new need that she had experienced only once before at his hand. Directed by this need, she felt the hidden kernel of her sex demand satisfaction, and she began to arch her hips slightly to relieve the pressure there.

"Oh, Jesus, honey," Slade breathed raggedly. *"Now!"*

His command caused her movements to increase in earnest. Leaning forward, her hips ground against his thrusting groin in driving, undulating rhythm. The pleasure she knew then was so intense she was amazed and delighted to experience it. Tiny spasms began to explode and radiate throughout her, growing to the peak of their intensity as he suddenly stiffened and spilled his seed into her and she was enveloped in an incandescent glow of mindless, sublime ecstasy.

Still glowing, she limply fell forward onto his broad chest, gasping for breath. Their bodies, drenched with the sweat of their exertions, began to cool under the slight breeze which drifted in through the open porthole. With the gentle swaying of the ship to guide them, they both drifted off into a brief, satiated sleep.

Slade was the first to awaken. He looked down into Raine's peaceful, upturned face and felt a love he'd never thought possible for another human being. He had said the words aloud, and had meant them, but he was only just now realizing that the emotion of love was a real and tangible thing.

She meant so much to him it was frightening. The thought of her not being with him forever caused a chill to crawl up his spine, and he shuddered. The sudden movement awakened her, and her eyes blinked for a moment before she turned and smiled up at him.

"Did we fall asleep?" she purred drowsily.

"Yes, but not for long," he murmured, pulling her close to him so that her pale, golden head was nestled beneath his chin. "How do you feel?"

"Mmm . . . complete," came her soft reply. "Is that how you're supposed to feel after something like that happens?"

"I imagine it is." He chuckled, more than pleased with her answer. Yes, he was complete, too. Completely whole, and no longer the half-empty shell that he'd been before. "It's how I feel, at least."

A moment of blissful silence ensued; a moment in which they both lay there, enjoying the feel of their heartbeats thudding in unison. They were two halves, finally joined together as a whole after a lifetime of separation. It was almost as beautiful as the loving experience they'd just shared.

Raine moved then and Slade did nothing to stop her. Her hand slid across the flat plane of his belly to find his bandaged hand. Capturing it with hers, she dragged it back across him and placed it on the gentle swell of her belly.

"Slade?"

"Mmm?"

"How . . . how do you feel about becoming a father again?"

He was so unprepared for the question that he laughed outright. "Well, I know it was good, sweetheart, but don't you think that's presuming a bit too much too soon?"

"Not at all." She sat up in the bunk, turning to face him. Her hand, still in possession of his, pressed it more firmly against her belly. "In fact, it's already happened."

"You mean, just *now*?" It was very hard for him to keep a straight face and the laughter out of his voice.

"No," she negated with a slow shake of her head. "Manila."

"Manila!" His smile faded in an instant, and his ardent gaze began to devour her lovely form. There was a difference all right, not a very big one, but one that was noticeable, now that he saw it. Her breasts were slightly fuller for one thing, and the tips were no longer the pale pink they had been but were a dark rose in hue. "My God, Raine! Why didn't you tell me sooner?"

"I was going to, but the time never seemed to be right."

"Time! What the hell has that got to do with it?" he demanded, jackknifing upright beside her.

"Everything, Slade. You don't just go up to a man in the middle of a hurricane or interrupt him when he's arguing with someone and casually inform him that he's going to become a father. If you'll recall, we've been through a lot of that these past weeks. This is the first real chance I've had."

"How long have you known?"

"For only a few weeks now, that's all. I merely suspected at first, but by the time we landed at the island, I knew it was a certainty. That's why I was so angry when you told Ruaita that I was your woman. I mean, I hadn't even had the chance to tell you I was carrying your child and you were announcing to total strangers that I belonged to you."

There was a long, silent pause then, and Raine could not tell by Slade's blank expression what was going through his mind. Eventually, she was forced to ask, "You aren't angry, are you?"

"No! Why should I be?" he countered.

"Well, some men would be."

"I'm not *some* men." He grinned. "Fact is, I think I'm damn proud!"

"Are you . . . really?"

"Yeah! You bet I am, sweetheart. But what about you?"

"What do you mean?"

"Do you want the baby?" The question, huskily phrased, was wrenched from him.

"Yes! Oh, Slade, I want this baby more than anything in the whole world. It's a part of *you*. How could you even ask such a thing?"

A look of sadness filled his eyes before he averted his gaze. "Annalise gave away Davey. Hell, my own mother didn't want me! She ran off with some merchant when I was just a kid, and Papa and my Aunt Cathy had to raise me and my older brother."

"Slade, I'm not Annalise, and I'm not your mother, either."

Remembering the hell she had gone through to get her own son back again, he nodded. "I know, sweetheart. But being abandoned by your mother is a hard thing to forget. That's one of the reasons why I've told Davey that *his* mother is dead. I didn't want him to have to suffer the bitterness and guilt that I did."

There were a lot of questions Raine wanted to ask, but now was not the time. He would tell her, in his own time and way, the rest of his painful past. She would just have to be patient, and wait.

"Our child will have both his parents, darling. I'll never leave you willingly."

"Oh, God," he groaned, hugging her to him fiercely. "I love you so much it scares me."

"I know, darling. I love you, too. But there's no reason to be frightened. You should be happy, and thrilled about all of this. We're a family, the four of us. Well, five, I guess I should say."

"Yeah." He chuckled at last. "We are, aren't we?"

"We have been for quite some time now. I think of David as my . . . well, he's much too old to be my son, so I guess I think of him as my younger brother. And you're so good with Adam, it won't be too hard for you to treat him like your own, will it?"

"He already calls me Daddy, why wouldn't I?"

"Oh, Slade! We have so much, so very, very much."

"I know," he murmured against her hair. "That's what frightens me. In the past, whenever I've gotten to the point where I'm beginning to feel happy and content, something, someone always comes along and takes it away."

"Not this time," she vowed in earnest. Pulling out of his embrace, she captured his bearded face with her hands. "This time nothing or no one will destroy what we've got. They wouldn't dare!"

Slade ground his mouth against hers, absorbing into his soul the very essence of her faith and assuredness. But in the back of his mind, the niggling doubt continued to linger. Out there somewhere was that nameless, faceless entity that would threaten his newfound happiness with Raine. He could feel it!

Chapter Eighteen

TREHEARNE STOOD AT THE PROW OF THE *SEA GULL*, his left eye pressed to the viewing end of the spyglass. To the naked, untrained eye, the speck on the far horizon would appear to be only that and nothing more. But with the aid of his glass, he could clearly see that it was a ship, and the ship they'd been searching for at that. Allowing himself a secretive smile, he collapsed the glass with a firm, resolute push.

"It's the *Mary Ellen*," he announced, turning to the man beside him.

"You're certain," Roger challenged.

"Oh, aye!" Trehearne nodded. "She's a three-masted barkentine with her name clearly printed on her hull. But by the looks of her, I'd say she's been damaged. That storm took off part of her mainmast."

"I hope that's *all* that's wrong with her." An acute pain tore through Roger's gut at the thought of his son—or Raine, for that matter—being injured.

"You'd best be going below and telling your . . . er, friend that we'll be coming alongside her in a couple of hours."

"No," Roger negated in a low voice. "Not yet. He's waited this long; he can stand to wait a while longer."

Now that the moment was almost upon them, he knew he was going to have a fight on his hands. But getting his son back again was going to be easy compared to keeping Hardy in line. These last weeks at sea had been pure hell. Hardy had been like a man beset by demons, alternately ranting and raving at anyone who crossed him one minute, and wailing out his fears and apprehensions to Roger the next.

Somehow Hardy had sensed that he was no longer useful to Roger and that their relationship was slowly coming to an end. What he hadn't realized, though, was that their affair had been over long before they had found Yang, the Cantonese houseboy who had worked for Raine. Luckily for them, the little Chinaman had directed them to Macao, where he had last seen Raine, for it was there that they had found Trehearne who was looking for passengers. Or did luck have anything to do with it?

In any case, Roger thought with a dispirited sigh, he wasn't looking forward to tackling Hardy's unpredictable temperament.

"How long before the sun sets, Captain?" he queried.

Trehearne turned to face the stern, his eyes estimating the hour by judging the distance between the bright ball in the sky and the edge of the water. "An hour and a half," he finally responded. "Maybe two."

Two hours to get to the *Mary Ellen* and two hours until sundown, he mused before suggesting, "Perhaps we should delay our joining the *Mary Ellen* until after nightfall." Those two hours would give him enough time to prepare Hardy—prepare him with the nearly full bottle of Scotch they still possessed. But then again, Hardy was about as unpredictable drunk as he was sober.

"I'll have to hoist my colors, in any case," Trehearne said, "to let them know we're a friendly vessel."

"Do whatever you must, Captain."

Trehearne bobbed his head as a sly smile tugged at the corner of his mouth. Then he pivoted his hulking body and ambled toward the stern.

Had he been more observant, Roger would have noticed the Cornishman's expression and questioned it. But as he gazed out to sea, his thoughts were too preoccupied with Hardy, his son and Raine for him to see.

What a fool he had been. A blind, besotted fool for choosing Hardy over Raine. Looking back on it now, he knew he should have never left her or taken their son. It was the worst mistake he'd ever made, and he would give anything if he could go back and erase the past.

Still, he thought, it wasn't a total loss yet. If he played his cards right, he could get her back again, because of the two, Raine was by far easier to manage than was Hardy. And he missed her, dammit! Missed her soft, husky voice, her low-pitched laughter when she was happy, her pliable, comforting body. She may not be as exciting in bed as he'd hoped, but with a little instructing she could be. After all, she had been willing enough the first time.

Roger took a long, deep breath and gazed one last time at the tiny dot on the horizon. There was another problem to be faced first, though, before he could confront Raine. And Hardy, he knew, was not going to be the most reasonable man to tackle.

"They're hoisting their colors, Mr. Dennison!" Hanging onto the rigging high above the deck, Davey called down to the first mate below.

The ship, which had been following them for some time now, had finally drawn close enough for the crew on deck to see it without the aid of a spyglass.

"Looks like we'll be having visitors before the day is out," the first mate remarked to Tex. "Better inform the captain."

With a brisk nod of his bright auburn head, Tex leaped down from the bridge as Mr. Dennison began giving orders to the rest of the crew to prepare for boarders.

Once he'd arrived outside Slade's quarters, Tex rapped his knuckles sharply on the door. "Clipper spotted off the starboard stern, Cap'n!" He waited for a response, hearing muffled voices from inside the cabin before the door swung open.

Slade filled the opening, his bandaged hands holding his unfastened trousers together at the waist. But a movement behind him drew Tex's gaze and the seaman blushed furiously. It was Raine, dressed in one of Slade's too-large shirts and nothing more, her long legs bared to his astonished gaze.

"Uh, I—I hate like hell to bother you, sir, but— but Mr. Dennison thought you ought to know," he stammered uneasily.

"Any idea what they want?" Slade bit out, knowing by Tex's expression what was going through the man's mind.

"No, sir, sure don't. They ain't in trouble, though, that's for sure. Mr. Dennison seems to think they just want to visit."

"Hmm." Slade nodded. There was nothing unusual about that. Ships at sea for long periods of time often broke the monotony of their voyages with brief visits between passing ships. "Well, maybe we'll be lucky and they'll have a preacher aboard."

"Sir?" Tex's gaze sliced away from Raine and back to Slade. "A preacher?"

"Yes. You're the first to know outside the family. Miss Sheridan and I plan to be married."

"Well, hey!" Tex beamed and clapped a hand across Slade's shoulders. "Ain't that nice! Congratulations!"

"Thank you, Tex." Raine smiled.

"Yes, thank you," Slade rejoined.

"Well, I'll get on back up topside then. Married! I'll be durn."

Slade closed the door only to lean against it, laughing. "Did you see the look on his face?"

Giggling, Raine nodded. "He was certainly surprised, wasn't he?"

"Yeah." Slade moved into the cabin, stopping when he stood directly before her. "You won't mind, will you? Being married here at sea instead of in a church?"

"No, of course not. But what if there isn't a minister aboard the other ship?"

"Then we'll get the captain to marry us. It'll be legal either way."

Raine ran her hands up his broad, hair-covered chest and let the tips of her fingers weave through the crisp mat of curls there. She felt the nubs of his brown male nipples harden under her touch and smiled. "You could marry us, couldn't you?"

"I suppose," he conceded, winding his arms about her waist and pulling her close to him. "But I've never performed a marriage ceremony before."

Sliding her hands down the length of his chest to his belly, Raine began to fasten his trousers with infuriating slowness. The gentle brush of her slender fingers there caused him to groan audibly. "If you don't hurry up, lady, you're going to be taking them off again instead of buttoning them up."

"My, my! You're a lusty old devil, aren't you?" she teased.

"Lusty, hell! I'm downright horny."

"*Again?* Why, Slade, I would have thought that a man your age would be rather exhausted after making love twice in one hour."

"Any other man my age would be, but then I've got you to excite me, don't I? My friend there . . ." he glanced pointedly down to the growing bulge in his trousers, ". . . seems to have a mind of his own."

"Does he now?" With her violet eyes locked to his green eyes, she slowly slid her hand inside his pants. After she found that part of him which she searched for, she played an enticing, arousing tune across his burgeoning flesh. "Yes," she agreed huskily, "he does seem to be saying something to me."

"Raine," Slade cautioned in a throaty moan. "You're asking for trouble."

"This kind of trouble I can handle, darling." Her fingers gently curled around his swollen member.

Unable to stand her delightful tormenting any longer, Slade's mouth swooped down, claiming her lips in a hungry kiss. She did not object, but welcomed it joyously. His tongue thrust like an ardent rapier into her soft mouth, finding a competitor of equal prowess within. Her smaller, more feminine foil grazed the underside of his tongue until he withdrew it slightly, then she easily took command of the moment by immediately gaining entrance through his lips. It was a teasing, warring game they both played to the hilt while the fires within their souls burned out of control.

Somewhere in the back of Slade's dazed, preoccupied mind a little voice called out to him. *Duty*, it said. But he refused to listen to its warning. There would be plenty of time for duty later. All he could think of now was satisfying himself and this lusty little creature he held in his arms.

"You are, without a doubt, the damnedest woman I've ever known," he confessed some time later, as they lay sated in each other's embrace.

"I'll take that as a compliment." She laughed on a husky breath.

"Better make it a complaint," he parried. "I've got guests coming aboard any minute now, and here I am, still in bed with you. You make me forget my obligations."

"Well, nobody forced you, you know." Her violet eyes blinked back at him with mocking innocence.

"Ha, the hell they didn't!" Chuckling, he rolled away and got out of bed. He stood there for a moment, letting his gaze rake every inch of her glowing beauty, only too aware that she was admiring his nakedness as well. "When you've finished checking over the merchandise, you wanton hussy, you can get your lovely little fanny out of that bed and help me get my pants on."

Like some sleek, golden, well-fed cat, Raine sinuously uncurled her long legs and slid her feet onto the deck. As she brushed past Slade to find his trousers, he thought he detected a purr coming from the direction of her long, creamy throat. He smiled, pleased with her teasing movements.

"It's not that I don't like what you've got on now," he began, stepping into the dark, tight-fitting pants she held for him. "Because I *do;* I like it a lot. But have you given any thought to what you're going to wear?"

"Oh, I thought I'd resurrect old Angus Mac-Dougal, or the nun, or, perhaps the mysterious Mrs. Cavanaugh. We haven't seen them for some time."

His green eyes narrowed to impatient slits at her mention of the characters she had portrayed. "Be serious, Raine. It's not everyday that you get married, you know."

"Yes, darling, I know." She smiled, holding his snowy white shirt while he shrugged it over his shoulders. "But I would hate to spend an inordinate amount of time getting myself and Adam ready and getting Hetty all excited, merely for nothing. Why, we aren't even sure that there is a minister aboard the other vessel, are we?"

"Just get your drawers on and let me do the worrying about that, okay?"

"Whatever you say," she conceded with a dutiful nod.

Married. Mrs. Slade. The Captain and Mrs. Quentin Slade.

Those delightful titles continued to rattle around in her head as she saw Slade out of the cabin moments later. All of them had a decidedly pleasant ring, she thought, stepping over to the cabinet that had become her wardrobe. And all of them would suit her quite admirably.

With a cautious, critical eye, she surveyed the neatly folded garments there, rejecting one after another with a disgruntled shake of her head. Nothing seemed appropriate for the occasion to come. The yellow was far too simple. The rose-pink was much too flashy. And the skirts and blouses she'd been wearing everyday wouldn't do either.

Then her questing fingers grazed the gown on the very bottom of the stack and a smile crept to her lips. Yes, of course! Her white silk cheongsam that she had worn the day she met Slade. How very prophetic; how very right. Why hadn't she thought of it sooner?

Hetty burst into the cabin just as Raine fastened the last button on her *broderie anglaise* camisole and petticoat. Adam sat on the ledge of the woman's outthrust hip, his favorite thumb stuck in his mouth.

"What on earth is going on?" Hetty demanded. "Are we to have visitors here in the middle of the ocean?"

"Yes, isn't it exciting?" Smiling, Raine pulled on a filmy wrapper. "Tex told us that a clipper ship is in the vicinity and we're going to have them aboard for dinner."

"The whole crew!"

"No, no. Probably just the officers. I'm not sure exactly what the protocol is."

"Well, I should think that it would be more correct if it were the other way around—we go aboard *their* ship and have dinner with *them*. After all, theirs is the larger vessel of the two."

"Yes, but Slade thought it wiser for us to do it this way. Come to Mummy, darling," she cooed, gathering Adam into her arms. "We need to get you changed and washed up."

"He isn't dining with us, is he?"

"Why not? His table manners aren't too atrocious, and besides . . . it isn't everyday his mummy gets married." She waited pensively for the outburst and winced when it came.

"*Raine!*" Needless to say, Hetty looked thoroughly scandalized. "You aren't seriously considering marrying that . . . that *American*, are you?" She pronounced it as if it were a filthy social disease.

"Hetty dear, under the circumstances, it's the wisest thing for me to do."

"What circumstances are you talking about?"

"Well, we love each other, for one thing."

"But you can get over that!"

"And for another . . ." Raine paused, giving her old friend a beatific smile, ". . . I'm carrying his child."

With a melodramatic groan, Hetty dropped onto the unmade berth, shaking her gray head with despair. "How could you, Raine? How could you make the same mistake a second time? I would have thought that that catastrophic alliance with Roger had taught you a lesson."

"Hetty, my loving Slade is *not* a mistake. And I will thank you not to mention Roger's name ever again. He's a part of my past that I would rather forget."

"But how can you when you're carrying around his offspring?"

Raine peered down at Adam's flaxen head and hugged him closer to her heart. "Slade is Adam's father now, and I intend to see that he grows up knowing *only* him as such."

"And his title," Hetty injected doggedly. "What are you going to do about that? Your son is an English nobleman now. Although he's only a lowly baronet, he's still a nobleman just the same. You can't possibly think of denying him his birthright."

"There are enough Ashleighs in England, Hetty, just waiting for the chance to carry on the lineage where Roger left off. You know that as well as I do. Adam will be a Slade, just as soon as his father and I can make it legal—an American, Hetty!"

"If only it were that simple. But it isn't, my child, it isn't."

Raine turned her back on her old friend and proceeded to wash and dress her son with angry, jerky movements. It was useless to try and make Hetty see things from her perspective. The woman did have a point, though, but she wasn't going to dwell on it now. There would be plenty of time to decide about Adam's title and future later on, after they reached America.

At the sound of the door opening, Raine whirled around, wanted to mend the rent between them. "Hetty."

"Yes?"

"Please . . . be happy for me, if only for today. I do love Slade, you know."

Hetty looked at her for a moment, her rigid expression fading slowly to one of patient acceptance. "I know, my dear. I know."

A million stars twinkled overhead as Slade stood by the port railing, waiting to greet the newcomers who were now boarding his ship. The clipper *Sea Gull,* anchored a short distance away but still clearly visible in the early evening twilight, might well be dwarfing his *Mary Ellen* with its more impressive size, but Slade was positive that his crew could match her efficiency any day. They stood like proud sentinels at their posts behind him while he stepped forward to welcome his guests.

Salutes were exchanged with Trehearne, the first to board and introduce himself as the *Sea Gull*'s captain. But it was the other two men who followed that had Slade more than a bit confused. It was plain to see by the cut of their clothes and their demeanor that they were not seamen. One was tall and angular with a thatch of well-groomed blond hair, while the other was of a slighter build, with dark hair and swarthy coloring. The co-owners of the *Sea Gull*, perhaps?

"It's good of you to have us aboard, Captain Slade," Trehearne proclaimed as his eyes cautiously canvassed the crew about them.

"Our pleasure, Captain Trehearne," Slade rejoined.

"I see you suffered some damage in the storm. No injuries, I hope."

Slade lifted his bandaged hands, cocking his head to one side. "Only minor ones, I'm glad to say. Rope burns." He shifted his gaze to the two non-seamen behind Trehearne. "I hope you gentlemen will understand if I decline to shake hands with you. I'll allow my first mate, Mr. Dennison, that honor, if you don't mind."

Stepping forward as he was expected to do, Mr. Dennison gave Captain Trehearne a smart salute then extended a hand in turn to the other two men.

"Captain Slade, Mr. Dennison," Trehearne began smoothly. "My passengers: Sir Roger Ashleigh and his companion, Mr. Gerhardt von Koenig."

The shock of the Cornishman's introduction registered with Slade, momentarily shattering his outward composure. But with his first mate holding everyone's attention, he had time to pull himself together and school his astonished expression.

Good God in heaven! Obviously Raine hadn't killed the man as she had thought, because this wasn't a ghost standing before him, he was flesh and blood. They had come after the boy. He knew it and had to think of some way, something, in a hurry to protect her. She would probably fall to pieces, and Fong would—

Fong!

It hit Slade then with a force that overwhelmed him. All of the missing puzzle pieces finally fell into place, all of the unanswered questions were suddenly, clearly resolved. Von Koenig had stolen the figures from Fong, and Fong had used Raine as bait to lure him here into his conniving clutches. God damn the man! God damn his miserable, manipulating soul!

Trehearne was part of Fong's scheme, too. Slade was sure of it, because he knew the Cornishman's reputation; knew that he had been in trouble in the past and owed somebody a favor for helping him out. Fong was that somebody.

Quickly he scanned the deck and finally located the face he sought in the starboard shadows. *If I could get my hands on you,* he thought, *I'd make you pay for this.* But he couldn't reveal his newfound knowledge now, because, as usual, Fong held the upper hand.

"Captain Slade?"

"Yes." Reluctantly, he shifted his gaze away from Fong, altering his expression as the taller of the other two men approached him. "Sir Roger, isn't it?"

"Oh, please, drop the 'sir.' Roger will do. There's no need for formalities out here."

Slade nodded his head in agreement. "As you wish. What can I do for you?" By all outward appearances, Raine's former husband looked much like any other man. There was not one thing even remotely effeminate about him that Slade could see, though he knew otherwise. Ashleigh's rugged, cleancut good looks, his deep, booming voice, his gentlemanly behavior were all so misleading, Slade could easily see what Raine had found attractive in him.

"I understand that you have passengers aboard," Roger remarked cautiously. "A woman and a little boy."

It was on the tip of his tongue to lie to the man, but Slade knew he couldn't do it. No, in this situation, the truth would have to do. "As a matter-of-fact, there are two women and a boy aboard. Why? Do you know them?"

"I might. Tell me, are they all right? I mean, they weren't harmed or injured during the storm, were they?"

"No," Slade began, lifting his bandaged hands, "the only one injured was—"

"Oh, damn, Roger," von Koenig snarled drunkenly. "Get on with it! Forget about that bitch and her whelp and find out about the figures."

"Figures?" Slade frowned from one man to the other, hoping his feigned confusion was convincing. He halfway expected Fong to jump out of the shadows and take control of the situation—in fact, he wanted him to. But when he didn't, Slade knew he would have to continue stalling until Fong decided to make himself known.

"Hardy, I'll handle this," Roger bit out angrily. "Just stay out of it, please." He turned back to Slade with a long, indrawn breath. "You must forgive my companion, Captain. He has been somewhat out of sorts lately and has had to find solace in a bottle."

"Only because you've been so damn preoccupied with finding your son!" von Koenig snapped.

"I mean it, Hardy. Shut up!"

It was easy to see that all was not well between the lovers. Slade made a mental note of this and vowed to put it to good use later on, if and when he needed to. But right now, he had a more pressing problem on his hands: keeping Roger away from Raine. And Adam, he tacked on mentally.

Down below in the galley, Raine's only problem was in finding a suitable place for them to dine.

"The salon just ain't gonna be big enough, Miss Sheridan," Cookie explained with a slow shake of his head as he chopped at a chicken carcass. "It won't seat more'n eight men at one time, and we don't know yet how many extra mouths we gotta feed tonight."

"Well then, why don't we dine on deck? There is plenty of room up there. Some of the crewmen could carry up the tables, and I'm sure we can find the extra chairs we're going to need." It was a really wonderful idea, she thought. A wedding, followed by a feast under the stars. Oh, yes, wonderful and very romantic!

"I'd need to okay it with the cap'n first, though. But if it's all right with him, it's all right with me." Cookie raked the last of the chicken remains into the big refuse bucket and grabbed the handle before starting for the passageway. "I gotta go feed the sharks, then I'll speak to the cap'n."

"Feed the what?" Her half-giggle held a note of surprise.

"The sharks," he repeated. "Ain't you ever seen

them fins in the water after we dump garbage overboard?"

"No, I haven't."

"Well, they'll be there, sure as shootin', just as soon as all this blood and guts hits the water. Draws 'em like flies from miles away, it does. But better to feed 'em chicken innerds than an arm or a leg, that's what I always say."

Raine shuddered at the thought and followed Cookie out of the galley. But where he continued on up to the main deck, she lingered below, checking up on Adam and Hetty. The baby was sound asleep in Hetty's bunk.

"It looks as if he's going to miss the wedding after all, doesn't it?" Hetty observed.

"And are you going to miss it, too?" Raine queried.

Hetty stood there for a moment, looking at Raine, then she released a long breath and slowly shook her head. "No, I'll be there."

"Oh, Hetty, don't be this way," Raine begged. "I'm happy. Be happy for me."

"It will be difficult . . . but I'll try."

Smiling, Raine embraced her old friend and bestowed a kiss upon the woman's wrinkled cheek before stepping back. "Thank you, Hetty. You don't know how much your approval means to me." Odd as it seemed, Hetty was like a second mother to Raine. "Well, I must be off. Here I am, soon to be the captain's lady, and I haven't even greeted our guests yet."

"The captain's lady." Hetty sniffed. "You make it sound far grander than it really is."

Closing the door behind her, Raine had to giggle. Hetty would never thoroughly approve of Slade, no matter what, so her half-approval of him, given grudgingly, would just have to do.

Holding the straight skirt of her cheongsam above her ankles, she climbed the short flight of stairs to the main deck. She didn't have to look for Slade, for he stood nearby, his imposing back turned to her as was Mr. Dennison's, who stood beside him. She hated to interrupt this obviously all-male gathering, but she had to make herself known.

"Excuse me, gentlemen. I'm sorry to have taken so long." Stepping toward the group, she held her head proudly and smiled serenely as if she were in fact the captain's lady. "But I was seeing to our dinner, you see, and I—"

Breaking off in midsentence, she inhaled a horrified breath as the man standing behind Slade moved into her line of vision. With a sickening lurch, the deck shifted, suddenly disappearing out from under her and she felt herself falling into a deep, dark abyss from which there was no light or retreat.

"No, no, you're dead!" she whimpered before the dark cavern walls closed in on her.

Chapter Nineteen

SLADE WAS BESIDE RAINE IN ONE LONG STRIDE, breaking her fall with his outstretched arms before she could hit the deck. A half-step behind him was Roger, looking more surprised than any of them at this American who was holding his wife.

"Raine?" Slade's worried voice called out to her as he straightened, cradling her like he would a child. With relief, he saw her heavily lashed eyes begin to flutter. "Sweetheart, it's going to be all right."

Sweetheart! Roger threw Slade an incredulous look as all the color drained from his face. He felt as if someone were reaching down into the depths of his soul and ripping out his heart.

"He's dead," Roger heard Raine mutter. "I killed him."

"No, my love, you just thought you did." Slade crooned, starting for the quarterdeck gangway.

"You see, you needn't have worried about the bitch after all." Von Koenig's slurred ramblings penetrated the roaring in Roger's ears. "Women like her always land on their feet."

"Shut your filthy mouth, or I'll shut it for you," Roger turned on him in fury. "There's only one bitch aboard this ship and it isn't her." The sight of Hardy made him sick to his stomach and all he wanted to do now was get away from him.

"Where do you think you're going?" von Koenig called after him.

"To my . . ." Wife? No, she wasn't his any longer and never would be. She had been once, but he had tossed her aside when she had served her usefulness and now the American had her. "To Raine," he ended with as much pride as he could muster, turning to descend the quarterdeck steps.

Slade was sitting beside Raine on the bunk when Roger quietly entered the cabin. He was murmuring soothing words to her as she whimpered, "But the fire, Slade. All that blood. He was *dead*. I know he was. I saw him!"

"Sweetheart . . ."

"I only wanted my son. I didn't mean to kill him. God, I didn't want him to *die!* I just wanted Adam back."

"I know, my love. I know." Slade held her head against his chest, gently rocking back and forth with her as she continued to weep pitifully.

Roger could only stand there and watch, his traitorous conscience slowly crucifying him. *He* had done this to her; he and no one else. His greed and his lust for Hardy had overriden his decency and now she was suffering for the cruelty he had inflicted.

Long moments passed before Raine's sobbing

finally began to subside. Roger wiped his brow and cleared the guilty knot from his throat. Slade's head jerked around at the sound, his eyes narrowing to icy slits of green. "What are you doing here?"

"I was worried about Raine," Roger intoned weakly.

"Worried! Jesus Christ, man, haven't you done enough to her already? You see how she is, now just go on and get the hell out!"

But Roger didn't. He stepped further into the cabin until he could clearly see the woman in Slade's arms. "I'm not here to cause you trouble, Raine. I—I didn't know that my appearing this way would affect you so. Believe me, I didn't. I only wanted—"

"I know what you want, Roger, and you're not going to have him!" she cried. "He's *my* son! You took him from me once, but you won't do it again."

Roger slowly shifted his gaze to Slade. "May I have a few minutes alone with her . . . please?"

"Hell, no!" Slade growled, holding Raine tighter. "I would be crazy to leave her here with you. You've done enough damage as it is. I'm not going to let you do anymore."

"I only want to talk to her, nothing more, I swear it."

"Whatever you have to say, Roger, can be said in front of Slade," Raine declared. "We have no secrets from each other."

Roger winced. "I can see that. But there are a few things I think we should discuss."

"Such as?" She pulled away from Slade and stood up.

"Percival," Roger replied bluntly.

"His name is Adam!" she bit out.

Roger clenched his teeth tightly and held onto his temper. "All right, Adam then. He is my son, Raine. I've gone to a lot of trouble to find him, and I'm not going to just give him up."

"Neither am I!" she cried.

"Suppose—suppose we try sharing custody of him," Roger suggested hesitantly.

"That's impossible," Slade interjected with a shake of his head, a challenging gleam appearing in his eye. "Unless, of course, you're planning on living in America, too, that is."

"America?" Roger frowned.

"Yeah! That's where *we're* going to live. What did you think she was going to do after she married me? Move back to England so you and that . . . that lover of yours could humiliate and degrade her some more?"

"No! I've never degraded her!"

"What do you call having her declared an unfit mother and stealing her son, then?"

The bluntness of Slade's words hit Roger like a hard blow to the chest, but he refused to back down. "He's my son as well!" he bit out defensively, his nostrils flaring. "Whatever has happened in the past, I am *still* that boy's father, and not you or anyone else can change that fact. But how can I expect you to understand? You're not a father."

"But I am," Slade rejoined with a smoothness that surprised Roger. *"My* son is aboard with me at this very moment. So don't try giving me some cock-and-bull lecture about the responsibilities of fatherhood. I could probably tell *you* a thing or two."

"Then, as a father," Roger began slowly, "I'm sure you can understand my position. I want my son with me and I intend to have him."

"So he can grow up to be like you?" Slade jeered. "Fawning over other men instead of courting women like a normal young man should?"

"Now, see here—"

"No, Roger, *you* see here!" Raine boldly stepped between the two men, having stood silent as long as she could. "Granted, Adam is your son and I'm willing to believe you love him, but is that enough? Is it? What Slade just suggested is true; you are *not* the perfect model for a child to pattern himself after." Taking a deep breath, she tried to reason with her former husband. "You confided in me once, a long time ago, about how unhappy your childhood was. Do you want that sort of childhood for your own son, too? Do you want him to be as confused about himself as you were? I don't think so, Roger. Neither of us, I'm sure, want that for Adam."

A brief look of dejection crossed Roger's handsome features as his lean, upright body slowly relaxed. "No, of course I don't. My life was a nightmare, a living hell until Hardy came into it. It's not much better now . . . without you. Believe what you wish, Raine, but I did love you in my own way."

Feeling Slade shift uneasily behind her, Raine reached back and grasped his hand in hers, squeezing it gently. The movement, undetected by Roger, told Slade that Roger's declaration had meant nothing to her, that she still loved him. His fingers, curling into hers, assured her that he understood.

"I know you did, Roger," she voiced softly, "but it wasn't enough. If it hadn't been von Koenig, it would have been someone else, some other man. I just didn't have the capacity to give you the kind of love and happiness you wanted. I doubt if any woman could."

In one, smooth, premeditated movement, Roger cupped her chin with his fingers and smiled sadly down at her. "You understand me so well, don't you? Yet you don't condemn me. Thank you," he whispered as his head swooped down, claiming her lips in a brief, tender kiss. When he pulled back, he shifted his gaze straight into Slade's cold green eyes. "Guard her well, Captain. She is truly one lady worth cherishing."

"I know," Slade agreed almost gruffly, his fingers tightening about Raine's.

Knowing that he had the two of them convinced that he would be giving up his son to them, Roger breathed an inner sigh of relief. They were so stupid, so sure of themselves. But he was still going to take his son away with him when he left this ship. No child of his would ever be raised by this gullible, upstart American.

But then he suddenly remembered Hardy and grimaced audibly. "Oh, damn! I completely forgot about Hardy and his obsession with those damn figures."

As it had done earlier with Slade, the last puzzle piece fell into place within Raine's head. She whirled a startled face around to Slade, her violet eyes wide with comprehension. "Fong! *That's* why he's here—"

"Fong Chiang is aboard this boat?" Roger demanded.

"You know him?" Slade challenged.

"No, not the way Hardy . . ." He broke off with an expressive shudder and turned toward the door. "I've got to get up there before Hardy finds out. As crazy as he's been behaving lately, there's no telling what he might do."

Slade was right behind Roger, with Raine bringing up the rear, as they made their way topside.

Nightfall had at last descended completely. The lanterns, their only source of illumination on this moonless night, cast ominous shadows on those about the deck; more ominous than the tense air of expectancy which surrounded them all.

Fong, a good many inches shorter than Trehearne, stood next to the Cornishman as von Koenig, tight-lipped and seething, trembled nearby. His plan had worked! He had lured the German here and now he was going to extract his revenge as he had so carefully planned.

"I've carried out my end of the bargain," Trehearne said to him. "I've brought von Koenig to you just as you instructed. As I see it, we're even now. I'm no longer in your debt. Agreed?"

Fong bobbed his hairless pate in a slow, affirmative nod and heard von Koenig hiss, "Set up! The two of you set me up for this, didn't you?"

Dark, hate-filled almond eyes slid around to face his accuser. "I would have confronted you in Hong

Kong, but there are authorities there that I would rather not deal with. This is just between you and me, von Koenig. But no one steals from me and gets away with it," Fong growled, the icy timbre of his voice causing Raine to shrink back. "Men like you, who rob from my dead ancestors' graves are a blight on humanity."

"You're no better!" von Koenig argued. "Don't think you are. You've robbed just as many graves as the rest of us, and have profited by it, too!"

"Ah, but for a different reason. My people have benefited as well. You . . . *your* kind steal for the sole purpose of personal gain. My country has been raped and pillaged for centuries, our treasures taken from us without a thought as to what *we* might derive from them. But no more! That is going to come to an end—if not now, then very, very soon."

"Hardy." Roger's pleading voice cut through the heavy silence that followed. "Give it up. Can't you see that you're outnumbered here."

"No!" von Koenig snapped viciously. "Those are *my* Hindu statues, and I intend to have them back. This . . . this pitiful excuse for a man is no match against me."

A ghost of a smile crossed Fong's lips and Slade nearly groaned aloud. The fool, he thought, had done the wrong thing now. But he was glad it was the German and not himself on Fong's bad side.

"Maybe so," Fong admitted. "Maybe not." Then he tilted his chin ever so slightly, and as if they had been given a silent order, a dozen or more men stepped forward into the light, making themselves visible to von Koenig. "You may be deluded in thinking that you can overpower *me,* but can you take on all of my men as well?"

Von Koenig panicked. Like a wild animal who had suddenly found himself trapped, he reached into his coat and produced a revolver, aiming it directly at Fong. "Tell them to back off. Now! Or I'll put a bullet right between your slanty little eyes."

Slade's only thought at that moment was to protect Raine and his son, Davey, who unfortunately stood right in the line of fire on Fong's other side. With a subtle jerk of his head, he motioned for Davey to get out of the way. Aware of the dangerous position he was in, the boy slowly obeyed, moving deeper and deeper into the shadows of the bow. The instant Slade saw his son disappear into a crouch, he turned and started to grab for Raine.

Startled by the movement, von Koenig whipped the gun around and squeezed the trigger, sending a bullet through the outer flesh of Slade's arm. With the deafening ring of the shot still reverberating in the air, Fong's unshod foot lashed upward and kicked the weapon free of von Koenig's hand so that it sailed, still smoking, onto the bridge. But rather than overpower or subdue his now unarmed opponent, he crouched into an ancient martial arts stance —his feet parted, his elbows bent, his hands curled into odd-looking claws near his chest—and smiled.

"You're a dead man, von Koenig." He laughed maliciously. "You simply do not realize it yet."

A strangled cry ripped through the night as Raine suddenly noticed the red stain spreading over Slade's white shirt. "Oh, no, you've been shot!"

Unwilling to avert his gaze from the tense tableau before him for long, Slade quickly glanced down at his bleeding arm and slapped a bandaged hand over it. "I'm all right. Get below," he ordered bruskly, only now feeling the pain begin to throb in his shoulder. "Davey! Go with her."

"I'm not leaving you here," Raine maintained stubbornly. "You're hurt."

"I said *get below,* dammit!"

"Come on, Miss Sheridan." Suddenly Tex was beside her, wrapping an arm around her and pulling her toward the hatchway.

"No! Not without Slade." But her protest was no match against the Texan's greater strength.

Just as they reached the opening, though, Hetty burst out with a sleepy-looking Adam on her hip.

"What on earth is going on?" she demanded of no one in particular. "I thought I heard a gunshot."

The unexpected arrival of the child and the other woman took Fong's attention away from von Koenig for a brief moment. But it was all the German needed to make his move. In two quick leaps, he was up the bridge ladder and in possession of the gun again. Neither Fong nor his men, who were rushing toward him, could stop the inevitable from happening.

Point-blank, von Koenig aimed the gun and fired it. As the bullet tore through Fong's lean side, the impact forcefully knocked him and the men behind him onto the deck in an ungainly heap.

"Now, *you,*" the German cried, turning the gun on Hetty. "Get over here!"

"No!" Roger and Raine screamed in unison.

"Not my son, Hardy!" Roger persisted, starting toward the bridge.

"Stay out of this, Roger," von Koenig warned. "I don't want to hurt you, too."

But Roger didn't listen. He stepped in front of Hetty, only glancing down briefly at the son he loved so much before turning his full attention back to von Koenig. "Don't do this, Hardy."

"I have to," von Koenig proclaimed, his crazed glance darting to the people who were now surrounding him. "He's my only chance of getting out of this alive. You heard Fong. He wants to kill me." Slowly, cautiously, he made his way down the bridge ladder, the gun pointed toward the baby's head.

"But Fong can't hurt you now," Roger stressed with forced calm. "See? You've shot him."

Von Koenig glanced down at the unconscious, bleeding Oriental then back at Roger, who had taken a step closer to him. "It doesn't matter," he insisted. "I still have the rest of them to contend with. They want me dead, too."

"No, they don't," Roger replied. "Just give me the gun."

"But the statues, Roger. You know I've got to have them."

Raine was trembling from head to foot, worried what Roger might do next. *She* dared not move to try and protect her son from the demented madman, because his gun might go off and shoot Adam. She could see the insanity in his face and knew he was on the verge of doing something rash. But with Roger's back to her, she couldn't see his expression or know

what he was thinking. Their lives—*Adam's* life—
were in his hands now.

"I'm not going to let you touch my son," Roger
declared firmly, his forward steps slowly closing the
distance which separated him and the German. "I
can't, Hardy."

"Stay back!" von Koenig barked. "I don't want to
have to shoot you, too."

"Then for God's sake, put the gun down and
forget this madness."

"I am not mad! I want only what is mine." He
began backing up toward the railing, the angle of his
steps giving him a clearer range of Hetty and the
baby. "I stole those statues and 'to the victor goes
the spoils.' You know that as well as I do. They'll
bring me a fortune back in England. I may not be
able to buy back my inheritance, but at least I can
live in the manner to which I belong and not have to
depend on wealthy lovers like you for my support."

Roger paid no attention to the man's demented
ravings. He muttered a silent prayer then took a
deep breath and lunged at Hardy in a flying leap.

Von Koenig pulled the trigger the instant Roger's
feet left the deck. But the bullet didn't go where he
had intended it. It went no further than the center of
the younger man's chest.

Roger knew only a brief moment of agonizing
pain before the deadly bullet stopped his shattered
heart from beating. His body, still moving forward,
fell heavily against von Koenig's and they both
tumbled over the railing and into the fathomless
waters below.

Dozens of running feet rushed to the side where

tortured screams began to fill the night air. Slade, one of the first to reach the railing, glanced down then quickly turned away just in time to stop Raine from witnessing the carnage below.

"Don't look!" he ordered grimly, holding her head tight against his chest.

"But Roger—!" she began, twisting in his arms.

"Was dead before he hit the water," Slade ended solemnly.

The German's screams continued to rip through the souls of all who watched for a moment longer, then, thankfully, they ceased. The only sound that followed was the thrashing of fins against the water as the sharks ended their frenzied feeding.

More than a dozen crewmen rushed to various spots along the railing and emptied their heaving stomachs into the drink. The sight had truly been a sickening one. But Slade looked heavenward and thanked God that he had at least spared Raine that.

When all was silent once again, she turned her tear-filled eyes up to his. "He did it for Adam."

"I know," Slade soothed, pushing back her loosened blond hair with his bandaged hands. "I know, sweetheart."

"He—he died, saving his son," she sobbed.

"Shh. Try not to think about it. It's all over now."

Slowly he led her over to where Hetty stood with the baby. He could see the tears streaming down the older woman's cheeks, but the proud erectness of her carriage assured Slade that she was holding up better than most of them. After all, he surmised, she was a survivor.

Releasing her hold on Adam when Raine reached

out for him, Hetty opened her mouth as if to say something. But thinking better of it, she closed it again, sniffed once, then turned on her heel and went below.

Raine buried her face into her son's blond curls and allowed her sobs to begin anew. He was all she had left now of Roger, the man she had once loved, the man who had hurt her so deeply. But that didn't matter anymore; the painful past was no longer important, because she now saw him in a different light. Never would a day go by that she wouldn't be reminded of his love. She would forever see it in her son's face until the day she died.

But, she vowed silently, she was not going to let what transpired here tonight warp her reason. She couldn't! For nestled within her was the product of her love for Slade. A love that surpassed any other on earth.

With one last sniff, she inhaled deeply and looked up at the bearded man beside her. A weak smile tugged at her lips, and was instantly mirrored in the sad, dimpled grin that he returned to her.

"Are you going to be all right now?" came his soft query.

"Yes." She nodded. "Yes, I'll be just fine."

He dropped his uninjured arm about her shoulders and gave it a comforting, reassuring squeeze. In her own way, Raine was as much a survivor as the rest of them, he concluded.

But, hell, he couldn't stand here philosophizing the rest of the night, much as he would like to. There was still a lot they had to do, take care of; his bleeding arm for one, and Fong's wound for another. Already the Oriental had regained consciousness, he saw, and was loudly cursing in his native tongue as his men helped him to his feet.

"Looks like we're not going to have our wedding tonight after all, doesn't it?" he remarked dryly.

"It wouldn't be right," Raine murmured quietly. "Not after what's just happened. Couldn't we . . . I mean, wouldn't it be better if we waited until we got to Hawaii?"

"Sure, if that's what you want."

"It is, darling."

Solemnly he nodded his dark head then looked around as Davey stopped beside him. There was an obvious, unmistakable pallor to the boy's face. "Are you okay, son?"

"Yeah, I'm all right, Pa." Davey managed a feeble smile before his gaze drifted to Slade's bleeding arm. "But what about you?"

"Oh, hell! This is just a little flesh wound. It's not even worth worrying over. I've suffered worse and lived to tell about it."

"Slade!"

Three heads turned in unison as Fong called out. He was standing by the railing, his weight being supported by Captain Trehearne and one of his crewmen.

"Yeah, what do you want?" Slade returned cautiously.

"It has been an interesting evening, old friend. But I am afraid that I must take my leave now."

"It's about time," Slade agreed on a low growl. Then louder, "You going without your little statues?"

"Oh, I already have them. They haven't been aboard your ship since the night we landed at the island."

Slade shot a questioning look at Raine, who looked back at him with astonishment written on her face. "I never thought to look for them after I moved into your cabin," she confessed.

Fury instantly welled up inside of Slade. "You sneaky little son of a bitch!" he snarled and started toward Fong to wring his scrawny little neck. But before he could take more than one step, two pairs of hands quickly reached out and stopped him.

"He's an injured man, Slade," Raine reminded him.

"Yeah, Pa," Davey agreed. "And so are you."

The oaths Slade swore caused Raine to blush. But his rage soon diminished and he was left breathing raggedly.

"One of these days, Fong," he pledged with a jeer. "You just wait! One of these days, I'll get even with you for what you put us through tonight."

Fong threw back his hairless head and roared with laughter, then immediately doubled over and gripped his bleeding side. "Ah, old friend," he said at long last, "I will hold you to that."

Treharne and one of the other men helped Fong over the railing. But as his head slowly disappeared out of sight, Slade heard him say, "Until that day, though. . . ."

Chapter Twenty

RORY SHERIDAN HOPPED AGILELY OUT OF THE HIRED carriage and scanned the busy dock around him. There were ships of every size and description nearby, many of them were probably barkentines. How on earth was he supposed to find the *Mary Ellen* among this bloody lot?

"Hey, mister," the driver called down to him from his perch. "You want me to wait, or what?"

"Yes, wait, please," Rory directed him over his shoulder.

"How long you gonna be?"

"I haven't the foggiest. But I'll make it worth your time, I assure you."

The driver shrugged carelessly and settled back in his seat, pulling his wide-brimmed hat down over his face to hide it from the glare of the hot August sun.

Rory adjusted his topper over his unruly blond curls and started off down the dock in search of a three-masted barkentine, whatever that was. One ship looked like another to him, but Raine had said she would be arriving on a barkentine, so that's what he would look for. He'd received her letter only weeks ago, from Hawaii of all places, informing him of her approximate date of arrival in San Francisco. What she had been doing on that island, or indeed in that part of the world, she hadn't said, for the letter had been little more than a note, very short and to the point.

Knowing his sister as he did, though, she had probably gotten herself into some kind of difficulty and was now expecting him to bale her out. If there was one thing he could always count on Raine doing, it was the unexpected. She'd been that way even as a child.

A grizzled-looking longshoreman caught Rory's violet-blue gaze and he decided to shorten his search by asking him where the *Mary Ellen* was moored.

The man pointed. "Just right up ahead, young fellah. She got in last night, just before the fog rolled in."

With a nod of thanks, Rory turned and sauntered off in the direction the man had pointed. Fog, he thought with a rueful shake of his head. In that respect, San Francisco was a lot like London. One could always count on the fog rolling in just after sundown and rolling out again shortly after sunrise.

"Ah, there we are," he murmured with relief, spying the barkentine he sought. "Now to find little sister and discover what the hell all this is about."

No sooner had he started toward the boarding steps than he saw the group assembled on deck, and he stopped in midstride, thoroughly dumbstruck. The slender blonde surrounded by the group of tall, brawny men was definitely his sister Raine, but she looked considerably different from the last time he'd seen her. She no longer possessed that dewy-eyed, untouched look of innocence that he remembered her having. Instead, she now looked happy, content and quite serene. And she positively glowed, too. But what was she doing with all those men?

"Raine?"

Whirling about at the sound of her name, Raine saw her brother start across the deck toward her. But he got no more than a few steps when she cried out his name and rushed over to him, throwing herself in his arms. He lifted her off her feet and swung her around in a wide circle, letting his love pour out to her in his tight embrace. He had missed her even more than he imagined.

"Oh, it's so good to see you again!" She laughed tearfully, her feet once again touching the deck.

"It's good to see you, too." Holding her at arm's length he surveyed her slender, lilac-clad figure. "You certainly don't look any the worse for wear. But what in the world are you doing here of all places? And what were you doing in Hawaii? The last time I saw you, we were in London, and you were planning to marry that rogue Ashleigh."

Raine's smile, which had begun with his spate of questions, faded somewhat at the mention of Roger. But she recovered and said, "I'd rather not talk about him, Rory, if you don't mind. Come, let me introduce you to my family."

"Your family?" Wearing a puzzled frown, he allowed her to pull him across the deck.

"Yes. Well, they're actually your family, too, brother dear."

Rory's confusion began to mount as she proceeded to introduce him to a lad on the brink of manhood with a slight Eurasian look about him—his step-nephew? But the towheaded cherub in the older boy's arms couldn't be Raine's child! She said he was, though, and there was a definite likeness between the two of them.

"Ah, there he is." Raine smiled, dragging Rory's attention away from the two boys. "Rory, I want you to meet my husband, Quentin Slade. Darling, this is my older brother, Rory."

To say he was astonished by the sheer size of the American before him would be an understatement. But what really astounded him more was the fact that the man was talking to a tiny bundle in the crook of his arm. Certainly not the sort of thing one would expect a man of his size to do. At least, not in public.

"How do you do?" Rory's polite greeting reflected his cautiousness, yet he extended his hand to shake the American's outstretched one.

"So you're Rory," Slade remarked with a wide grin, the grooves deepening in his teak-brown cheeks. "Raine's told us so much about you, I feel as if I already know you."

"Has she! Well, I—I wish I could say the same," came Rory's vague reply.

"Oh, here, sweetheart," Slade murmured, placing his tiny bundle into Raine's waiting arms. "She started fretting a while ago, and I thought I'd better bring her to you."

"She?" Rory let his perplexed gaze drift from the American down to the bundle and then up to his sister, who was busy unwrapping one end.

"Yes, Rory. Your niece. Isn't she an absolute

darling? She looks just like her father, dimples and all, don't you think?"

Peering over his sister's shoulder, Rory thought that the baby looked a good deal like his sister. Yet where Raine possessed honey-gold locks, the baby had a head full of dark, curling hair. Two huge violet eyes, surrounded by a thick fringe of dark lashes, blinked up at him as an angelic, dimpled smile stretched her tiny rosebud pink mouth. No, she was undoubtedly the American's as well.

"My niece, hmm? What's her name?" Thoroughly captivated by the infant, he extended a finger to caress her creamy, downy-soft cheek.

"Louisa Catherine," Slade supplied proudly. "*I* wanted to name her Raine, after her mama, but your sister wouldn't hear of it."

"And for a very good reason, too," Raine inserted. "No child should have to go around with the same name her parent has. It's much too confusing. And besides, I think Louisa Catherine suits her. I know our mother would have liked knowing we named our daughter after her, and so would your Aunt Cathy," she said pointedly to Slade.

"Daddy," the towheaded cherub suddenly called and reached out for Slade. The tall, Eurasian youth willingly released him.

"Yeah, go to Pa! You're getting too heavy for me to hold."

"You're . . . David, right?" Rory asked the boy.

"Yes, sir. But you can call me Davey, if you want."

"Davey . . . and Adam." Rory frowned and

scratched the back of his neck. "I must try and remember all these new names."

"Oh, you'll have plenty of time to get used to them," Raine assured him.

Catching her subtle intonation, he inquired, "Oh, then you're not just passing through."

"No," Slade said. "From the looks of it, we're going to be here a long time." The look he exchanged with Raine did not escape Rory's notice.

"Well, good!" Rory beamed. "It'll give us a chance to really get acquainted, won't it. Oh, and you're more than welcome to stay at my house. I've plenty of room just going to waste."

"We wouldn't dream of imposing," Raine demurred quickly, a teasing glint appearing in her eye. "But since you've offered. . . ." She let her meaning sink in and smiled at her brother.

"Yes," Rory drawled, recognizing the old Raine lurking beneath the new. "After all, what are families for?"

It took a while to unload all their bags off the ship and onto a wagon nearby. They had accumulated a lot during their voyage . . . and lost a lot as well.

"It's a shame Hetty didn't make this leg of the voyage with us," Raine remarked as Rory's hired carriage made its way into the heart of the city. "It was the most pleasant by far."

"Hetty!" came Rory's cry of surprise. "Was she with you?"

"Well, she was until we landed in Hawaii," Raine admitted, then turned to Slade to see the difficult time he was having in keeping a straight face. She nudged him with her elbow and warned amusedly, "Shh! Don't start giggling now, Rory will think we're unbalanced."

Looking at the two of them battling to keep a straight face, Rory knew they were sharing a private secret. But he remarked with a frown, "Well, I know Hetty's a bit stubborn and singleminded, but—"

The muffled chuckles exploded into uproarious laughter. Even Davey joined in. And Adam, who sat in Slade's lap, cackled with delight and clapped his little hands.

Until the laughter died down, Rory had to sit there, feeling decidedly the odd man out.

"Forgive us, Rory," Slade begged, still chuckling.

"Yes, dear, we didn't mean to get so carried away." Raine lifted a gloved hand to wipe her cheeks. "It's just that it's . . . it's so funny! Hetty, I mean."

"Well, what about her? Let me in on it, please."

Slade cleared his throat and began. "You see, Rory, we had this cook on board the *Mary Ellen* who was . . ." he paused, groping for the right word.

"Smitten," Raine supplied.

"Yeah," Slade agreed. "He was sort of smitten with Hetty, but she must have taken it as something much more serious. Anyway, when we landed in Hawaii and Raine and I found a preacher to marry us, Hetty started giving Cookie these fairly expressive looks at the wedding."

"Hetty?" Rory queried with surprise. The Hetty he knew had very little to do with men, other than on the stage of course.

Slade nodded. "Yeah, but Cookie didn't want any part of what she had in mind. He told me once, a long time ago, that that was the reason he went to sea in the first place, 'to get away from some blame woman,' he said. Anyway a day or two before we were going to sail, he jumped ship. And Hetty went right along with him. She said something about finding the little weasel and making an honest man of him before he could get too far away."

"Poor blighter," Rory responded, feeling his own lips twitch.

"Exactly," Raine agreed. "But you know how Hetty is when she has her mind set on something. And she was determined to catch Eugene."

"Eugene?" Rory frowned.

"Cookie," Davey explained, grinning.

"Oh!" Rory nodded, understanding.

"Well, she had the crew unload all of her stuff, lock, stock and birdcage, and that's the last we saw of her," Slade ended with an amused shake of his head. "God help Cookie if she finds him."

"You mean *when* she finds him, darling," Raine supplied. "Our Hetty has a way of getting what she wants. Doesn't she, Rory?"

Their laughter continued until they reached Rory's tall, Victorian house near the top of Russian Hill. At Raine's first sight of the imposing brick structure, she released an "Ooooh!" of pleasure.

"How did you ever find it?" she asked her brother as Slade helped her out of the carriage.

"A business acquaintance helped me to acquire it," he explained, leading them toward the tall flight of wooden steps. "Don't worry about the bags,

301

Slade. One of my staff will see to them when the wagon arrives."

"You've a staff as well?" she remarked, letting her gaze scan the lovely bay-windowed structure.

"Yes, they sort of came with the house, I suppose you could say," Rory added.

"Business must be good, huh?" Slade wondered.

"*My* kind is," Rory informed him with a sly wink.

Slade looked suitably impressed and entered the house behind his wife. "Just what kind of business are you in anyway?"

"Well, it isn't the theater. At least, not the acting end of it," came Rory's glib reply. "You see, through a chance of good fortune, I found myself on the winning end of a card game. A high-stakes card game, at that. When the debts were settled, I discovered myself the possesser of a hotel, a restaurant and this house here."

"You don't say!" Slade's attention was well and truly caught with this admission.

Seeing the unmistakable glimmer in her husband's eye, Raine felt an ominous, sinking feeling inside. "Darling, you wouldn't—"

But Slade wasn't listening. He let Adam slide down his long body to the polished hardwood floor, remarking, "You know, Rory, that's exactly how I came to be captain of the *Mary Ellen*—a high-stakes poker game."

"Well, well!" Rory beamed. "It seems you and I have quite a lot in common after all, doesn't it?"

The two men started toward a pair of tall, opened doors which led into Rory's study just inside the entrance.

"Now, wait just a minute," Raine called sharply, stopping them in midstride. "You can't just leave us here."

"Oh, forgive me." Somewhat flustered, Rory turned back to her. "I sometimes forget myself."

"Yes, I can see that," she chided.

"Rosa! Li-Po!" Rory called loudly. "Come out here! We have guests!"

No sooner had the cry left his lips than two people suddenly appeared through a doorway hidden beneath the stairs. The woman, Rosa, was a slender, middle-aged Mexican, dressed in a multicolored skirt and snowy peasant blouse. Li-Po, as his name implied, was Oriental. He was garbed in dark, loose-fitting trousers and coat.

"Take my sister and the children upstairs to their rooms, will you, please?" This to Rosa. Turning, he addressed Li-Po. "Get one of the other boys to help you with the bags when they arrive. They should be here shortly."

The two servants nodded at Rory's instructions and Raine found herself being led up the stairs as her husband remained below, "to discuss business," he said.

"I can see that I'm going to have a problem with your father," she murmured to Davey as they mounted the stairs.

"You can handle him," the boy assured her with a wink.

The rooms Rosa led them to, though sparsely furnished with just the bare necessities, were quite comfortable looking. Bright paper covered the walls, while heavy, mahogany furniture partially filled the carpeted floor.

"I put the *muchachos* across the hall, *si?*" Rosa asked with quirked brows.

"Oh, yes, that will be fine. You don't mind sharing a room with Adam, do you, David?"

Looking down at the little boy who held his hand, Davey grinned. "No, of course not. Come on, squirt."

Raine had to smile as the two of them left her room. They were such opposites, in age as well as looks, yet there was already a brotherly bond between them. Without having to be asked, Davey had already put himself in charge of Adam. Though fourteen years separated their ages, they had developed a fond camaraderie for one another that most natural brothers never acquired in a lifetime.

A tiny whimper of complaint brought Raine's attention back to the baby in her arms. Having slept through most of the journey from the boat to the house, Louisa Catherine was now wide awake and demanding to be fed. She was wet, too, but until their bags arrived, she would just have to stay that way.

"Be patient, precious," Raine murmured lovingly. "Mummy will have your dinner for you in just a minute."

She closed the door before settling herself in the large stuffed chair placed before the wide bay window, unbuttoning her bodice as the baby continued to voice her frustrations. At last, when her breast was finally free of the confining bodice and camisole, Raine brushed her dripping nipple against her daughter's cheek, then chuckled when the baby voraciously latched onto it. She was such an uninhibited infant, not unlike her father in many ways, and Raine loved her all the more for it.

Silence soon fell over the room, broken only by the loud grunts, gulps and smacks of the nursing child. This, Raine had to admit, was the part of motherhood she cherished most—the part she had been denied with Adam. Recalling the differences between her two children's births, she reflected back on the moment her daughter made her debut into the world.

Slade had been with her, nervously wiping her brow as he whispered words of encouragement to her. And he had stayed by her side from the moment she began her short, undifficult but painful labor, until the moment of delivery was actually upon them. Then he had moved to stand between her parted, upraised legs and had caught their bawling daughter in his large, scarred hands as she slid out of her mother's womb.

It was even-odds as to who had been the most surprised, herself or Slade, for neither of them in their wildest dreams had ever anticipated the baby would be a girl. With two sons already between them, they had been certain beyond a doubt that it would be a boy!

From the first, though, Slade had been entranced by his tiny daughter. He had stubbornly held onto her and cleaned her while Hetty had looked after Raine. And only with great reluctance had he given his precious little girl to Raine so that she could nurse her. At the time, Raine had thought with much amusement that if God had furnished Slade with mammaries, he would have fed the baby himself. His fascination with Louisa Catherine was that immense.

Though he had many obligations to occupy his time on the voyage from Hawaii, Slade had managed to spend a goodly number of hours with Louisa Catherine, talking to her in babytalk, playing with her and changing her diapers. But he never forgot or ignored his two other children. It was as if, with the arrival of the new baby, Slade had developed a larger capacity for loving and sharing with his family.

Until now, that is.

Raine peered out the bay window, a speculative scowl gently contorting her soft features. What were Rory and Slade up to? Oh, she had suspected beforehand that they would come to be friends, but she hadn't imagined that their bond would be like this. Not so soon, at any rate.

A sound brought her attention sharply around to the door. Slade stood there, leaning against the jamb, a smile dimpling his handsome face.

"Her ladyship was hungry, hmm? I thought I heard her crying a minute ago." He pushed away from the frame and sauntered over to where Raine sat, squatting down on his haunches so that he was eye-level with his wife.

All thoughts of verbal retribution fled from Raine's mind as she noted Slade's loving look. There would be time enough later to find out what mischief he and Rory had been plotting. Right now, she just wanted to enjoy this moment of intimate silence with her beloved.

Slade smoothed the dark curls off his daughter's moist brow as she continued to grunt and gulp noisily. A glimmer of lust appeared in his eye a moment before he moved his fingers up to cover the swell of Raine's breast.

"Slade?"

"Hmm?"

"She doesn't need any help from you." But Raine gasped as his fingers slid across her creamy skin to capture her other breast in his cupped palm. His long forefinger and thumb encircled the nipple as milk flowed out of the tiny pores and onto his knuckle.

With an almost sensual slowness, he brought the finger to his mouth and licked the liquid away with his rough tongue. "Mmm! Good stuff."

Raine was tempted to tell him that he could have a more substantial sampling of it later, after their daughter's appetite had been appeased, but her remark was interrupted by a pint-sized, towheaded whirlwind.

Adam burst into the room and threw himself upon Slade's unsuspecting back. Wrapping both his arms and legs around Slade's neck and chest, he began bouncing up and down excitedly. "Daddy horsey! Go ride!"

Red-faced and gasping for air, Slade managed to loosen the toddler's stranglehold around his throat so that he could breathe again. "Whoa, pardner!" Then to Raine, "I'm getting too old for this."

"Too old!" Raine laughed. "Why, darling, you're just getting started."

And then Davey suddenly made his appearance,

his look of concern vanishing as he took in the scene. "Golly, Pa. I turned my back on him for just a minute and he was out the door and gone. I was afraid he'd fall down the stairs or something and hurt himself."

As the older boy stepped further into the room, he noticed his stepmother's state of undress and stopped, suddenly finding himself unable to go any further. "Ooops!" he blushed furiously. "Sorry, I didn't know you were—"

"Oh, that's all right, David," she murmured without a hint of reproach, calmly draping one of the baby's lacy blankets across her bared bosom. "Please, do come in."

"We're a family now, son," Slade reminded him as he slowly got to his feet. He held Adam in his arms rather than on his back. "You're going to have to get used to seeing your mother feed your little sister. And you, young man," he turned to address the child in his arms, "are going to have to limit your horsey-back rides to your big brother there. Otherwise, I won't live to see the age of forty."

A wonderful feeling of blissful contentment descended over Raine as she continued to listen to her husband gently scold their younger son. Slade was so right; they really were a family now, and a loving one at that. No matter what the future held in store for them, she was certain that, as a family, they would be able to handle anything that happened. With all of the love they possessed for each other, how could they not?

About the Author

Born and raised in the Dallas, Texas, area, Carol Jerina has always been an avid reader. It was only after the birth of her last child though that she seriously began her writing career. Now, when she isn't creating a new book with exciting, colorful plots and characters, she spends her free time acting as head cook, housekeeper, chauffeur and referee for her four sons and husband of fifteen years.

Tapestry

HISTORICAL ROMANCES

Breathtaking New Tales

of love and adventure set against
history's most exciting time and
places. Featuring two novels by the
finest authors in the field of romantic fiction—<u>every month</u>.

Next Month From
Tapestry Romances

DAUGHTER OF LIBERTY
by Johanna Hill
CHARITY'S PRIDE
by Patricia Pellicane

POCKET BOOKS